CORBIN KOHL

ADRIFT IN HELL

Also by Megan Bledsoe

Glitching the Matrix: *a novel . . .*
The Metanaut: *a supernatural thriller*
Girl, Incorrupted: *a love-horror story*

THE *CORBIN KOHL IN HELL* SERIES
fun low-fantasy mysteries
Corbin Kohl Adrift in Hell
Corbin Kohl Baited in Hell
Corbin Kohl Cornered in Hell

MEGAN BLEDSOE

CORBIN KOHL ADRIFT IN HELL

Arched Brow Books

VANCOUVER

CORBIN KOHL ADRIFT IN HELL

Copyright © 2025 by Megan Bledsoe

The moral right of the author has been asserted.

Published by Arched Brow Books
Arched Brow Books is a trademark of Arched Brow Publishing

Designed by Megan Bledsoe

Cover design elements by Toon and Logo (man falling), PavelVectors (flames), and iconsy (flame) via canva.com, and by padrinan (texture) via pixabay.com
Cover and text typefaces by Vernon Adams (Anton), Georg Duffner (EB Garamond), Steve Matteson (Open Sans, Tinos), and Pria Ravichandran (Palanquin) via fonts.google.com

Bledsoe, Megan, 1980–
Corbin Kohl Adrift In Hell / by Megan Bledsoe.
First Edition. | Vancouver : Arched Brow Books, 2025.
FICTION / Fantasy / Action & Adventure.
FICTION / Fantasy / Humorous.
FICTION / Fantasy / Cozy.

Summary: Hang out with Corbin Kohl as he navigates his new life in a place that might be Hell—except it's awfully fun.

ISBN 978-1-969265-04-4 (paperback)
ISBN 978-1-969265-99-0 (epub)

For DWS
Thank you for the assignment!
(My concrete detail was *knees*.)

CORBIN KOHL

ADRIFT

IN HELL

1

The hotel's sliding glass doors slid open with a soft whir, letting in a fresh whiff of sulfur. It stunk, but I was getting used to it.

The woman who stepped inside had beautiful knees.

Most people's legs have funky joints. You notice that kind of thing around here, in the City. Either the knee fails to connect the thigh bone to the shin bone in one smooth, straight line, or the joint is so swollen it looks like a big gnarly burl on a heat-worshipper tree.

Not this woman. Excellent knees.

She walked them toward me, heels clacking on the lobby's pink marble floor.

I was sitting in a cushy red wingback chair, one in a circle of four set between two pillars, just beyond the end of the front desk. Behind me, the lobby opened up to the elevators. A breakfast room stood off to my left. They'd served me a pretty good French toast earlier. I could still taste the syrup.

I wiped my hand down my mouth to remove any sweet,

sticky dribbles and sat up straighter in my chair—then reminded myself to act casual.

It was hard. The Hotel Burning Bright's concierge and front desk attendant had both looked up from their posts, to my left, to watch the woman stride past. Their uniforms were pale red, a gauzy lightweight material I'd noticed last night when I'd checked in but was coveting now. The early morning weather girl on Channel 7 had said the day was going to be another scorcher.

No way... ya think?

I'd woken in my room on the eighth floor in the middle of the bright night, in part thanks to an extra heady whiff of the perpetual rotten-egg stink of sulfur; in other part thanks to the construction crew on the street below starting up their front-end loaders and jackhammers well before the witching hour. As if they could beat the heat.

Maybe they knew something I didn't.

Right now, outside the hotel lobby's floor-to-ceiling windows, the morning was already so hot that last night's rain (or what passes for it) was evaporating from the sidewalk in rainbow-tinted rivulets, like steam off a boiling pot.

So not only was it hot out, it was humid.

I'd dressed in blue Bermuda shorts, the kind with a zip fly and five pockets, like pants only hemmed above the knee, and a white polo shirt, the three buttons undone. Both were a thick, chafing cotton. I'd chosen form over function, thinking it would help me fit in with the hotel's clientele. So far, so good. In the hour I'd been sitting here, I'd seen only a handful of guests in the lobby, and all of us were wearing our sweat-worthy best.

Except the woman.

The woman wore a white cable-knit sweater and gray wool skirt, a thick winter weight. Strange choices, but high quality. Clearly, the woman knew how to get ahead around here.

I'd been wiping the sweat from the back of my neck every couple minutes, already wilting in the heat, but I didn't see any perspiration on her. Her wavy, sun-blond hair was still light and bouncy at the roots. Her legs still dry, even in that wool skirt. The hemline skimmed just above her bare knees. It had a slit on one side, and as she walked toward me, a sliver of the skirt's white lining flashed with every other step.

Flash.

Flash.

A gray thread dangled from the top of the slit—it was coming undone—and the slit's extra length revealed that her legs did indeed flow in one straight yet supple, curvy line, from hip bone to the tips of her toes—the nails of which were painted white and peeping out of strappy white heels.

She raised a hand and waved, her face brightening into a smile. She was probably late twenties, maybe thirty. She had a heart-shaped face and a heart-shaped mouth, but her nose was on the prominent side, and it had a droopy tip that didn't quite gel with her other features and yet only made her face more interesting.

She wasn't waving at me, of course. But I was spared the

internal debate about whether or not to sneak a glance behind me to see who she was meeting, when a man stepped out from behind my left shoulder. From the elevator, probably, except I hadn't heard it ding.

He had on a long-sleeved cream linen shirt, khaki pants, gloves, one of those wide-brimmed hats with a flap to protect the neck, and dark sunglasses. Inside. I cracked a smile.

Could be that my first real assignment was nothing more than a final test.

Or a prank.

Back home, I would've camouflaged my smile by running my finger up the screen of my phone, pretending to be amused by some piece of content rather than the mark, but I didn't have a phone here. So I rubbed my face like I'd had one hell of a night and was still working on destroying the evidence.

The man, still wearing his doofy hat and glasses, gestured to my right, to where a half wall separated the lobby from a dimly lit bar. The bar's neon lights on the back wall were off, and no one stood ready to tend guests—service wouldn't begin until two o'clock that afternoon—but the area itself, with its black high-top tables and chairs, was still open to lobby spillover.

The woman nodded and veered course toward the bar—without first greeting the man in the hat with a hug or a kiss or even a handshake.

Interesting.

Especially since she was still smiling wide.

Was it a real smile? I supposed it could be, depending on what she was here to exchange. Not being close enough to read her eyes, I couldn't make an educated guess.

I wasn't worried about the man seeing me, not with that giant hat blocking his motion perception. But I waited for the woman to walk close enough to the bar that her back was to me to start scanning her legs, the backs of her knees, her calves, and, as I leaned to the left just enough to peer around a red wingback chair, her ankles.

And there it was.

A tattoo.

But the circular design was not what I'd expected. The woman's white shoe straps wrapped around the ankle, making it hard to see the detail, but if her tattoo was indeed of a sea-goat, then its horns were depicted curved, following the line of the sea-goat's spine and transformation into a fish tail. The design looked like a circle from afar.

As the woman walked further away from me, I squinted, trying to make the tattoo appear as I needed it to be. Was that circle a sea-goat?

But it had to be it, right? This had to be her. How many people willingly tattoo their Achilles tendon? The spot had to be painful. Not to mention, how many women were meeting someone in the Hotel Burning Bright this morning? The only other people I'd seen in the last hour or so, aside from me, doofy-hat guy, and hotel personnel, were a handful of tired people trudging to and from the continental breakfast or checking in at the front desk.

No, this was her. It had to be. Right place, right time, right tattoo as far as I could tell, right location on the ankle.

Which meant I was truly in the presence of Amlathea.

Whoa.

But was this the right guy?

Amlathea reached the bar first and stood just inside the entrance, waiting for him to get there, too.

Still no physical contact. For some reason, that seemed odd to me.

Again, the man in the hat held out a hand and gestured her further inside the bar, toward a table in the back right corner. She complied, and as he followed her, the man looked over his shoulder and scanned the lobby—the bellhops carting luggage in from valet, the marble pillars holding up the second floor. As his sunglasses-covered gaze passed over me, I heaved a bored sigh and shifted my weight to the other hip, switching up which leg was crossed over the other. *Nope, I'm not expecting to get up any time soon.* I rested my chin in my palm, my elbow on the red wingback's armrest, and kept my eyes focused on the sliding glass doors, letting my peripheral vision take over.

Amlathea reached the table in the back corner and attempted to scooch around it, to take a seat that would put her back against the wall. But the man slithered an arm around her waist. She looked over her shoulder at him, her brow wrinkling in confusion, but she let him pull her away from the table, closer to the wall—and out of my sight.

Ah hell, they were making a run for it. I launched out of my armchair and ran for the bar.

The bar's side wall was decorative, dimly backlit rock. But a vertical rectangle of much brighter light was shining down its middle, revealing the sidewalk outside the building and the street beyond. The rectangle quickly thinned into a sliver, until the hole in the wall disappeared completely, the bar's temporary exit closing behind them.

Right man. Definitely the right man.

For a split second I thought about running back through the bar, across the lobby, and out the front door. But that would only work out for me if they, too, were running around the building toward the hotel's front entrance.

Unlikely.

I heaved a heavy sigh, resigning myself to act on my only option.

I'd had success with sliding glass doors during training. Sure, glass was the easiest material to work with, but it still hurt like a mother.

But I'd done it.

I could do a hotel wall, too. Sure I could.

Here I go.

Watch me do it.

I bounced on my toes and flicked my hands, preparing to do it. The bar's decorative wall was very cool, the color and texture of desert rock. Or maybe it *was* desert rock. At least two layers of it, all craggy and pocked and backlit so that the pockets of empty space popped with light. Very cool. But admiring it wasn't helping me any. Not at all, in fact. I squeezed my eyes shut and grimaced, bracing for the pain. I groped the wall with a hesitant hand. (It *was* rock, smooth yet gritty). Then reminded myself that it's best to just barge through with the shoulder. I tilted to the side.

2

And I ran through the wall.

Well, I say *ran*, and I did amble as fast as I could, but the motion was more like walking through molasses and being stung by jelly fish and electric eels. The yielding rock sounded like chalk scraping on sidewalk. Musty dust tickled my nose. I'm told that the old guys can pass through walls in an instant, but I was still hoping I wouldn't be here long enough to get that good at it. I gritted my teeth and groaned at the sharp pain as I pushed my way through the wall.

Outside, the sulfur smell ramped up immediately, and it was bright out, always bright out. Once I had enough of me out of the wall that I could put all my weight on one foot, I yanked my other foot free. I stood there for a second, shaking off the pins-pricking sensation and trying to shallow breathe so as not to inhale too much of the sulfur scent. My shoulder hurt like hell. My shoes sizzled on the sidewalk.

I'd breached the wall just in time to look right, look left, and see Amlathea wobbling down the sidewalk in her strappy white heels, Victor pulling her by the elbow around the corner of the building.

Yes, Victor. Had to be. Doofy neck-flap hat and gloves or not, only Victor Kane could've parted the bar's wall like that.

I had to give him props, though, and not just for the stunt. He hadn't sent an underling to meet Amlathea. He'd actually put on a disguise and come himself. He'd made his first public appearance in years, all in the hopes of making it back to his lair with her.

I grinned, wondering if that confirmed all the rumors.

I took off after them.

I'd come out in the relative shade of the hotel, of course—because the hotel's back side, like the back sides of all buildings in the City, faces away from the Pit—but sweat still gushed from my skin. Even my forearms were sweaty.

It wasn't even eight o'clock yet. And no breeze would be coming to wick the sweat away any time soon, not today. Not even as I ran. I looked down as I wiped the back of my neck. The soles of my shoes were mingling with what was left of last night's rain. Every step spurted steam out the sides and left sole residue on the sidewalk.

So *that's* how the City's sidewalks had gotten its marbled effect. I'd been wondering.

I turned the corner. Victor and Amlathea were halfway down the sidewalk, running toward the front-entrance side of the hotel. The blinding light from the Pit was spewing up glowing pyroclastic clouds several blocks away. I picked up speed, scanning the end of the block for trouble. But the glare of the Pit clouds on flat surfaces is ten times worse than that of Earth's sun. I could barely see the street.

But also, I'd been told to observe an exchange. Nothing more. Chasing people down the street was exciting and all, but what if I had the wrong woman? Or gave myself away? Or tipped them to Management's mission? What if this was none of my business?

Ahead of me, the woman stumbled. The strap on her shoe broke and came loose. Revealing more of that circular tattoo.

It had to be her.

Which meant my target was indeed meeting Victor Kane.

If I didn't know any better, I'd say I was about an hour away from receiving major bonus points from Management.

Too bad those weren't the points I was most interested in earning.

I was gaining on the two of them with each step. So I lowered my gaze to Amlathea's ankles, trying to get a better look at the tattoo, trying to confirm that the circle was indeed a stylized sea-goat.

But I was also reaching the distance where the body instinctively knows to straighten the dominant arm and reach out for the target's shoulder.

My fingers brushed Amlathea's hair.

Victor looked back at me and grinned.

In a few more steps, the shade from the building across the street would abruptly end in a clear—and bright—

demarcation line on the sidewalk. We were almost at the street corner. I didn't know what Victor had planned, but it couldn't be good for me.

"Victor…"

He stepped behind the woman and shoved her into the street just as a yellow construction front loader rumbled toward the intersection. The front loader's black scooper had a bunch of stickers on the side, and it was riding low and flat to the ground.

Amlathea stumbled forward in those strappy shoes of hers, arms waving. She tripped over the side of the scooper, strappy feet in the air. She scrambled to upright herself as the front loader lifted its scoop—with her still in it.

The woman with the ankle tattoo was my target.

But the front loader was hauling her away fast and picking up speed. I wouldn't catch her on foot. And I was convinced that Management had never considered her contact would be Victor Kane himself.

I watched the woman for a split second, noting she wasn't calling for help, then turned back to Victor.

But the shoe-residue-marbled sidewalk where Victor's feet had been was already sealing closed.

3

"What happened?"

My boss, Terry Peaches, fortyish, had the whiniest voice I'd ever heard. Every short-*A* vowel sound of his came out like a baby's cry. *Whaaa, what haaappened?*

"They had a clever getaway car," I said. "Hidden in plain sight at a construction site and modified for speed. No license plate, granted the right-away... and Amlathea wasn't exactly struggling or calling for help."

Terry flinched at something I'd said.

Despite the constant heat, Terry had worn a shorts suit every time I'd seen him so far, every one of them a shade of blue. Today's was royal blue with a red tie. His chin dropped to his barrel chest, blond hair falling over his forehead, and he bit his thumb as he paced behind his desk, the top of which was glass, generally clear of things, and hid nothing. He had tiny feet, but he stomped them around like he was a big man.

Terry's office was on the twenty-first floor. Behind him,

his office's floor-to-ceiling windows offered a view of the Pit, about five blocks away. The smoke rising up from the burning red caldera was white, almost clear. Which meant the air was easier to suck into the lungs, but the smell was particularly sulfurous.

And yet Terry's office always smelled worse than it did outside. I had no evidence yet, but I'd swear on a copy of *The Wrath of No Man* that he piped the stench in direct. Terry thrived on it. Of that, there *was* some evidence, but only circumstantial.

"But did she make an exchange?" he asked.

I puzzled at him. There were no visitor's chairs in Terry's office, so I stood in the middle of the room, equidistant between the door and the glass front of his desk. The carpet was like that plastic, outdoor-grass stuff I remembered from back home, only red. It rustled beneath Terry's footstomps.

"I mean, yeah, don't you think? Maybe not the kind we were expecting. No hand-off or anything. But she gave them herself. She was the exchange."

Terry grunted, his chest puffing in a *humph*.

"And one other thing," I said, dreading this next part. And what might come after it. Would I be kicked off the case? Or would the case become my life? Either way, I was in for more change. And given what passed for my life these days, I hated change. "The contact was Victor."

"Victor?" Terry stopped pacing and frowned at me. "Victor Wally?"

The guy who'd descended into the Pit's caldera and lived to tell the tale, to Terry's dismay and embarrassment.

"Uh, no, Victor—"

"Victor Tamales?"

The guy who'd diverted the Pit smoke toward his food cart, across town, harnessing it as free energy and pissing off Terry in the process. Me, I kinda liked the tacos being so cheap he'd been willing to give me one in exchange for a quarter. And the hint of sulfur on the tongue wasn't bad. Kind of like that spice that tastes like death. Asafoetida or whatever. But Terry's angry reaction was part of why I thought he truly needed the sulfur smell to survive. If it was going to the taco truck, then it wasn't coming to him.

"Yeah, no," I said. "It was Victor—"

"Victor Sa—"

"Terry." I stop-signed him with both hands. There were enough Victors around these parts to take an eternity listing them all. "It was Victor Kane."

Terry's chin doubled as he tucked it back toward his neck in surprise. He groped behind himself for his rolling office chair and sat down. The chair's high back rose at least eighteen inches above his head, like a throne. Did I mention the faux leather is gold?

"Victor Kane? Are you sure?"

In training, they'd showed us pictures—mugshots, they looked like, but without the black height lines on the white backdrop—of people who had quote-unquote *other* skills. Skills beyond the ones our trainers were deigning to teach us. We were learning to do what, on Earth, had been impossible. But here, walking through walls was just part of Skill Set Level 1. Management didn't want us getting caught off guard by someone doing something even more unfathomable than walking through walls just because they hadn't told us the action was possible. Hence, the show and tell. Victor Kane had been mentioned as someone who could do a very rare something *other*.

Beyond the windows, the smoke rising from the Pit started to darken. It was just a coincidence, of course. But still. The next part of this discussion was the part I dreaded.

In response to Terry's question about whether I was sure it was Victor Kane, I sighed, shrugged. See-sawed my hand back and forth. Comsi comsa. "Ninety-five percent?"

Terry glowered at me. "Come again?"

"I couldn't see his face. He was wearing dark glasses and one of those hats that cover the neck. But he escaped the hotel by opening the wall."

"Opened... he didn't just walk through?"

"Definitely opened. I saw the light shining through the hole myself. And I counted at least three seconds before it closed behind him and the woman, Amlathea. But—"

He flinched again. "There's more?"

"He got away again by opening up the, um, the ground."

There. I'd said it. Nice and simple. No ambiguity. Management hadn't mentioned that little aspect of Victor's skill set, and given how much they'd rambled on about the variation of other people's skill sets, I had the feeling Victor's ground-opening skill had been left out of the presentation for only one reason.

Management didn't know about it.

Terry certainly didn't. He frowned at me. "Like a little caldera?"

"No." I frowned back. "Like a fissure," I said. "A crack. Like how the wall opened up, only in the ground."

Terry shook his head. And I couldn't blame him. Walls opened onto air. Inside or outside, there was space on the other side of a wall in which to find yourself. With the ground...

"It opened into—what?—fire and brimstone?"

"No," I said, hesitation coloring my tone. I had to admit this part was the problem, but I didn't want it to become *my* problem. "It was dark and loamy and... and moist."

Terry's upper lip curled in disgust. He was catching on, but he still looked puzzled. So I told it like it was:

"The hole was like digging up on the, uh, on the Earth's surface, like... like dirt."

Terry gasped and clutched a hand to his chest like a lady of manners—you see them around here sometimes—but then his eyes narrowed. "Impossible."

It wasn't my place to confirm or deny what was possible around these parts, and I had no clue about what was supposed to be possible or not, anyway. So I stood mute, rolling my right shoulder joint and rubbing the deltoid, trying to soothe the lingering pain of pins and needles— more like spears and pitchforks.

Walking through walls was nothing like walking through glass, I'll tell you that much.

Terry said, "I'll need you to do me a favor, Kohl."

Well, that sounded ominous. I didn't know much about

Victor Kane. But what little I did know made me wary of being assigned to checking him out. From what I'd learned in training, people didn't usually go missing around here. But on the rare occasion they did, Victor Kane's name was usually part of the theory.

I still hadn't figured out what I was doing here, in the City. So I wasn't too keen on possibly suddenly finding myself somewhere else. Somewhere else, in my recent experience, was never somewhere better.

"What about the woman?" I asked. "Amlathea?"

Certainly she was a safer assignment, right?

Terry gave me a pained look like he had no idea who I was talking about. Or like he didn't want *me* knowing who I was talking about. Probably that one. After all, I'd learned the target's name not from him but from doing my own research.

"With the tattoo?" I prompted.

"You saw it?"

"Sort of. It was partially covered by the straps on her shoes. It was circu—"

"Ah-ah-ah!" Terry warned. He pursed his lips and shook his head.

If this had happened a few weeks ago, on my first couple days on the job, I would've been more confused and more frustrated than ever. But over the past few days I'd gotten used to it. Or at least apathetic to it.

I was the rank of need-to-know. Fine. It made it harder to know which details were important and which weren't, but apparently making such distinctions wasn't expected of me. And anyway, I was learning the tells.

Still, I liked clarity. "So..."

Terry's phone rang. It was an old rotary dial. Olive green enamel. For better and worse, there were no cell phones here. At least not on a grand scale. Reasons included signal interference thanks to the Pit and heat too harsh for sensitive electronics. I'd heard that some people had makeshift phones, but I was told they were more like glorified walkie-talkies.

Terry let the phone ring a second time before answering. I hadn't been dismissed yet, so I waited. He glanced at me, then stood and walked to the window as far as the curly cord would allow. He spoke in quiet if terse tones, with his back to me... glowered over his shoulder at me a couple of times... finally hung up.

"Take the rest of the day off, Kohl."

My eyebrows rose in surprise—those glances he'd given me during the call had looked bad; he still hadn't told me if I was done with Amlathea; and what about Victor Kane?—but when it comes to a free pass, no one had to tell *me* twice.

And practically a whole day, too. What a score.

"Sounds good. See you later," I said on my jaunty walk out.

"I want you back here tomorrow," he called after me. "Nine o'clock."

I winced, stumbling a step and hunching my shoulders, but I kept walking.

And then he added, "Sharp."

4

The room outside Terry's office was windowless, with dark faux-wood paneling and the same red plastic carpet. Terry had an assistant, poor old guy, but his tidy glass desk to the right of Terry's office door, as you exit, was empty. I turned left and hit the elevator down button, just in case it happened to be waiting on this floor. But it wasn't. I can't stand being in Terry's red, windowless waiting room, so I hit the button several more times, just because, and then took the fire exit stairs.

It wasn't even eight yet. What to do with myself for twenty-five hours?

My footsteps echoed in the gray concrete stairwell, which miraculously smelled more like dust than sulfur. The metal handrail was cool to the touch. The stairwell spiraled slowly and sometimes steeply around the elevator, and on a few of the lower landings, which had fewer exit doors, I could stand in one spot without being spotted by anyone suddenly entering the stairs.

I pressed my shoulder, forehead, neck, underarms, underlegs—basically any body part I could finagle into contact with the rail, I pressed against the cool rail. It felt so good. What a treat. If the railing weren't heating up at my touch, I might've done this for my whole twenty-four hours.

I did it for about twenty minutes. Then finished my decent down the stairs to the ground floor, braced myself, and pried open the door.

First came the heat. Like opening a pizza oven back home. The wave of heat rolled in at me, so thick I had to step aside to get out of its way. After the heat came the glare. Like exiting a dark theater into a bright summer day, face first into the sun.

Except the glare here wasn't sun. The glare from the persistently yellow sky above was too bright to see for sure what the source was, and no one I'd hazarded to ask—namely, Terry and my training instructors—had been willing to tell me what it was. But I was developing some suspicions.

I'd been in the City for a couple of weeks now, but I still felt like a tourist. I know, *tourist* has positive connotations—at least when you *are* the tourist, maybe not so much when you're *dealing* with the tourist—but I mean it. If you like people-watching, strange architecture, new things, different things—and I do—then the City's not that bad. And it's big enough that I'd probably, hopefully, never get to see it all.

But the weather was something else.

Hot. Always hot. At least it had been the last few weeks. But, like I said, the City wasn't on a planet orbiting and wobbling in a solar system, like back home. So I wasn't holding out much hope for a change of season.

I darted out of the stairwell, into the bright of day, and crossed the four-lane street, into the relative shade of an old apartment building. It was four stories tall with slender windows evenly spaced throughout the upper floors. The street-level occupants were all stores, or the backs of stores, anyway. This being the side of the building furthest from the Pit, the relative-shade side, there were no front entrances. All the stores had dull gray rear entrance doors. Some of them single doors, some of them double doors. For larger deliveries, maybe.

Simple black-and-white signs above the doors identified the names of the stores. The third sign from the right was for a store called *Physical Services Parlor*.

I was still feeling a little raw and raggedy from running through the hotel wall after Victor and Amlathea. In particular, my shoulder was killing me. I was told the ache wears off eventually, but there were procedures and therapies to speed up the process. So why wait?

That decided the first hour of my free day.

I tried the parlor's back door, but it was locked. Hmm. Cautious choice or a Pit penalty?

And did I really want to find out?

I could have walked the City streets and found another parlor to help me with the aftereffects of walking through walls, but that would have meant more glare and heat. And curiosity always gets the best of me. I can't turn it off. I love to learn. *Why, oh, why, store, have you locked your back door?*

At the edge of the building, I turned the corner, keeping my head down as I walked into the glare of the Pit. Terry's office was five blocks away, which made this block less than four blocks away. The heat was something else and the glare was blinding. I took to reverse blinking—opening my eyes for a split second and otherwise keeping them closed—as I made my way down the sidewalk.

It was still pretty early in the morning and no one passed me. Only a few cars puttered by. There's no rush hour here. At least not in any predictable sense, according to any time of day. The City's inhabitants don't all go to work at nine and leave work at five. Some do—mainly those who are closer to the Pit than others, in the metaphorical sense—but most people do not.

And here Terry wanted me back in the office tomorrow at nine o'clock sharp. Not a good sign. I racked my brain for something punishable I had done but came up with nothing.

I turned left at the front of the building. The hottest, brightest part. The Physical Services Parlor was three doors in, poor souls. My hair, brown and cut in one of those cool-boy styles once upon a time, was now a sweat helmet on my head. I could actually smell myself without sniffing an armpit. I picked up speed to a fast walk, stopping just a gear short of adding the hop in my step that would have made my gait a run. City folk take Community Watch to a whole new level. And you don't want to be caught running or appearing to be running from the effects of the Pit. By anyone. Bad things can happen.

5

The parlor's entrance was one of those single glass doors with a silver metal handle across the middle that made me think of old malt shops and pharmacies from the 1950s back home. I opened it slowly and heard an electronic buzzing sound, like hair clippers or a beard trimmer, coming from somewhere deep inside the store, but then a little doorbell rang over the top of it—*ding*—and the buzzing stopped. I smiled and relaxed. Nostalgia. It's the little things, you know? The little things that let you know you're gonna like the people you're about to meet.

Door all the way open now, about to step inside, and I felt a rush of air conditioning. Hmm. Locked back door. Air conditioning. And the room I was stepping into was empty and only twenty feet wide by ten feet deep, if that. The back wall was made of pressboard. I could see the texture of the layered flakes beneath its thin coat of green paint. The green paint was a good sign—green, to induce calm and creativity, which was how I hoped to be feeling in an hour—but the construction work was shoddy. No way was it sanctioned or up to code. The green pressboard wall and the empty waiting room, without a help desk or even art on the walls, seemed more purposed toward keeping the likes of me from seeing the rest of the store space than welcoming me inside.

Now I know I just complained about Community Watch tattling about petty things, but this place was looking like something bigger and worth mentioning. Back home, I would've said it was a front for drugs or some such. But drugs aren't really a thing here and *some such* could be anything. I was too new in town to know, yet, about all the shady opportunities.

So the next step I took was back out the door, back onto the sidewalk. Nothing to see here folks, and nobody here to see it either. I'd just be going now.

Except I wouldn't be.

I'd like to say I was spotted on video, that some kind of hidden surveillance system had caught me. But it wasn't. It was the bell. The comforting, damning, welcome-into-the-shop doorbell. I'd heard its *ding* and stood there reminiscing like an idiot.

It was one of the more subtle, more cruel ways that the City showed you, demonstrated for you, exactly where you were. The Pit, the heat, the sulfur smell. The nostalgia that turned against you. Nobody ever confirmed it, never even came close. But with hints like these, how could you not know exactly where you were?

The left side of the green back wall shook, revealing a

crack. A door. For a moment it jiggled in place, like it was stuck. Then it burst open.

A big dude, the kind with no neck to speak of and lats so big his arms hovered at his sides, dipped his squared head under the green pressboard door frame and stepped inside the little room with me. He had unsettling light-hazel eyes.

Sure, I could've left, could've turned heel and ran. But, as mentioned, around here that's a solution akin to jumping from the frying pan and into the Pit.

I stepped fully inside the little waiting room like that had been my goal the whole time and I was just slow getting to it. I let the door close behind me. The bell deep inside the store somewhere finished its jingle: *dong*.

In my head, the jingle kept going. *Dong-dong dooonnnng*.

"Can I help you?" the man said. His tone was kinder and his voice not as low as I'd expected. He was wearing a yellow tank top, the kind from the eighties with the thin shoulder straps and a scoop neck that came down halfway between his pecs and his navel. He might've been from the eighties himself, for all I knew, what with that muscle head and the squinty eyes and the neck rolls so big they were peeking out at me from the side.

Maybe his storefront was hiding a gym.

But I didn't think so. His pants weren't gaudy fluorescent spandex; they were dirty khakis cut off above the knee. He had massive calves. And he'd shoved his bare feet into some brown plastic slides. I could see the dude's toes. Gross.

"Uh..." I looked around for a service menu, but the green

walls were bare. What had I come here for? Oh, yeah. I'd first heard the technique's name during training, after our first test run through a glass wall. Some people make it through. Other people hit their heads at best, and at worse, end up on a table having glass picked from their skin.

"Can I get a Cellular Twist?" *But not from you. Please.*

"Been walking through walls, huh?" The dude raised his muscular arm and groped at the green pressboard wall to my left. I could see cracks, but they formed a rectangle that was smaller than the dude's door. More like a hidden compartment. Either way, it, too, was stuck. The dude tried digging a sausage finger into the cracks, but that wasn't happening.

He hit the green wall with his meaty fist. I flinched back a step, and it was a good thing, too, because a flap of pressboard dropped where I'd been standing, right between us, stopping parallel to the ground at waist level. His, not mine.

An old piece of orange rope held the makeshift desk in place, but I wouldn't have put any weight on it.

The dude reached inside the resulting wall compartment and pulled out a book. He opened the book and flipped its pages until he got to the one he wanted. A weekly scheduler. He ran his finger down today's date. I don't know what he was looking for. There wasn't a single handwritten word on the page.

But, ah, the appearance of respectability.

6

"**S**ure," the dude said, "I think Angela's free. Come on back."

Do I have to?

He turned and ducked back through the pressboard doorway. I had to step over the bottom door frame, but the top was at least eight inches above my head. No ducking for me.

I entered a hallway that smelled of cold disuse. Couldn't complain about the cold, and it almost made being here, facing an uncertain future, worthwhile. But the disuse was a bit of a quandary. I mean, at the very least, the big dude was using the space, and after walking in his wake through the plywood door, I could tell you he did not smell like cold disuse; he smelled like my shorts after a heated game of basketball played on the rim of the Pit.

Maybe his khakis *were* hiding gym spandex.

The hallway ran the whole length of the store and was lit with exposed bulbs strung every four feet. At the end was the locked exit door I'd tried to open earlier. The left wall was concrete, and the right was another plywood wall, also green, but still not doing much to help me stay calm.

The dude said, "Shut the door, will ya?" Then, "Yo, Angela."

I turned back toward the waiting room to shut the door, pinching my fingers in the plywood and getting a sliver in the process. I stuck the tip of my finger in my mouth and sucked it out. The air conditioning had dried my sweat into salt, and the splinter removal tasted as such.

When I turned back around, a woman was standing in the hallway. She was dwarfed by the dude, but I figured her for close to my height, close to my age. Long dark hair in a messy braid hung over the front of one shoulder. Tight black tank top. White baggy linen harem pants sat low on her hips and cinched at the ankles. Arms crossed, no smile.

"This is Angela," the dude said. "She'll take real good care of you."

Before I could say *thanks*, the dude turned heel and mosey'd down the hall, arms hovering at his sides. When he reached the end of the line, he looked back at me, just a hint of a smile, and then he vanished into the green wall.

Whether he pushed open another hidden door or walked through the pressboard like a pro, I had no idea; I was too far away and standing at too narrow an angle to tell.

Nor could I decide whether I was happy or not to see him go. My gaze traveled from the spot where he'd last been standing back up the hallway to where Angela still stood, about ten feet away from me. Arms crossed, no smile.

"We don't have to do this," I said.

"You have keys?"

"Uh..." I assumed she meant something akin to cash money. "Not yet—"

She rolled her eyes.

"—but..." I reached into the back pocket of my Bermuda shorts. My skin chafed against the shifting damp waistband. I pulled out my wallet and spread open the cash compartment. "I've got a few dollars left. American."

I pulled out a five, held it up for her to see.

She scowled at it, didn't take it. Just turned and shoved her way through the green wall.

The pressboard swung forward into another room and then swung back out at me, hinged like a saloon door. A third type of door, different from the dude's door down the hall, and the door to the waiting room. Like floor models. Maybe they made doors here... when they weren't doing Cellular Twists.

Yeah, probably not.

"You coming?" Angela said.

"Oh." I'd thought she'd left me, intending me to show myself out.

I pushed through the saloon door into a room that left a lot to be desired. I found a waist-high table draped in a white sheet, yes, but no ambiance. The room was unfinished. Concrete floor, exposed two-by-fours, and just enough room for the two of us to walk around each other without touching. Barely.

"Lie down," she said, flipping her braid behind her, out of her way.

I hopped up on the massage table—the cushion wasn't half bad—and lay on my back. She squatted down in front of the table and ducked beneath the sheet. I heard rustling and felt the table wiggling beneath me. I rolled toward the edge and pulled the sheet up further to see what she was doing.

The massage table was more like a cushioned kitchen island with shelves. A flimsy one at that. I couldn't see what all she had in there, but she came up with something I recognized, although it was on the small side.

A Cellular Twister looks kind of like a hair dryer. Functions like one, too—to the layman, at least, which I still was.

"Lie back."

I did, as she pulled up the sheet near my head and plugged in the Twister. Standing over me, looking down, her face less than a foot away, her breasts even closer, she said, "Is it your shoulder?"

"It hurts all over, but, yeah, mostly in the shoulder."

Mostly a lot in the shoulder. I squeezed my right deltoid, which had led the charge through the hotel's wall.

Angela turned on the Twister. It made a low humming sound, not unlike a tuning fork. I didn't feel any heat or force of air against my skin, as with a regular hairdryer, but I did feel a tingling sensation deep in my muscles and joints.

When I'd had this procedure done back at training, after making it through the glass wall, the tech had been this guy wearing weird goggles, and his Twister had been this pro-industrial-looking thing, attached to this big unit about the size of an air conditioner that rolled around behind him. He'd held the Twister's blower-end a couple of inches away from my body, and he never touched me himself.

Angela held her portable Twister about a foot away, bending her elbow to maintain the distance as she put her other hand on my shoulder, and her fingertips pressed into my skin, like she was checking for lumps or sore spots.

She must've seen my confusion on my face, because she shook the Twister and said, bored, "I'm disillusioned. This is all I need."

If I'd been confused before, I was even more confused now. And there was so much to unpack. My brows pinched together tighter.

"Oh, jeez." She removed her hand and aimed the Twister at the floor as she stepped away from me, but only for a second, only long enough to sigh before stepping right back into position. "You don't know what I'm talking about."

It wasn't a question, but I still shook my head. What's disillusioned? What do big, rolling Twister jet pack things do and why, oh, why didn't she need one? But first, "What's disillusioned?"

It was a term I'd heard before, in training, sort of, although I'd felt like the instructors were talking around the concept instead of explaining it. It had to do with why some people here, and only some people, could walk through walls. The gist was that the walls were an illusion. Kind of like back home, where everything is made up of atoms that are mostly empty space—except here people lean into the emptiness.

Figuratively and literally.

But not everyone can get beyond the Illusion. They think it's real. And that's why they can't walk through it.

And that's where my training on the subject had ended.

But I'd been thinking about it ever since. I'd been thinking about the people in my class who'd taken one look at the wall and shaken their heads with fear in their eyes. Even after watching someone else do it. *Yeah, sure, that guy can do it. He's the trainer. But* I *can't do it.* Seemed to me that it wasn't so much that people *thought* the wall, the Illusion, was real. It was that they *feared* it was real. They feared that walking through the wall was going to hurt. That even trying to go through it was going to make them look like idiots. And so it did.

Thing is, it *does* hurt to walk through walls. So if you feared that, you weren't wrong. And as you started to push through the wall, you felt that pain. For some, it was the tingles of making progress. For others, it was the pain of jabbing their finger into a hard and unyielding surface that felt pretty damn real for an illusion.

For the people who made it through, something within them was trumping the fear. Not a hundred percent. Pretty sure my fear, the first time through, was a solid 49.9 percent, and whatever had trumped it was 50.1 percent at best.

But that was good enough.

If you could manage it.

And if you couldn't... well...

"I can see the Illusion," Angela said, her tone still bored. Like a chastised kid who was only answering my questions now to avoid a talking-to about rudeness from some parental authority figure later. She probed my shoulder with her fingers. "I can see where your cells are still twisted out of place from when everything in you shifted to accommodate the wall. It's worst here."

I'd been grabbing my deltoid, where the cup of my palm curved perfectly around my shoulder, but Angela was pressing against the skin that was lower down on my arm, where I'd gotten vaccination shots as a kid. The muscle aches were similar. And now that she'd mentioned it—and was pushing on it—that spot did feel a little closer to the most tingling pain as well. Which I could tell now was radiating outward from deep inside.

"You led with your shoulder, didn't you? Pressed this part right into the wall."

"Yeah."

"Was the wall rock?"

"...yeah..."

"And backlit?"

"Yeah. How'd you know?"

"You've got some rock dust left behind and..." She grimaced, one corner of her mouth skewing to the side as her upper lip curled outward.

It was not encouraging.

My pulse raced.

"And what?" I asked. Something more? Something worse than rock dust? How bad was rock dust?

"Hold on." She set the Twister on the massage table, aiming the vent at my shoulder, and bent down next to me, lifting the massage table's sheet up over her head. The table jostled as she rustled things around on the shelves beneath me.

"Here we go." She popped up with something that looked like a hand-held vacuum cleaner. Plugged it in next to the Twister. Turned it on. It sounded like a hand-held vacuum cleaner. She applied the suction end to her own hand, seemed satisfied, and then aimed it at my shoulder.

Pain. I grunted.

"Sorry," she said. "Guess I should've warned you."

But she didn't look sorry. She Mona Lisa smiled, like she kinda liked it.

The suction didn't hurt so much that I couldn't take it, but it wasn't the kind of vacuum suction I'd been expecting, where your skin moves like little waves toward the pull and it's nothing more than fun and funny when you're a kid.

It was like bits and pieces of something in me were being sucked out. I'd never had a kidney stone, which, given the body part involved, was probably worse, but I imagined this pain was similar. Something not supposed to be in me and too big to pass without notice was leaving abruptly. Many somethings. I could hear the faint ping and thud of each vacating bit as it hit what I presumed was a filter in the vacuum.

I looked over at it. The suction end was black plastic. A red and black patterned bag collected all the debris. The model name was *Dust Devil*.

Of course it was. I snort-chuckled and shook my head at my life. Some people cry over what happens to them and shrink into themselves over time, and other people laugh amidst their bewilderment and then make the best of their new normal. I tended toward the latter.

The initial shock of the dust-removal procedure waned, and soon after, so did the pain. What was left behind felt like my usual shoulder. Functional and there when I needed it, but otherwise not something I had to pay much attention.

"I think it's working," I said.

Angela grimaced again. "For the rock dust, yeah."

Huh. But not for the something else. Something else was still in my shoulder. And it still had Angela concerned. Which meant it was probably worse than dust, even though the dust hurt and the something else didn't.

Great.

"What else do you see?" I asked.

Angela didn't answer. I thought maybe she couldn't hear me over the Twister and the Dust Devil. She had one in each hand, aimed at my shoulder, her face pinched in concentration. Lips puckered. She had great lips. The bottom one a little fuller than the top.

She turned off the Dust Devil first, then finished with the Twister, probing my shoulder with her fingers again, before turning it off as well. She took both pieces of equipment, lifted the sheet, and stashed them under the massage table.

"Sit up," she said.

I did, on the right side of the table, leaning forward to

grip the cushion's edge and letting my legs dangle over the side. The concrete floor had a sheen, but it was dull right below my feet.

Angela hopped up and sat next to me. Her braid fell to the front of her shoulder.

"What's the diagnosis, doc? Am I gonna live?"

I was hoping for a laugh, an immediate affirmative response.

Angela sighed and hung her head. "About that..."

My stomach clenched, my muscles tightening, my body suddenly on high alert. I whipped my head to look at her straight on. She was staring down at her hands, rubbing her thumb.

Oh, this was not good. This was *not* good.

"No candy coating," I said, the tone of my voice rising in pitch. "Just give it to me straight."

Angela nodded, her shoulders relaxing. She glanced at me but then looked down again. "You're, uh, you're not gonna die."

I sighed with relief as she said:

"Yet."

I froze, muscles tense as my eyeballs darted around in their sockets trying to find a meaning to her words that might make them more palatable.

"You have something in your shoulder."

"No kidding. What? Light?"

She nodded. "There's light, but that'll take care of itself in time. It's not a problem."

"Well, that's good. So, what else is there? You asked if the wall was rock. You asked if it was lit. You didn't ask about anything else."

And never mind that no one at training had mentioned any types of wall material posing a particular problem.

Some training.

"Yeah," Angela said. "That's the thing. I don't know what it is."

My body was so charged, my head hair was standing on end. I felt like my scalp was pulling away from my skull.

"Well, then, how do you know it's gonna…" I couldn't say the words. Wasn't gonna, and you couldn't make me. If I refused to say them, then maybe they'd never come true.

"The rock dust is gone. The light is fading, working itself out. All your cells are reoriented properly; they're no longer twisted out of place. But some of them are…" Her palms rotated skyward and her fingers curled as if she was grasping for the words.

"Are what?"

She glanced at me. Before she could look back down again, I grabbed her chin and held it in place. Her eyes were a coal black, and I'd never seen a pair that held more worry.

"Just tell me."

"I'm trying. If you'd needed sugar coating, this would be taking a lot longer. I'm not good at sugar coating. I'm—"

"Stalling. Just say it. What's going on in my shoulder?"

She shook her head. "That's another thing. It isn't just your shoulder."

I let her go and looked at my lap, feeling weights behind my eyes. I swallowed hard.

She hopped off the massage table.

"You're leaving me?"

She met my eye. An eternity passed before she spoke. "I need to talk to Darryl."

"Who?"

"The guy who let you in."

"Talk to him about what?"

"Just wait here."

I nodded. At least she wasn't kicking me out.

Yet.

I couldn't sit up anymore. The effort to both sit up and hold myself together was just too much. I twisted my butt a quarter turn, bringing my legs back up on the table, and lay back, flopping my forearm over my eyes.

"I'll be back in a second," Angela said.

It was a lot longer than a second. And in that time I ran through what had happened that morning, what I had done, at least a dozen times. I'd pushed through the wall. I'd led with my shoulder. I'd done what they'd said to do, how they'd said to do it. But no one had mentioned anything in training about dying. Cells twisting? Sure. They'd mentioned that. But not even *that* was a guaranteed consequence. I'd been told that with practice even that could be avoided. I was told it was all safe.

But why shouldn't I expect some misinformation? It's not like this place was by and for and composed of the virtuous. For all I knew, Management and their training protocol was the least virtuous of all.

Angela pushed the saloon-style door open and came in with a pep in her step and a pad of paper in hand.

"Okay. I think we can get you an appointment with Cherise Montaire."

Cherise Montaire? It sounded vaguely familiar. "Why do I know that name?"

She smiled at me. It was a strange smile, but it was the first one I'd seen on her. And it made her very pretty. I wondered what she looked like smiling at full watt.

She said, "You ever meet someone whose face looked familiar, but you couldn't place it? And every time you see that person, they look like someone other than who they are, but you can't remember who?"

"I guess."

"You probably don't remember too well, because that's the point. They don't want to be recognized. They don't want to be remembered. Well, Cherise Montaire takes that to a whole nother level. Even her name is like that."

"Huh. And she can help me?"

The smile faded. "Well, it's the best Darryl and I could come up with."

I wasn't sure I trusted Darryl at all, let alone to help me, but I kept my mouth shut. I had no other options and no one to ask. Terry wouldn't be any use.

"What's your name?" Angela was saying.

"Corbin Kohl."

"How do you spell that?"

"First name, C-O-R-B-I-N. Last name, K-O-H-L."

Angela wrote it on her pad. "I'm going to make the call. I think it's best. She can be... well... Do you have a phone number?"

"Yeah. Answering machine, too." I gave her the number. "When do you think she can get me in?"

"No idea. Hopefully soon, you..." She shook her head. Like she'd said too much.

"I what?"

"You should go do something that calms you down."

"That's not what you were about to say."

"No, but it's still what you should do. I'll leave you a message when I've got your appointment."

She turned to leave the room.

"Wait? That's it?"

I didn't want to be alone. I was already alone here. Hadn't thought I could get much more alone. But there's not much that's worse than facing a problem alone.

Angela reached for my hand and squeezed. I fought the urge to get a better grip around her fingers and never let go.

Now was the time most people would say something like *You're gonna be okay.* Or *We're gonna get you through this.*

But Angela didn't say anything. Just squeezed my hand and left.

7

I pulled open the parlor's glass front door, nose wrinkling instinctively at the sulfur smell, and turned left, down the shoe-goo-marbled sidewalk in full glare of the Pit.

I was headed nowhere in particular. Just letting myself bake in the heat and the bright glare of the yellow sky, hoping it might all drown out the other stuff I was feeling.

Two hours down, twenty-three more to go. I wondered how much more trouble I could get myself into.

On the plus side, I had no more pain. Had no idea what was going on in my body that was slowly...

Wait.

Slowly?

Angela had never said anything about speed. In fact, she seemed in a hurry to get me an appointment. In fact, it was her urgency that made me okay with leaving the appointment-making in Angela's hands.

Ah hell, how fast was this thing gonna play out? How

long did I have left? And what would happen to me once it was done?

Because, okay, I didn't really like to think about it. But the fact was, I was pretty sure that I was already D-E-A-D. I mean, I was here, wasn't I? Not sure how I'd gotten here. Not even sure where here was. One day I was mowing the lawn for my parents' elderly neighbor; next thing I knew, I was waking up on a table under bright lights with people from Management looking down at me.

At first I figured I had been kidnapped and taken to some unfamiliar place. But it didn't take long to realize I was no longer on Earth at all. I mean, four blocks over, a giant Pit was spewing fire and brimstone into the air. There's a crater on Earth, in the Middle East, that's been burning since the early 1970s. It's big, a couple hundred feet across at least, and when the light's just right, around dusk or dawn, the crater glows red with rivulets of fire snaking up the craggy walls. It's impressive.

But it's nothing like the Pit.

And I'm not talking just its hellfire appearance.

The Pit is more than ten times the size of the crater burning on Earth; it's four thousand feet across, at least, over three-quarters of a mile. It throws up flames ten stories high, spits burning embers, coughs up smoke.

But I'll say it again: it's more than just the Pit's appearance.

Case in point: Just by thinking about it, and with nowhere else in mind to go, I found myself crossing a four-lane street and heading toward it.

You'd think the buildings would become dilapidated the closer you got to the Pit—who wants to live there, right?—but the architecture actually becomes more grand. The materials more luxurious. It's like penance and a status symbol all in one, living and working near the Pit.

Three blocks to go, and the street I crossed next was six lanes wide. People choose to drive past here. On purpose. Even if they don't have to.

Two blocks to go, and the park that surrounds the Pit came into view. Purgatorium Park. Believe it or not, it's lined with trees. Heat-worshipper trees. They're not like any trees I ever saw back on Earth. They're shaped like coned popsicles, like evergreens with the bottom branches trimmed away, but the trunk is smooth—except for the ones with giant gnarly burls—and they've got big, waxy leaves, like magnolia trees. No blooms, though. And they're resistant to heat. More than resistant, they love it. They all lean toward the Pit, like sunflowers following the sun.

I reached the edge of the park and stopped. Technically one block to go, the park block.

The park grounds is made up of packed black dirt. Gritty. Charred rock bits, probably.

Inside the circle of heat-worshipper trees, the rim of the pit, the caldera, rises maybe forty feet above the park. About as high as a three-story building.

People were standing up on the edge like it was some kind of tourist attraction. I had yet to get that close. And I didn't think I'd be getting that close now.

I made it as far as one of the trees and leaned against the

trunk. Another weird thing about the heat-worshipper trees? They sweat. So I slid down the trunk to my butt faster than I'd intended, hitting my tailbone hard enough to knock some wind out of me. I caught my breath. Put my forearms on my bent knees and clasped my hands together. Let out a sigh.

I could hear the Pit bubbling and popping, pumping out heat and spewing smoke and embers. I tilted my face up to the Pit, hoping it would burn away all the dross.

But none of me was dross. Not here. Not to the Pit. Like the trees, like the people who lived and worked in its closest blocks, I was unharmed by the Pit. Uncomfortable? Sure. Hot and sweaty? Absolutely. But not harmed. Sitting this close would not burn my skin or bake my insides.

I rubbed my shoulder, wishing the heat could fix what was happening inside my body. But that, too, was unlikely. I had a feeling nothing good happened here, in the City. Nothing got better. Things only broke down.

Only changed for the worse.

And just when I was getting used to my new normal. Meeting people. Developing my routine.

I was really starting to hate change.

But at least I had the whole rest of the day and night before I had to appear in Terry's office at nine o'clock tomorrow. I checked my watch. Twenty-one hours. Twenty-one hours to do—what? Tackle my bucket list? Too late for that. The only thing I knew of to look forward to around here was my appointment with Cherise Montaire. And that anticipation was less joyful excitement, more dread and necessity.

The Physical Services Parlor wasn't exactly on the way home, but I figured Angela had had enough time to make the call, and I had time to spare, so I stood and made my way back, figuring I could get my appointment details before grabbing some lunch.

But the massage parlor's glass front door was locked. No *ding-dong* for me. And no one came to the door when I pounded like a madman.

8

If the Pit were a clock face and the Management Building was at six o'clock, then I lived at one o'clock.

I had a studio apartment on the third floor of a five-story apartment complex. The building was old stucco construction and falling apart, but it had its perks. For one, two bus lines stopped right outside the front door. For another, it was thirty-six blocks from the Pit. No prestige for me, but there were times when I thought I caught a whiff of fresh air.

Fair trade. Totally worth it.

For a third perk, the complex predated the mandate about building orientation relative to the Pit—all entrances should face the Pit; all Pit-facing windows should stretch floor to ceiling; all living-space dimensions should be widest on the Pit side, that sort of thing. My pre-mandate apartment bucked all those requirements. I had an interior entrance and all my windows faced away from the Pit, which helped keep my studio... well, not cool, exactly, but less hot for sure. Helped me sleep better, too. There's no real darkness here, no night per se, but I'd managed to maintain some semblance of a circadian rhythm thanks to my studio's relative coolness, my windows facing away from the Pit glare, and a hefty set of double-layered blackout curtains that had been left behind by the previous tenant.

My apartment was simple. Mostly wood and beige. The front door opened onto a short hallway. Walk-in closet to the right, bathroom to the left. Then a wide open room with a kitchenette on the left wall.

On the right, just after the closet, I had a twin bed, an empty passthrough bookshelf that acted as a wall and held an old bunny-ears, color-tube-style TV, which sat on a lazy Susan. And then I had an old wood coffee table and an old brown-and-orange-plaid couch, set right under the windows. All the furniture was all here when I got here.

I didn't have much by way of decoration, or stuff. Just the basics. For instance, my phone sat alone on the coffee table. The phone was beige, a corded handset and answering machine combo with an extra-large tilted display screen, big buttons, and a red message light.

And right now, the message light was refusing to blink.

I picked up the phone receiver and held it to my ear. Dial tone. So it was working. I set it down again, fast, just in case Angela chose that moment to call.

But the phone remained silent.

I checked my fridge. The shelves were empty save for condiments and a few slices of bread still in the plastic bag and stored next to the cooling element to keep them fresh as long as possible. I could've made myself a mustard sandwich, but I wasn't much hungry.

Still no phone ring.

I spotted the phone book sitting on the beige laminate kitchen counter. It had been gifted to me as part of my move-in welcome package, along with some coupons to local restaurants. Back home, I would have recycled it immediately. Here, my studio was bare. I had nothing. It was nice to own something. And a lonely phonebook on the kitchen counter couldn't exactly qualify as clutter.

I flipped to *M* in the white pages. Cherise Montaire wasn't in the phone book.

I closed the book and rapped my fingers on the cover. Should I chance missing Angela's call?

I sat on my plaid couch. My knee bounced. My fingers gave themselves a nice fidgety massage. My lungs heaved heavy sighs, hundreds and hundreds of them before I finally decided I should do it, I should chance missing her call. Because, really, she might never call. And the waiting was torture. The waiting, alone, could kill me.

I dialed directory assistance, but the person on the other end could not connect me to a Cherise Montaire.

"I have no record of that listing, sir."

I hung up. Checked my watch. A little after two o'clock. Nineteen hours left of my free day.

So much for spending it on fun.

9

I headed back outside.

There is no hottest part of the day here, because, as I've said, there is no sun around which the City is rotating. There are no rhythms of light and dark, of cool and hot.

There's only light.

There's only hot.

The only thing that might have a rhythm is the spewing of sulfur from the caldera. Sometimes it's thick, sometimes it's barely present. Sometimes it's white or gray or black as coal.

But if it had a rhythm, I hadn't figured it out yet.

Right now, as I waited for the bus on the sidewalk corner outside my building, the ever bright yellowish-white sky overhead, I couldn't see it, I couldn't see the smoke. Across the street from my building was a self-storage facility with clear glass exterior walls that revealed nothing but orange doors and the untold crap hoarded behind them. Ten glorious floors worth. It almost completely blocked the Pit.

And even standing right in front of my building, with my back pressed against the wall, I was still in the storage building's shade, glorious shade.

But I could smell it.

The sulfur.

If I had to guess, based on smell, I'd say the smoke was approaching coal level. Thick and black. I could feel dust clinging to my nostril hairs. A quick rub of my nose—yup, my thumb was smeared with black grit.

And forget your clothes. You might put on a pink or yellow shirt in the morning, but when you got home that night, it would be gray.

My white polo shirt was already gray. My Bermuda shorts were too dark blue to show the dust, but they felt grimy. I was still wearing them, though. My closet's as bare as the rest of my apartment.

I spotted the Red bus trundling down the three-lane street and stood up off the wall, made my way to the curb.

The Red buses resemble the old yellow school buses of my youth, only painted red for easy identification, and instead of windows, they're open to the air. The seats are high-backed like I remember, too. All I needed was a backpack and a bully to try to take it from me, and it'd be almost like twenty years ago. I climbed aboard and slid into the red vinyl seat right behind the driver. The backs of my legs started sweating immediately. It's just a theory I have, so far, but it's like the City is made up of the worst experiences from Earth.

I still didn't know my way around very well, let alone by bus, but if I lived at one o'clock on the Pit's clock face, then the place I was headed to was at eight o'clock and a lot closer to the Pit. According to the colorful bus map posted behind the driver, it would be about a forty-five-minute bus ride.

Back home, only people with lower incomes rode the bus. People who couldn't afford a car. Or at least couldn't afford one yet.

But here, in the City, pretty much everyone rode the bus. There were people who had cars—I'd seen them driving around—but I didn't know how they'd gotten them. And not just because I had yet to see a car dealership anywhere. Same as I didn't know how people got luxury apartments close to the Pit, and not just because I had yet to see a *For Sale* sign anywhere. Not that I wanted to live closer to the heat and the smoke and the sulfur smell, but still. I understood these things held appeal. Status. Convenience. And I bet the couches were comfy, the TV's bigger and flatter, too.

How did someone move up in this world?

I had no clue.

This bus? I didn't pay to get on. I just waltzed right up the stairs. The bus driver didn't even look at me. Just shut the door after the last person stepped on. So, if I didn't pay to get on the bus, then how was the bus driver getting paid?

My guess?

He probably wasn't.

My job? It was less a carrot situation and more of a stick situation. I wasn't getting paid. I was given a studio apartment and told that I could keep it if I kept coming to work.

Food was another matter, though. I'd gotten restaurant coupons as part of my welcome package, right? Coupons imply an exchange. Food for something. But what kind of something? Back home, I would have said money. Around here? I had no idea.

But I wasn't starving. Not quite. The Management Building had a cafeteria on the second floor. I could eat there for free. But I could not take food out. I knew this, because I tried once. I got banned for twenty-four hours. There's no security or anything. Nobody stopped and frisked me at the exit. But when I got home, my answering machine's red light was blinking. Terry had left me a message, telling me to call him back.

"You took a ham sandwich out of the cafeteria today."

"Yeah, why? Is that a problem?"

"It is."

"Oh. Sorry. I'd give it back, but I just ate it for dinner."

"Well, I hope it was filling. You can return to the cafeteria day after tomorrow."

The next morning, my stomach rumbling, I tried to stop at the cafeteria anyway, but the door wouldn't open. Elevator or stairwell. (And the escalator only exits down.)

I wear no kind of identity bracelet. I carry no magic key card. Unless they put a chip in me—and I'd inspected every inch of my neck and arms and found nothing—then I had no idea how they were keeping tabs on me. But they knew my every move.

Although, without money, I didn't make many.

The air thickened quickly with smoke and the smell of

sulfur as the bus entered the six-lane road that circles Purgatorium Park. City traffic flow is designed like the spokes on a bicycle wheel. You drive toward the center and circle the Pit until you find the spoke that'll take you back out in the direction you want to go. I supposed it was efficient. But if I had a car, I'd weave through the back side streets.

The Red bus circles Purgatorium Park, stopping at each spoke, and then heads back out toward my apartment building, on the one o'clock spoke. I stayed on until the eight o'clock stop, where I told the driver thanks and hopped off the bus. After the bus trundled off again, I ran across the six-lane street and hoofed it from there.

Management's Training Facilities building stands seven streets from the Pit, takes up an entire block, and looks like a big white cube, like an old Masonic lodge, kinda, but with floor-to-ceiling windows on the Pit side. Mirrored glass. It didn't do anything to keep out the glare or the heat, but it did keep pedestrians from gawking.

I entered through the sliding glass doors. The lobby stretched the length of the mirrored windows and the ceiling was four stories high, the height of the building—but it wasn't very deep. Maybe twenty feet at most. In that sense it reminded me of the narrow green lobby at the Physical Services Parlor. Oversized paintings of boring landscapes hung on the walls, and a bored receptionist greeted visitors from a half-wall desk just inside the entrance.

He stood to assist me, but I waved him off. "I know where I'm going."

I didn't know if that would fly. There was a good chance he'd sit back down and call for someone to come take care of me. So I hurried around his desk to the bank of elevators behind him—four to the right, four to the left—and pushed the call button. One of the eight bays opened immediately. I stepped inside and pushed the close button.

The elevator could take me up four floors, but it could also take me down to a dozen more below ground. Maybe more than a dozen. There was a mysterious keyed button below the B12 button.

I hit B4. The elevator dropped and opened onto another bay. I stepped out.

One door to my left, one door to my right. Neither one marked. Every surface white. Everything soundproof. Like if you weren't supposed to be here, then Management didn't want you figuring out where you were.

But I'd been here a few times, after wall walk-through trainings, and after getting disoriented the first time, even with an escort, I started paying more attention to things like elevator buttons and right or left turns. The people I needed to talk to were on this floor, behind one of these two identical doors at either end of the elevator bay.

And I'd gotten on an elevator on the right side of the bank.

Which meant Cellular Twist services was to the left.

10

Like the rest of the silent hallway of eight elevator bays, the door to Cellular Twist services was white, opaque.

Uninviting.

But I didn't bother knocking. If this was the right door, they wouldn't be able to hear me anyway.

I turned the knob, opening the door a crack, and immediately knew I'd picked the right room. The sound roaring out at me was like a dozen hair dryers all blowing at once, and the fetid air reeked like a high school weight room after practice.

I slipped inside the room and shut the door behind me, then stood against the wall.

Cellular Twist Services, like the rest of the building, was stark and white. But being underground did not keep it cool. If anything, it felt hotter down here than it was upstairs. For one thing, the humidity was higher. For another, I wouldn't be surprised if the inferno that fueled the caldera also cradled the Training Facilities' basement floors.

All ten of the Twister service stations had a patient stretched out on a waist-high bed, with their feet pointed toward me. The beds were all metal tube construction, like gurneys but without the wheels or rails, and the mattress pads were an ugly lime yellow that was forgiving about stains. Good thing too, because everyone was sweating. Not a dry shirt in sight.

The techs all wore big goggles, big steampunk-looking things, and they all held Twisters connected by cords to waist-high machines that rolled around behind them as they moved around the service bed. The machine's purpose had never been explained to me—even when I'd asked—so I'd decided to think of it as a jet pack.

The techs' Twisters were twice as big as Angela's, and the techs stood further away from their patients when they used them. Seeing the room from this perspective, against the wall, not being worked on, it looked clinical, like quarantine, like the techs had been advised not to touch us, not to get close. The techs weren't wearing protective suits, just their own regular clothes. Shorts and T-shirts mostly. But their body language had the feel of being clad in a protective suit.

Most techs were aiming their Twisters at their patients' shoulders, but a few were aiming at their patient's head or hand, or at a foot. It all depended on what body part the person had led with, what they'd used to break the surface of the wall.

At the farthest station to the left, my favorite tech, Big John, was storing his Twister atop his machine. His patient was sitting up and scooting off the table. I couldn't hear them over the roar, and they were probably too far away for me to hear them regardless, but they made hand movements like they were saying bye to each other, thanks. The patient then walked my way, stopping just short of me to take a seat in one of the chairs along the wall. Trainees never wandered about alone. They were escorted everywhere.

I nodded hello at the guy as I scurried past him.

"Hey, John?" I said as I reached the foot of the bed. Big John didn't hear me, though. The rest of the stations were still doing their noisy thing, and John had his back to me, doing something with the jet pack.

I stepped closer and reached up to nudge his shoulder.

He startled and slowly turned around to tower over me.

"Corbin? Hey, man. What are you doing here?"

As far as I knew, nobody called him Big John to his face, but if you said the name Big John in mixed trainee company, everybody knew who you were talking about. Big John was a big guy. Just big. Six foot five at least. Four hundred pounds at least. The bottom of his T-shirts never quite reached the top of his gym shorts. He had a dimpled chin and was generous with the smiles. His service goggles were pushed up on his forehead, but his eyes were still rimmed with pressure marks.

I glanced to my right. The other nine service techs were all still working, but they'd begin finishing up soon, which meant the escorts would be here soon. And there was also the chance that the receptionist upstairs had been given one of those luxury apartments by the Pit, and so cared about keeping his job, which would mean that someone like security could show up any second as well. So I got to the point.

"Could you take a look at me? I walked through a rock wall this morning."

"Oh, yeah, that can be rough. Sure thing. Climb aboard."

I crawled atop the yellow mattress, lay on my back, and got comfortable on the bed. John pulled his goggles over his eyes. Looked down at me. Not for the first time, I tried not to laugh. His goggles pinched his nose and pulled at his top lip, making it curl up, and his eyebrows stuck out above the goggle frames. In previous sessions, I'd never seen his eyebrows move, but right now they seemed to be trying their darnedest to puzzle together.

"See anything?" I asked.

"Uh..." He cocked his head to the side. "Yeah. Or, well..." He leaned closer—but not too close, I noticed. "Yes and no."

My heart rate sped up. I hadn't realized just how much of me had been hoping for an all clear.

He said, "Did you already have a service done?"

"Yeah. Why?"

"Where'd you go?"

"The Physical Services Parlor. Over off Spoke 6, about four blocks up."

"Near the Management Building?"

"Yeah. Why? Is it bad? The store was sketchy as all get."

"No," John said, and then he reached his hand out. Didn't touch me. But his outstretched palm hovered over my right shoulder, then traveled over my chest. "Did Angela do it? Dark braid? Surly demeanor?"

"Yeah," I said. "How'd you know?"

"Did she send you here?"

"No. She—"

"Didn't think so," he said with a chuckle. "What did she tell you to do?"

"So I should listen to her?"

"To Angela Ruiz? Yeah. You should listen to her." John looked over his shoulder and then leaned closer to me, spoke quieter. "Even with these goggles we're all wearing, she's a way better Twister than anyone around here."

He stood up straight again, took off the glasses, set them on the jet pack. Then he motioned his hand for me to sit up. I did, dangling my legs over the side of the table. He perched on the edge, one leg bent and dangling like mine, the other fully extended and touching the ground.

The roar of the rest of the Twisters started quieting down as more techs finished their services.

John turned to me, his hands folded in his lap. "What did Angela tell you?"

"She... she said she got all the rock dust but that there was something else in..."

"Inside you. Yeah." As was typical of Management personnel, John's tone and expression didn't reveal much. "What did she tell you to do?"

"What would *you* tell me to do?"

"Me?" John sat up straighter, puffed his cheeks, blew out a breath. "Officially or unofficially?"

"Seriously?"

He shrugged. "Officially, your cells are all oriented properly and I see no debris left behind, so our work here is done."

"Unofficially?"

He looked out at the other nine service stations, the other nine techs. If monsters be among them, I didn't notice any paying much attention to us.

But John must've seen things differently, because he leaned back and spoke behind my ear.

"Unofficially, there's something in you that shouldn't be there. But I'm not smart enough to tell you what it is, other than it looks like it's slowly eating away at you. Like a cancer, but without the tumor. What to *do* about it?" He shrugged. "Unofficially? Meaning don't let anyone here know I said this. I would've sent you to Angela. Whatever she told you to do, you need to go do it."

11

There's something in you that shouldn't be there.

I'd heard the same diagnosis from Angela, but having it confirmed by the Twister service guy I trusted most had my body itching like crazy. As I rode the elevator alone, up the twelve floors to ground level, I scratched aggressively at my arms and shoulders, leaving a crosshatch of red welts behind—and knowing it wasn't doing any good. The culprit was too down deep inside me, too entwined with my cells.

I left the Training Facilities without incident. The receptionist didn't even look up when I came off the elevator and walked past his desk, my steps echoing in the cavernous lobby.

It was getting close to dinner time. Not that I could tell that by stepping outside. The sky overhead shined yellowish-white, as brightly as ever. But the outdoors entered my nose and lungs easier than usual. Seven blocks away, the Pit was steaming up clear rivulets of heat rather than plumes of smoke. I stood on the colorfully marbled sidewalk and breathed deeply, wondering if the air quality had any effect on my prognosis.

Officially or unofficially?

Back home, I'd know the answer.

Here, it could go one of three ways.

But I was learning to fear the worst.

My stomach growled. The Training Facilities had a cafeteria, as well as dorms and other amenities, but, as easy a time as I had getting in, I didn't want to push my luck. On my last day at the facility, when I'd graduated, so to speak, they'd made it sound like it would be best if I forgot the place. I saw a lot of people during training, but we were kept busy, housed separately, ate separately. I didn't really have a chance to make any friends. Unless I counted Big John as a friend. Which, given that he'd just helped me unofficially, I supposed I could do. What kind of guy might Big John be outside of work? A sports bar guy? A D&D guy? Maybe a cooking guy or a saxophone guy?

Back home, I'd been an outdoor guy. Hiking and camping and that kind of thing. That wasn't really an extracurricular option around here, aside from the hiking-as-walking bit. I didn't mind hiking the pavement and exploring the City, but while glass and concrete jungles might be a thing, it's not trees.

The Management Building and its cafeteria was five blocks from the Pit, off Spoke 6. As the wheel turns, that wasn't too far. So I walked two blocks closer to the Pit, and then took a right and walked to Spoke 6.

This part of the City is mostly office buildings and apartment complexes with stores on the ground floor. Most of them five or six stories tall. A lot of the buildings in the City have the same number of floors as the number of blocks they stand away from the Pit. But that wasn't a hard and fast rule. The Management Building's thirty-three stories, and the huge, multi-colon digital clocks that topped it on all four sides, towered above its neighbors.

A few lucky people with cars put-putted past me. The curved streets seemed to slow people down. Or maybe it was that most people drove modest four-door sedans with no power. Most people. Right after I moved into my studio, I saw a fire-red sports car zoom past my building. Don't ask me what make and model it was, let alone why or how it exists at all, because I have no idea.

Yet.

I couldn't help thinking that word. I'm a curious soul. Given enough time, I would solve the mystery. But a bigger part of me hoped that my being in the City was all a mistake or a dream, temporary, and I'd be home again soon. The more days I spent here, the less likely it seemed that would eventually happen, but I was nothing if not hopeful about getting back home. Tomorrow morning would be good. I used to keep my room chilled to sixty-eight degrees. I imagined myself waking up in my old bed, all snuggled in my favorite blankets, not having to deal with this thing happening inside me.

Whatever she told you to do, you need to go do it.

Before I left, I'd asked John if he knew a Cherise Montaire.

"The name sounds familiar," he'd said, scrunching his face up in thought.

"Angela told me to make an appointment with her."

"Then why are you here?"

At that point, John's next patient had approached and he'd ushered me away, lest I get caught. I didn't have time to tell him that, actually, Angela had said that *she'd* make the appointment, but hadn't gotten back to me yet.

Although, for all I knew, my red message light, back at my studio, was blinking in my absence.

It's slowly eating away at you.

When I reached Spoke 6 and the Management Building, I wasn't feeling as hungry as I'd thought, so I crossed the street and headed to the front of block five and the Physical Services Parlor. I pulled on the glass door's metal crossbar handle, but it wouldn't open, wouldn't *ding* for me. But I was definitely feeling the *dong*.

Dong-dong donnng.

I put my face up to the window and shielded my eyes with my hands. The hidden door in the green pressboard wall was closed, as was the hidden compartment. Nothing to see here but a small, empty room.

Still, I stood there with my forehead pressed to the glass for longer than I can say, like if I just kept a vigil, the hidden door would open and Angela or even Darryl would appear and tell me they'd gotten it all wrong.

Like a cancer, but without the tumor.

I stepped back and considered returning to the cafeteria, because all I had at home was the makings of a mustard sandwich, but I wasn't sure I'd ever be hungry again. All I wanted to do was get back to my studio and check my messages, plan my trip to see Cherise Montaire, assuming the messages were good. Otherwise I'd call it a night.

Assuming I could sleep.

12

Five blocks away, outside the floor-to-ceiling windows of Terry's red carpeted office on the twenty-first floor, the Pit smoke rose from the burning caldera like a slippery black serpent undulating into the air, amidst glowing red embers. I'd never seen so clearly the line where thick smoke ended and fresh air began.

I didn't think Terry had either. It was a few minutes past nine. Terry had been sitting at his glass desk, in his rolling gold chair, watching the smoke when I'd first stepped into his office. He'd swiveled to look back and acknowledge me and then swiveled right back around to face the window. Neither one of us had said a word yet. The scent of sulfur was less pronounced than usual, both outside and in Terry's office, but the heat was almost unbearable. Sweat was dripping from my armpits down my ribs.

"What's it mean?" I asked about the smoke.

He didn't answer me. But the question seemed to break the smoke's spell on him. He turned in his chair to face me.

But he didn't look at me. He looked at his hands in his lap. He looked somber.

"Close the door."

"Um, okay." Nerves in my belly started undulating upward, into my chest, not unlike the smoke outside Terry's windows. This was the first time he'd ever asked me to close the door. Back home, being asked to close the door would have meant bad things far more often than not, so I could only imagine how bad the next few minutes with Terry would be.

I scurried to the door, rustling the plastic red carpet beneath my feet. Terry's assistant, a wizened old guy with dark gray hair slicked back with sweat, was slouched in his desk chair, arms resting on his sternum, teeth cracking a hard peppermint candy.

His eyelids fluttered open.

I smiled awkwardly at him as I reached for the knob and pulled the door shut.

I returned to the center of the room, equidistant between Terry's glass desk and the door and stood at parade rest, feet hip-width wide, hands clasped behind my back. Shoulders back, head high. I stared not at Terry but above his head, through his window, at the undulating black smoke.

At least my body *looked* ready to handle whatever came next, even if I, myself, was not ready. Because mentally, I was not ready at all.

There had been no blinking red light on my answering machine last night. No messages, no appointment instructions. I'd stripped off my soot-soiled shorts and polo shirt and done my best to hand-wash them in the sink. (Don't ask me where the water comes from, but the water pressure's not great, and it smells and tastes like sulfur. The tenant before me left behind a water filter in the fridge, and I was very grateful.)

I'd laid my washed clothes out on the kitchenette counter to dry. I'd taken my phone from the coffee table and threaded it through the passthrough bookshelf so that it would be easier to answer if Angela called. And then I'd closed the blackout curtains and climbed into my twin bed, pulling my thin, lone blanket over my head. I didn't think I'd be able to sleep, but I'd closed my eyes anyway and lengthened my breathing, pursing my lips on the exhale. Next thing I knew I was throwing off the sweaty cover and stretching out of the fetal position.

For a second it had been a good morning. But then yesterday's events came flooding back into my mind on a wave of fearful thoughts:

Something in me was eating me alive.

Angela still hadn't called about my appointment with Cherise Montaire.

And I had to be in Terry's office by nine o'clock *sharp*.

The clothes I'd left on the counter had dried stiff to the touch. Not that I had to wear the same thing two days in a row. I'd received clothes from the training facility in an event that reminded me of shopping with my mom at a by-the-pound store on fifty-percent-off day. I'd managed to score a few shirts and a few pairs of extra shorts that fit me pretty well. So I was now dressed in a pair of shiny purple basketball shorts with matte yellow stripes down the sides and a green T-shirt that read *Lucky*.

You gotta find support where you can get it.

Terry put his hands on the glass desk, palms down, fingers spread. Like he, too, was bracing himself for what was next.

Oh, this was not good. This could not be good.

Terry looked up at me and smiled. Sort of. His mouth was very tight. Today's suit was navy blue with a light blue tie. His blond hair, combed up from the back, had listed off to the side.

"How long have you been here, now, Kohl?"

"I don't know. When was I taken? *Why* was I taken? How long was I out for before I woke up on the table?"

"It's three weeks of training, right?" Terry said, like I hadn't spoken at all. "And you've been in your studio, what, five days?"

"Counting today? Sounds about right."

They'd given me a couple days to get settled in and teach myself the bus system before expecting me in Terry's office and giving me my first assignment: watch for an exchange between a woman with a sea-goat tattoo on her ankle and a person unknown, at the Hotel Burning Bright, expected to happen between six and eight in the morning yesterday. They hadn't said to make contact. They hadn't said to stop the exchange. They'd just said to observe. I had observed.

But I'd run after them to do so.

"I wasn't supposed to let them see me yesterday, was I?"

"What?"

"At the hotel. I wouldn't have been able to see what happened if I hadn't run after them."

"No, no. Management is quite pleased with your performance. Quite pleased."

Huh. *Management* might be, but Terry sure didn't sound happy about it.

And here I'd thought he and 'Management' were one and the same. Guess that made Terry merely *middle* management.

"What are you smiling at?" he asked.

"Nothing. So, if I did a good job, what's the problem?"

"Same problem. New details."

"So the problem's not with me?"

"Oh, I wouldn't say that. *Carl!*" he yelled, rising taller in his chair to do so. Then, slouching back down again, "Get the door for Carl, would you?"

I opened the office door and found Carl slowly rising from his chair, palms pressed heavily against his big, dark desk to support the ascent.

From his own desk, Terry called out, "The file for Kohl, Carl."

Carl nodded, having ascended toward standing enough that his palms were now rising off the desk surface.

There was only one file, a red manila folder, on Carl's desk. So I hazarded a guess.

"This it?"

Carl nodded, still working on reaching his full height. Which wouldn't be much taller than Terry.

"I got it," I said, taking the file. It was thin, a few pages inside at most. "Thanks, Carl."

He nodded again and began his descent.

I shut the office door behind me and returned to my spot in the center of the room, holding the file in both hands, like a dinner plate.

"You're dismissed," Terry said.

"Uh…" Normally, those were two of my favorite words that ever came out of Terry's mouth, but… "Aren't you going to tell me about the assignment?"

"Same assignment. New details. They're in the file. Which you can read elsewhere. Frankly, I don't think I can take looking at that shirt you're wearing any longer. *Lucky.* And green to boot. Sheesh."

My assignment had been to watch an exchange. I'd done so. Exchange over. The only thing that could continue was the participants. "So I'm watching for Amlathe—"

"Ah-ah-ah! Stop saying that name, would you?"

"Sorry, but… why?"

Terry sighed. "Just read the file."

I shifted it onto my left palm and opened the cover.

"On your own time," Terry said. "It should be self-explanatory. Now get out of my office."

I tucked the file under my arm and headed out the door, said bye to Carl as I pushed the elevator call button, and then, when the doors didn't open immediately, I took the stairs.

The stairwell was cool as usual, relatively speaking. I would have sat down right there on the steps and read the file, but the lighting wasn't very good. I could see the back of my hand, but not the details of my knuckles.

I figured I'd read the file in the cafeteria, alongside some breakfast, but I had to check something first.

I headed over to the Physical Services Parlor.

Still closed. Still nothing but an empty green room behind the glass door.

I sighed and turned toward the street, pressing my lower back against the silver bar door handle. The street was quiet. And you couldn't say the light was bad here. The sky was shining down on the City in whitish-yellow today, slightly easier on the eyes than its other variation, yellowish-white. The smoke was still rising into the sky like a black serpent, which seemed to be keeping the sulfur smell on low, the air fresher than usual.

I could think of worse places to read.

13

I slid down the length of the Physical Services Parlor's glass door, back scraping on the metal handle, butt hitting the *hot* cement, *hot hot* through my shorts. I dug my heels into the ground, my back against the glass, and pushed myself back up a tad. I pulled Terry's file out from under my arm, the contents from the red cover, and set the cover on the ground to protect my butt.

Ass burn averted, I settled against the door, legs bent in front of me. I jogged the file contents on my knees.

Three, maybe four pages.

But paper-clipped to the top page was an envelope.

The envelope was gray, like ash, like burned-out embers from the Pit. It was clipped to the papers, sealed-side up. Someone had squiggled a red pen along the triangular edge of the flap, zig-zagging over the seal. I sniffed it. I don't know why. But it didn't smell like saliva. It smelled like a fire that had burned itself out. Not unpleasant. Kind of nostalgic, in fact. My grandparents, dad's side, had had a wood-burning fireplace that would smell like that in the morning.

I flipped the gray envelope over.

FOR CORBIN KOHL'S EYES ONLY had been written in tidy block letters. Same red pen.

The pavement crackled under the wheels of a car. I looked up as a taupe four-door sedan passed by. There was nobody across the street. I looked left. Two women in shorts opened up shop at the end of the block, then disappeared inside, leaving the shoe-goo-marbled sidewalk empty again. I looked right and found it the same. Empty. Just me.

And my file.

My stomach growled. But that would have to wait. And not just because I planned on sitting in front of the Physical Services Parlor until Angela arrived.

I had the sudden feeling that I shouldn't be reading this file anywhere near the Management Building.

But here? I was hot and my skin was drying out, but it wasn't much worse out here than being inside, and this was probably a safe place to read the file. Better than my studio even.

But I was stalling. Hesitating. I didn't want to open the envelope. It was going to mean change. I knew it. And I'd had enough change. Just enough already.

Just enough already, Kohl.

I dug my thumb into the loose corner of the flap and tore open the envelope, revealing a fold of white paper. Thicker than a single sheet. I paused for a second, waiting for—I don't know—dust or something to fly out at me. But nothing happened. I thumbed the torn edges open wide and looked down deep on either side of the letter, but there was nothing else in the envelope.

I plucked out the letter. Unfolded it. The white sheet was, indeed, a letter. Written in that same red ink and tidy block letters. But what had made the fold so thick was a second sheet of paper that the letter had been folded around.

The second sheet unfolded to more than twice as big as the first.

It was light tan and thick, like parchment. Old. Dare I say, brittle. Like it shouldn't have been able to survive in all this heat, especially with its extremes of aridity and humidity.

Several dark brown spots, some of them as big as a dime, marked the parchment's upper left-hand corner. A few more smaller foxing marks speckled the parchment's edges. But other than that, the parchment had been well taken care of. Surprisingly, it wasn't cracking at the folds. At least not yet.

The parchment had a menagerie of hand-drawn markings on it. Flowing lines, squiggly lines. Shaded areas. Patches of upside-down *C*s and *V*s. As I studied the parchment's markings, goosebumps began rising on my skin, so many goosebumps that I shivered despite the Pit pumping its heat out at me from only four blocks away.

This parchment could only be one thing.

A map.

I love maps.

Love.

Love, love, love.

Adventure. Exploring.

Finding.

Discovering.

Holy hell. For my last assignment, I'd been given an address and told to sit in a hotel room all night long, and then sit in the hotel's lobby all morning.

Did this map mean that, for my next assignment, I'd get to go looking for something?

For what?

Treasure?

Holy hell. Only one way to find out.

I carefully folded the map and inserted it back into the envelope, wishing I'd been a little more gentle with it when I'd ripped it open. It would have offered the delicate map a little more protection. Oh well. I re-clipped the envelope to the meager stack of file papers, then turned my attention to the letter.

It was written in the same red pen, same tidy block letters as was on the envelope.

> *Your assignment, should you choose to keep*
> *living in your studio, has two parts.*

Above my head, something clicked, like a bolt unlocking. The door I was leaning against opened up behind me—*ding*—and I fell backwards into the Physical Services Parlor's green anteroom. My legs kicked out to counterbalance and slow me down, and I leaned to my right to land on my elbow instead of my back. As my forearm ground against the parlor's rough concrete floor, my hand fisted, crumpling the letter. The file contents and the envelope with the map in it slipped off my lap and scattered on the sidewalk. I scrambled to my knees and hurried to collect it all and shove it back into the red folder I'd been sitting on.

"Corbin?"

14

I held the reassembled red folder clutched to my chest, one shin on the marbled sidewalk, the other foot planted inside the Physical Parlor's open front door. Behind muscular calves and tapered ankles, the green anteroom's hidden door was open to the lit hallway beyond. I looked up at the kind tenor voice saying my name.

Darryl had one arm stretched out, holding open the glass door so that it didn't bang closed against me, but his lats were so massive that they and his massive triceps still touched. He wore a lime-green low-scoop tank top and a concerned look on his face.

I stood and dusted myself off, stepped inside the parlor. Darryl shut the door behind me. *Dong.* As with the last time I was here, it was cooler inside the parlor than it was outside.

"Is Angela here?"

Darryl turned and stepped through the hidden doorway, ducking under the pressboard frame. "Come on back," he said.

I followed after him, shutting the door behind me, wondering what to do with my folder. It was bright red and I had nowhere to hide it.

"Angela's making a house call," he said, as we walked past the room where she'd diagnosed me. We didn't go as far as the room Darryl had disappeared into at the end of the hall, though. Halfway between his door and Angela's, he pushed open a third door, into a third room. It was unfinished, with exposed two-by-fours, same as Angela's. Inside were old, beat-up metal filing cabinets and a desk covered with loose documents.

Darryl went around to the chair side of the desk, but he didn't sit down. He rifled through the documents, opened some desk drawers, rifled through the documents again.

"Here it is," he said, sliding out a sheet of lined yellow paper.

He handed it to me.

It listed a time in long form, with several colons, enough to include not only hours, minutes, and seconds, but also days, months, and years. It also listed an address.

"Is this my appointment?"

"Yeah. I know it's not for a couple days still, but you should count yourself lucky." He snorted a laugh. "Nice shirt, by the way."

I looked down at my green *Lucky* shirt, not feeling so much lucky right now as irritated.

"I've been knocking on your guys's door since yesterday. How long have you had this? Why didn't you call me?"

"She did call you. She got through to Cherise yesterday,

right after you left. She headed out for another house call after that, and then I think she went home. I don't know. I went to work out. But the message said to stop by and pick up the appointment info sometime this morning. We didn't want to give you the details over the phone. Isn't that why you're here?"

"You left me a message?" I shook my head. I'd slept with my big bulky phone right next to my bed. It hadn't rang once. And the answering machine hadn't blinked.

Out in the hall, door hinges creaked open, and then a heavy door slammed shut. Not any of the pressboard doors.

"Yo, Angela," Darryl called.

"What?" she called back.

"Office."

I stepped around the side of the desk, out of the way of the door. Angela pushed through it. She wore another tight black tank top and another pair of white pants, these ones flowy gaucho pants that stopped at her mid-calf. Tan flip-flops. She had a canvas beach bag slung over her shoulder, cream with black straps and a black bottom. How she managed to not only find clothes that matched but also maintain a consistent style from day to day was beyond me.

"Oh. Hey," she said when she saw me. Her gaze dropped to my hand, holding the yellow paper with the appointment details.

"I got you in two days from now," she said, setting her bag on the desk. The loose documents rustled under the bag's weight. Untold items clanked together inside the canvas. "That's a good time. We'd been thinking it might take a couple weeks, which would have been too..." She glanced at Darryl, who shrugged. "Anyway, two days is plenty of time, if you were worried about it."

"You left me a message?"

Angela frowned, looked at Darryl, then back to me. "Yeah. Yesterday. Soon after you left. I didn't think I'd reach her right away, otherwise I would've told you to stick around. Why?"

She seemed to be telling the truth. Darryl, too. I shook my head, confused.

Angela crossed her arms and settled her weight on one foot. "You didn't get it."

It wasn't a question, but I still shook my head.

She narrowed her eyes. "What else happened yesterday?"

Before I could recall what she already knew, she looked me up and down and noticed my red folder. I'd tucked it under my arm so that most of it hung out the back. But not enough of it, apparently. The visible edge was red against my green shirt.

"What's that?" she said.

The brown hairs on my head stood tall, as did the ones on the back of my neck. A vestigial show of fight-or-flight. Should I say thanks for the appointment and run? The file— the gray envelope, anyway—had said it was for my eyes only. I was pretty sure that excluded my boss's eyes too. There was no doubt it excluded Darryl and Angela's. I didn't feel comfortable sharing the file with them. Especially since I hadn't finished looking at it yet myself.

But the file wasn't my only problem. Something was eating me from the inside.

Like a cancer, but without the tumor.

And the way Angela was asking questions; the way Darryl was leaning on the desk, listening intently rather than leaving us alone; it told me that these two people may not know what was going on inside me, but they had their suspicions.

And if I played nicely, they might share them with me.

But more than that: I didn't have any friends here. And I needed some.

"Just a file from work," I said, tucking the yellow paper under my arm alongside it.

"Did you walk through that rock wall for work, too?" Angela said, her tone implying that she'd already guessed that I had.

I nodded.

Darryl said, "I take it you got the file this morning? A continuation of yesterday's assignment?"

"For your eyes only?" Angela added.

The skin on my forehead and around my eyes tightened. "Yeah. How do you know that?"

They shared a look again, Angela's eyes intense, one eyebrow arched high.

Darryl's bottom lip pushed out a tad, and, ever so slightly, he shook his head.

Whatever they could tell me, whatever they could do for me, they had decided not to.

"Your shoulder feeling okay?" Angela said, looking back at me. "You want me to take another look at it?"

I scoffed. "No," I said. I turned away from them and pushed hard through the saloon door. "Thanks for the appointment."

15

The cafeteria took up most of the Management Building's second floor. Wall-to-wall windows looked out onto the glass and concrete buildings across the streets, on three sides. The kitchen was at the back. The dining room's forty or so round laminate tables and beige plastic molded chairs usually sat unused, but today the space hummed with the din of multiple conversations. People in shorts filled the chairs. They leaned into their plates, tucking into something good. And the buffet line was way longer than usual.

There was no mystery as to why. The smell of Italian spices and tomatoes was somehow managing to cut through the ubiquitous smell of sulfur. I'd caught the whiff of deliciousness outside, on my way in, and the upper-floor office workers almost certainly smelled it too.

The digital menu on the wall behind the buffet bar said they were serving lasagna.

Score one for the *Lucky* shirt.

My stomach growled, loud enough that the woman standing in line in front of me looked back at me and laughed.

I shrugged and laughed with her. There was no more denying my hunger. I couldn't remember the last time I'd had a meal, but I was pretty sure it was way more than twenty-four hours ago. Back home, I'd eaten like I was still a growing teenager. But here? I don't know. I'd say I just wasn't as hungry, but I think it was more that food just wasn't as convenient or as tasty, and so wasn't worth pursuing unless I was starving.

The buffet bar stretched the length of the back wall. It was hot enough in here that the bar probably didn't need heat lamps, but a dozen of them shined down on the food, keeping it hot enough to steam up the sneeze guard.

I piled my plate with lasagna, bread, salad, fruit, roasted vegetables, more bread. At the rate I'd been going, it might be a while before I got to eat again.

But I didn't pile my plate too high. I couldn't take it with me, after all, and I didn't want to be tempted. Back home, I'd been a guy who was all about leftovers. A meal I didn't have to make or pay for or go anywhere for? Yes, please. Most of the time I didn't even bother to nuke it in the microwave.

At the end of the buffet, I slid my tray off the slide counter, careful to get my fingertips over both ends of the file so that it wouldn't flop down where everyone could see it. After leaving the Physical Services Parlor, I'd turned the red folder inside out. The inside was a muted pink. Still colorful, but not as eye-catching as bright red. I'd thought about putting it in my waistband, but I didn't want to risk it falling out and spilling the papers all over the place.

I'd come directly to the cafeteria, and as soon I got here, I'd picked up a tray and hid my folder underneath it. The tray was bigger than the folder, so the file would easily stay hidden until I had to bus the tray.

For now, I was good to go.

I scanned the dining room, tray in hand, looking for a place to sit. I'm not shy. Far from it, really. I kinda like a little chitchat, a little mental connection. Strangers, acquaintances, friends, family—at meal time, they're all the same to me. But on my previous couple visits to the cafeteria, I'd noticed that when the dining room is mostly empty, the few people in it sit with their backs to everyone else.

But that wasn't an option today.

"Corbin!"

I looked right, toward the sound of my name, and scanned the crowd for someone I knew.

At a round table at the edge of the room, right next to the corner windows, a tiny woman was waving her arm, making big arcs, trying hard to be seen. She had a tousled pixie cut, and her dark hair had a subtle purple tint. It really flattered her dark skin tone and brought out the apples in her cheeks.

I'd seen her before. At training. We'd smiled miserably at each other in passing. But I didn't know her name.

Checking to see that she meant me, I looked around, then looked back at her.

Yes, you, she mouthed, pointing at me, then smiling and beckoning me over.

Her table had eight chairs around it. Five of the seats were taken, but the other four people feigned disinterest in my joining them, either focusing on their food or whispering to their neighbors.

The woman with the pixie cut had a tray of half-eaten bread and vegetables in front of the seat that put her back most squarely against the corner of the room. The side windows looked down onto Spoke 6. Through the front windows I could see the Physical Services Parlor's back door, across the street.

A slouchy black bag sat on the chair to the right of the pixie-haired woman, but the chair to her left was empty. She pulled it out for me as I reached the table, then sat down, picked a chunk of roasted zucchini off her plate, and smiled at me as she popped it in her mouth.

She said, "Have you figured out where the food comes from yet?"

I laughed and sat down, careful to keep my folder hidden beneath my tray. The thick envelope made it lopsided. I twisted my plate, bringing the lasagna closer to me while subtly shifting the plate over the envelope's bulk to weigh it down.

"No. Have you?"

I forked into my lasagna. The six layers of noodles, loaded with cheese and sauce and sausage, by the smell of it, held together without spreading all over my plate. Like they'd made it yesterday and reheated it today, which made lasagna better, in my opinion. It smelled delicious up close and tasted even better. The tang of the tomatoes, the hint of heat in the spicy sauce, just the right amount of cheese. I looked up at the doors to the kitchen, behind the buffet, and sent mental compliments to the chef.

The woman with the purple pixie cut shook her head, picked up a roasted onion chunk. "I'd rather find out how to get a car. You think they have air conditioning?"

I thought of the cool air in the Physical Services Parlor. But nowhere else I'd been to, not even the Hotel Burning Bright, had air conditioning.

"Maybe," I said. "Any leads?"

"Nah. I tried to flash down a driver—ask the source, so to speak—but he kept trying to go around me and finally put the car in reverse and turned around. But there's no parking garage in this building. That's weird, right? My boss walks in the front doors, same as me. So I'm thinking cars might be reserved for, I don't know, some assignment beyond the bus system?"

"Could be. Have you been out that far?"

"No. Too scared to go alone. You?"

"No." I wanted to suggest going out there together, an adventure. But then I remembered my map, my assignment, the file beneath my tray that I still hadn't fully read yet. Not to mention my appointment with Cherise Montaire and the fact that I might not live—or whatever we were all doing here, in the City—much longer. My schedule was too up in the air at the moment to add anything to it.

"I'm sorry, but I don't know your name," I said instead. "How do you know mine?"

She laughed. She had a light, tinkling laugh, an easy laugh that invited you to join in or at least smile and relax. "No worries. I'm Annie. I heard you tell one of the Twister techs your name, before all the Twisters started roaring. I was in the bed next to yours." She ripped off a chunk of bread and stuck it in her mouth. Then she made a bewildered face, brows popping and brown eyes going wide. "Glass walls. Am I right?"

"You're not wrong. I walked through a rock wall yesterday."

"Shut up."

I laughed and nodded.

"Did it hurt?"

"Yeah."

"Worse than glass?"

"Lot worse. I don't recommend it."

"Why'd you do it?"

Annie wasn't exactly loud, but she was animated. I glanced at our four tablemates, wondering if they were listening. Aside from the file and being told not to say the name *Amlathea*, I'd never been told directly not to talk about my assignments. But the preference had definitely been implied. And clearly somebody was keeping tabs on me. Probably not anyone at this table, but still.

Annie waved them off. "Don't worry about them," she said, though her lowered voice undercut her words.

When I took another big bite instead of answering, she

said, "They've got me upstairs, assisting this horrid woman who only talks to me when she needs something. I sit behind this rickety old desk in this windowless room outside her office. Every surface is red. It's horrid. But two days ago, she tells me to go get her lunch. But not from here. Not from the cafeteria. She wants me to go to this little sandwich shop down the street, near Spoke 5. I'm like, money? She gives me this dirty little look—like I said, horrid—but then she digs into her purse and pulls out this."

Annie turned to the slouchy black bag sitting on the chair on her other side, opened up the flap, stuck her hand in, and came out with something small closed up in her fist. She passed her fist under, not over, our table, and kept her hand low as she opened her fingers.

16

In her palm was a wad of clear plastic, a baggie or plastic wrap or something. It could have been nothing more than garbage, but she looked up at me with excitement in her eyes.

I glanced at our tablemates. One of them was just finishing up, putting his napkin on his plate and pushing away from the table. A second looked like she'd soon be doing the same, and the two who had been whispering together before were still whispering now, their lasagnas half eaten and getting cold. Annie and I seemed to be in our own private bubble.

Still, I pushed my tray closer to the edge of the table to better hide whatever Annie was about to show me.

But in the process, the plate slid around on the tray, removing its weight from the bulging envelope in the folder underneath. The whole thing popped up half an inch, and the tray slid off the folder, revealing a sliver of muted pink.

I shoved the folder back under the tray and put the plate back over the bulge as quickly as I could, but no doubt anyone paying any attention to me had seen it.

I looked at Annie. Her observant gaze rose from the edge of my tray, where the folder had been visible, to meet my eyes. Her mind was definitely working behind those brown irises. But she didn't say anything. At least not with her words, not about the folder.

She took the wad of clear plastic in both hands and pulled it apart until it flattened out. The plastic looked like used sandwich wrap that had been folded over on itself a few times. Trapped in one of the corners was grit.

Red grit.

The longer I looked at it, the more I noticed it had a sheen. A glimmer.

I glanced at our tablemates again. Two had left, two were still whispering, and a new one had just sat down. I smiled at the new girl and then put my head down.

Whispering, I said, "Your boss gave you that to buy her sandwich?"

"More than this. She stuck her hand into her purse and scraped the bottom, like she was looking for loose change."

"Maybe that's what she found."

"My thoughts exactly. So I pocketed a little."

A very little. The biggest piece was maybe the size of a grain of rice.

When Annie didn't go on, I took my eyes off the red stuff in the plastic and looked up at her. She was watching me, like she was waiting for me to say one thing or another. I could only guess she was testing me, testing whether our moral compasses were aligned enough that we could be friends.

She'd essentially stolen from her boss. I wasn't sure how I would have felt about that if we were back home. Back home, I knew how money worked. I knew what the currency was. Back home, shiny red things in a baggie were more likely to be jewels and stealing them—or cavorting, after the fact, with someone who had—could land me behind bars.

But here? They'd taught us a few tricks, but then they'd left us to figure out all the important stuff for ourselves. And asking didn't yield any answers. Yeah, lasagna day was good, but I didn't want to eat every single meal in the cafeteria or else starve. So how else were we supposed to learn how to be more than hamsters powering someone else's wheel? How did we figure out how to get food and clothes and air conditioning for ourselves? It's not like they'd given us a more honest option. And anyway, considering I just wanted to go home, the City essentially already was a prison and Management was the warden.

"And?" I said. "What happened?"

She held out her hand, letting me take the baggie of red stuff. The bag rustled. I leaned closer to it, keeping my hand under the table. The red grit felt hard, sharp between my thumb and index finger.

Annie said, "So I take it to the sandwich shop. The sandwich guy's this big fella—like the floor behind the counter is a step or two higher than it is in front—white hat, white apron, looking bored, standing with his arm resting on the candy jars. So I'm placing the order, waiting for the sandwich guy to tell me the price, right? But he just looks at me. Like I'm supposed to know. Have you been in one of those shops? The menu is just the items, no prices."

I thought back to a few days ago, after I'd moved into my studio but before I'd received my Amlathea assignment, to when I'd gotten a taco from Victor Tamales. He'd given me one for a quarter. I'd been walking around my neighborhood, trying to get my bearings, when I noticed a crowd converging on a food truck. As I got closer, I overheard people walking away, talking about how they couldn't believe Victor had traded a shoelace for a taco, a zip tie for a taco. So I'd pulled out my wallet, figuring I could at least offer a quarter for a taco.

I didn't recall seeing a menu. I shook my head.

"So I hand the sandwich guy some of the red stuff, some bigger chunks. He takes it. Doesn't even blink an eye. Like a cashier accepting a five-dollar bill back home. No issue at all, totally standard. So he does something with it. Puts it down on the counter, counts it, weighs it, something. I couldn't see what, because the shop's counter came up to here on me"—she brought her palm between nose and eye level—"and there were jars of candy and whatnot on top of it besides. But then he says it's not enough. So I gave him some more. He gives me this weird little look, like a Popeye squint. Like the one eye of his is taking my measure, that kind of thing. I kinda got the feeling he wanted to swindle me. But he ended up giving me a few bits back. I figure

Sherry's likely to weigh it or whatever, too, so I gave most of it back to her, along with the sandwich. But this I kept."

I looked down at the baggie in my hand, pulling at the plastic so that it was taut over the red bits.

"What is it?"

"Got me. But it works like cash money. At least at the sandwich shop. You'd need a ton of it to buy a car."

I thought back to my first time in the Physical Services Parlor, right after Darryl had introduced me to Angela. Angela had asked me for something.

"Have any shops asked you for keys?"

Annie took the baggie of red stuff and put it back in her purse. "Keys?"

I shrugged. "After walking through that rock wall, I went to get a Cellular Twist, and before we got started, the woman asked me if I had keys."

"What keys?"

"No idea."

"You think it's money?"

"I don't know. I told her I had five bucks American and she just rolled her eyes at me."

"But she gave you the service?"

"Yeah. For free."

"Huh."

We sat there for a moment. Annie's plate looked about done, but I had some eating left to do. I forked in a few more bites of roasted veggies. So good.

"You got a phone?" Annie asked.

I nodded. "Answering machine, too."

"Me, too. Where do you live?"

"Spoke 1, thirty-six blocks from the Pit."

"Hey, that's near me. What's your phone number?"

She reached into her bag and came out with paper and a pen. We exchanged numbers and addresses and what floors we worked on. She was an assistant up on the twenty-ninth floor. Higher than Terry's office. I wondered if floor numbers related to seniority. Annie said that on a clear day, she could see far enough down inside the caldera to watch the edges of it bubble.

"Maybe I can sneak you up there sometime. For now, I should probably get back."

She stood and picked up her plate, and her gaze drifted to my tray.

My plate was becoming less and less heavy with every bite, and the bulge of the envelope underneath the tray was causing it to tilt.

"But give me a call later," Annie was saying as she walked away. She looked back at me over her shoulder and grinned. "We can talk about your red folder."

17

I sat on the edge of my plaid couch, elbows on my knees, chin resting on my fisted hands. Laid out before me on the coffee table, along with my phone and answering machine, were the yellow-lined paper with my appointment details, the red folder, the gray envelope, the letter, the parchment map, and three documents.

Not for the first time since I started looking at them, I forced a big breath of air through my lips, making a wubble sound.

I had no idea what to make of all this.

Behind me, I had the curtains open to let in some more light. My studio had overhead lights only in the bathroom, the closet, and right above the kitchenette, which was on, but it didn't extend to the coffee table. If I wanted more light in the big open room, I'd need to plug in a lamp, and I didn't have one.

Not that more light was going to help me figure any of this out.

I picked up the letter again.

> *Your assignment, should you choose to keep living in your studio, has two parts.*

> *We know you possess curiosity and initiative, because you managed to learn that the woman with the Capricorn tattoo is named Amlathea. Well done.*

On that excursion around my neighborhood when I'd gotten the taco, I'd also found a library. It was in an old building with tired storefronts on the bottom and what looked like small apartment windows on top. From the outside, the library reminded me of a small community library no bigger than its neighboring stores, with colorful handmade signs taped to the windows on either side of the door, telling me that I should *READ!* I was curious as to what books the City might *allow* me to read, so I went inside.

The front of the library was merely that, a front. It was set up like a shop, with what I could only guess at the time were best sellers prominently placed atop of small round tables and on five-foot-tall shelves angled to face the door. But I've never been a mainstream kind of reader, so I meandered over to the tall bookshelves lining the walls to see what else they had.

And I found a double door.

Make that a double doorway. An archway. It wasn't

visible from the library's front, popular section, but it wasn't hidden by any means. Anyone wandering the shelves could find it in the back.

And beyond the doorway was a real library.

I don't mean the kind with grand architecture, ornate ceilings, and strange sculptures that draw you in so that you can *then* notice the books. I mean the kind of place only a librarian could love.

Aside from the carpet, which was gray and completely silent to walk on, every surface was white and worked to make the room brighter than the dim lighting could do alone if the surfaces had been richer. All four walls, including the one with the doorway, were packed with stacks set perpendicular to the walls. On their ends, each shelf had a black, three-prong hand crank that, when turned, allowed readers to shift the shelves from side to side, removing any unused aisles and maximizing by a factor of ten, at least, the number of books that could fit into the space.

In the center of the room was a huge white staircase, with glass railings, that circled, by quarter turns, up to the second floor and beyond. Nestled under the staircase's highest landing was an old-fashioned card catalogue, also white. Around the staircase sat sixteen white laminate tables, two at each of the four sides of the staircase and two at each of the four corners, forming a square. The tables were rectangular and set up so that the long side sat parallel with the doorway. Each table had eight chairs with plush white seats one could sit in for hours—all of them empty of people.

It was a research library.

I climbed the stairs and found seven more floors, every one of them the same, white and full of books and empty of people. What I had thought were floors of apartments above a first level of stores was actually an eight-story library filled with stacks, with the windows painted black. The further up I went, the mustier the air became, but I didn't mind. I love the smell of old books.

I figured the oldest and rarest were on the top floor. I turned the crank on one of the rolling shelves, and it slid to the left, making the barest noise of gears grinding against gears and wheels passing over rails. It held scrolls, old books with raised bands on the spines, things that weren't books at all. The overhead light was diffused, easy on the artifacts but bright enough to read. Even the air felt somewhat cool. Maybe not as cool as the Physical Services Parlor, but definitely cooler than it was outdoors. Functional rather than ornate, whoever had designed this library had made every choice in service to the books first and then to the people reading them.

I wandered the stacks for hours that first visit, and I saw no one else in the library, not even a librarian. No one welcomed me. No one asked if they could help me.

But when I was told to go to the Hotel Burning Bright and watch for a woman with a tattoo, I'd taken the tattoo description to the library. I hadn't expected to find anything. Why would a library have anything to say about some woman's tattoo? I'd just wanted an excuse to use the library, to look through the old catalogue for something specific and follow its clues to the shelves. But the sixth floor of the stacks is dedicated almost entirely to tomes about the City and its residents. I easily found out who among the most prominent residents had a sea-goat tattoo.

And apparently that effort had been appreciated.

Score two for the *Lucky* shirt.

We know you are observant and resourceful because you managed to find your way back to Management Training Facilities and to its Twister Services center. Well done.

And we know you are personable and persuasive, because you managed to convince one of the Twister techs, John Carter, to help you after your encounter with the rock wall at the Hotel Burning Bright. Well done.

This was one of the things that was bugging me about the file. Management seemed to know everything about me, but the letter got this point wrong. I didn't go to Management Training Facilities to get a Twister after the rock-wall thing. I went to get a second opinion about what Angela had said about something else being inside me. And boy did I get one.

Like a cancer, but without the tumor.

And that was another thing. The letter didn't mention Angela or the Physical Services Parlor at all. I didn't know if that was a blindspot on Management's part or if they were withholding that detail for a reason, to lure me into some kind of sense of safety, of feeling incognito where Angela and Darryl were concerned.

I don't know. Maybe I was just being paranoid.

> *You will need to use these skills for your assignment. Which, as you may have deduced, is to find out what Victor Kane wants with Amlathea.*

> *Further, we want you to tell us who gave her that tattoo.*

So much for the letter. But that was a third thing. Why me? It's not like I'd been an investigator or a detective or some kind of, I don't know, cop back home. Yeah, I'm curious, I pay attention, and I like to wander, but such meager gifts do not a detective make.

As for the four loose documents that were in the red folder along with the gray envelope, they provided more information about Victor Kane.

The first document was an intake sheet. If I was reading it correctly, it said that Victor's name wasn't actually Victor Kane. His real name was Steve Larsen, and he'd arrived in the City the equivalent of about seventy-six years ago. That was surprising. The guy at the Hotel Burning Bright had moved like a guy in his prime. And the photo I'd seen of him during training—and in the file as document number two—looked the same: young.

Maybe that meant we aged slower here, if at all. I hoped so, because that would mean I'd have more time to figure out how to get back home. I'd hate to find my way back only to show up at age seventy-six, having missed most of my earthly life. That would suck.

But if I didn't ever find a way back, aging super slowly, if at all, would mean...

I blew a wubble at that thought and picked up document number two. Victor Kane's mug shot. It was the same one they'd shown us at training. Victor had dark hair, a cool-boy cut kinda like mine, and a prominent jaw. Good nose.

He was handsome. There, I said it.

But he had plotting eyes. This photo was taken during training. I knew that, because I'd posed for a similar photo soon after I'd woken up on the table. I looked tired in mine. I'd still been kinda groggy from however long I'd been out.

But Victor looked alert in his.

The third sheet was a report on how Steve Larsen had taken on the moniker Victor Kane. It had happened pretty quickly, almost as soon as he'd gotten out of training. The report made it sound like new arrivals always went one of two ways: either they ran on their hamster wheels, powering the cogs of Management in exchange for food and a place to sleep—or they didn't.

Victor was a name assigned to people who chose to go their own way.

Kane was added as the man formerly known as Steve Larsen's surname because he'd broken a branch off one of the heat-worshipper trees, one with a big burl on the end, and stormed the Management Building with it.

The report didn't say why he'd done it. Didn't say whether he was looking for something or demanding something, or whether he'd succeeded in his mission. Just said they named him Kane because he'd been carrying... a cane.

He almost certainly got away again, though, because he was still walking free, opening escape holes in hotel walls.

Come to think of it, I bet that's how he escaped from the Management Building. In fact, that was probably how Management had come to learn of his talent for opening walls.

The fourth document was almost certainly useless. It was a picture of an apartment building and an address. When Victor Kane had gotten out of training, he'd lived twelve blocks from the Pit, off Spoke 5... seventy-six years ago.

Thanks, Management!

The letter didn't give me a deadline. Didn't tell me whether I should update Terry with my progress, whether I *could* update Terry with my progress. Although, given the red-penned instructions on the gray envelope that the contents were for my eyes only and the fact that Terry had acted like he didn't want the red file anywhere near him, there was a lot of subtext to read between the lines.

I had the feeling that was going to be the theme of this assignment.

Take the parchment map, for example. I'd been so excited to see it. What was I going to explore? What was I going to find? The map alone didn't tell me anything. But the map in context with the letter and the four documents about Victor didn't tell me anything either.

Where did it start? Was it even in the City?

It wasn't even mentioned in the letter.

But it was included in the envelope, unlike the four documents. What did *that* mean?

And then there was the separate issue of the yellow notebook paper with my appointment on it. My meeting with Cherise Montaire. The address listed on the sheet, along with the appointment time, was Purgatorium Park, at Spoke 6.

It troubled me in more ways than I could count.

For one thing, it meant I couldn't go to her place right now and talk her into seeing me early.

For another, it meant she probably didn't have an office full of amazing potions or doohickies that could cure me.

In my heart, I had the idea that I would go and see her and she'd bop me on the head with her magic wand and fix me up, make me good as new.

But in my head, I kept coming back to the sketchiness of the appointment address. Angela had told me that Cherise Montaire was the best she and Darryl could come up with. Which probably meant she wasn't the best at all.

The best would be a panacea.

Or a false positive.

Or, I don't know, a doctor listed in the phone book.

Cherise Montaire was probably some old lady with a collection of chicken bones she shook around in a tin can before throwing them like Yahtzee dice and reading them like tea leaves.

You have two months to live, boy. Good luck.

Yeah, thanks, lady.

Not on the table, but in my pocket, was Annie's phone number. I pulled it out and added it to the rest of my meager information.

I'd left the cafeteria hours ago. It seemed long enough for Annie to finish work and get home, but for all I knew, she was still grinding away.

I wasn't ready to share the folder yet. And I wasn't sure I ever would be. I wanted to figure it out for myself as best I could first, and I wasn't sure how Management would feel about me sharing or what they would do to me if I did.

Was I really ready to become another Victor?

Victor Folder?

Victor Sharer?

Yeah, those names weren't cool enough to risk it.

But I did want to give my subconscious some time to work on solving the problem of my assignment, which meant I needed to give my front brain something novel to do.

I picked up the phone and called Annie.

18

Annie didn't answer, so I left her a message that said I'd be walking around the neighborhood between Spoke 1 and Spoke 2 for a while if she wanted to come out and join me.

Outside my apartment building the sulfur smell hit me hard. The Pit smoke, which had been black and condensed this morning, serpentining up from the caldera and keeping the air clearer than usual, had returned to its sooty state.

The particulate made the bright yellow sky look like brown mustard. Grit found its way into my mouth and onto my tongue. I thought about going back inside, but then I remembered Terry staring out his window, watching the thin, black line of smoke rise out of the caldera and into a clear sky like it had never happened before. Might as well start getting used to bad air again. I pulled the neck of my green *Lucky* shirt over my nose and mouth, but then let it drop and started walking.

I saw the occasional car, but no people. The neighborhood had many eyesores, starting with the storage facility across the street from my apartment building, with its glassed-in floors of orange doors. A few blocks later, the edge of a cracked and empty parking lot stretched into the distance, around a mall that was just this side of abandoned. Far and wide were old and probably mostly empty apartment complexes sitting atop of tired storefronts. Nothing was vandalized. No windows broken, no graffiti anywhere. That would all take effort.

And people.

It was just... dead.

Could have been worse though. They could have put me in a neighborhood with pastel row houses packed together so tightly you can't open your front door without banging your neighbor's elbow.

I found one of those off Spoke 12. Yeesh.

Annie lived off Spoke 2, thirty-two blocks from the Pit.

That sounds like it's near me, but the walk between spokes gets longer and longer the further away you are from the center of the City.

Math wasn't my strongest subject in school, but if the spoke streets are about ten blocks per mile, and if I add in the Pit's radius of about .4 miles, fudge all the numbers, and do a little guesswork, then that would make the radius at thirty-six blocks from the Pit about four miles.

Which would make the street that curved around the City at thirty-six blocks from the Pit a little over twenty-five miles all the way around.

Which would make the curved street between each of the twelve spokes at thirty-six blocks from the Pit about two miles between spokes.

Two miles between me, at Spoke 1, and Annie, at about Spoke 2.

Two miles was totally walkable for someone who likes to walk, but it was unlikely that Annie and I would find each other out and about by chance or on purpose.

Especially when I meant to meander but ended up walking like a man on a mission back to the library.

On my way there, I noticed something interesting.

Math was still on the brain, and I remembered back in high school doing some kind of measurement of our strides. I don't remember the point of the assignment, but my stride turned out to be thirty inches on the dot, which was an easy number to work with and so worth remembering. At thirty inches a step, I walk about 2,112 steps per mile.

The library is three streets closer to the City's center than my street, thirty-three blocks from the Pit, and it took me just over two thousand steps to get there.

And it got me thinking.

What if the library is exactly equidistant between Spoke 1 and Spoke 2?

If it was, it felt significant, like maybe I should go check out the halfway points between other spokes right around thirty-three blocks from the Pit.

The library was hidden, dressed up to look like an old apartment building with tiny windows no one would want to live in.

What if there were other gems hidden in the City?

And if there were, why were they there?

I could make a case for the library. My working theory

was that everything that sucked on Earth was present here. In which case, the library had to be some City resident's idea of hell. Or, given the big size of the library, maybe it was many residents' idea of hell.

But one person's hell was, in this case, another person's source of information.

And now that I thought about it, maybe it wasn't libraries themselves, all quiet and demanding of silence and full of boring books, that was hell. Maybe it was hell to some people that no matter how hard they tried, they couldn't bury all of the world's voices or hoard all of the world's secrets.

So what else might some people hate? What else might therefore have to exist in the City, at least in some representative form, that, with the right perspective, could turn out to be of great use to someone like me?

It was a question I'd have to explore another day.

And that was assuming my theory about the makeup of the City was anywhere near correct in the first place. Which, hey, it probably wasn't.

I made it to the little community library storefront and noticed new hand-made signs hanging in the two windows on either side of the front door. The last signs, if I wasn't mistaken, had just said *READ!*

The signs hanging there now said *BOOKS ARE MAGIC!*

Back home, that statement would have been nothing more than a nice metaphor. But here? Given the library hidden inside this old building, I wondered if it might be more literal than that. And if it was literal, what might it also mean that one of this world's secrets was being broadcasted to the masses, completely true and actionable, should any of us passersby choose to take it seriously? No one at training had mentioned any magic books. But no one at training had mentioned any massive libraries filled with resources either.

I pulled open the door and stepped inside. "Hello?"

I walked around the storefront's tables and shelves, but I didn't find anyone. Whoever had changed the signs, they were gone.

But when I entered the double doorway into the research library, I found more evidence that someone had been here. On the first white table I came to, the one in the center of the first row of three, someone had left a slip of paper and a little yellow pencil.

I don't know what I expected to find—a secret message? A secret call number?—but there was nothing written on the paper.

I chuckled at myself for thinking I'd find some kind of obvious clue to who knows what, but I picked up the paper and pencil anyway as I passed the table and made my way to the card catalogue nestled under the staircase's highest landing. I hadn't brought any paper or pen of my own, and having some would come in handy if I found what I was looking for in the catalogue.

The library's white card catalogue was huge, with more drawers than I wanted to count.

One of those drawers had been left ajar.

Just a little bit. It probably wouldn't have been noticeable to someone just passing by. But ten rows down, third column from the right, at about knee height, one of the little drawers was open half an inch.

That hadn't been the case last time I was here. I was sure of it. I hadn't seen an old-fashioned card catalogue before, except in pictures, and I'd looked at every inch of it. All of the drawers had been pushed in flush.

I knelt down before the slightly open drawer.

The first floor's catalogue was dedicated to searching by subject, and the open drawer was in the *S*s.

I pulled the drawer out to its full length, about three feet.

The cards had been split open on the subject of *Soil*. It was open to the header card, not any of the specific books on the topic. I flipped through a few of the cards that followed it, listing books about soil, but the titles suggested other topics, like if they said anything about soil at all, it was in passing. Which made sense. Aside from inside Victor's hole in the ground, I had yet to see any dirt.

I closed the drawer and moved down to the *M*s. Five or six drawers' worth. I opened the drawers and flipped through the cards, looking for *Montaire*.

Nothing. I moved up to the *C*s.

No Cherise Montaire.

But somehow, I found that comforting.

Sure, it might mean that Cherise Montaire wasn't a great enough healer to be listed as a prominent resident of the City.

But it might mean that she was so great, that trick she played on our minds with her name—it being familiar but unplaceable, unremembered—extended to books as well.

19

The next morning, I woke up with an odd feeling in my body.

Normally I didn't notice my body. It did what I wanted it to do and gave me no trouble. I had no aches and pains. And it had no aches and pains that morning. But still... I noticed it. Something about it. It felt odd.

Which couldn't be good. Not after what Angela and Big John had told me.

Like a cancer, but without the tumor.

My appointment with Cherise Montaire, two days from now, couldn't come soon enough.

I gave myself permission to start my day late. I had my own assignment now, one that gave me discretion, one Terry apparently had minimal say over. I was autonomous. And being anywhere by nine *sharp*—or earlier, in my opinion— was for people who were still being micromanaged.

I figured my options for getting started on finding out what Victor Kane wanted with Amlathea were to either visit his first residence in the City, which was probably a dead end, given that it was both seventy-six years old and handed to me in the file. I mean, if Management knew they could find Victor at his old apartment, why wouldn't they just go do that?

Or... I could follow my own lead.

I headed out about 9:05. What can I say? I'm a go-getter rebel.

It was stinky and hot that morning, but no stinkier or hotter than usual, really. I started sweating immediately. I'd had such good luck with my green *Lucky* shirt and my purple basketball shorts the day before that I'd hand-washed them both last night, set them out to dry on the kitchenette counter, and put them back on again this morning. The shirt was stiff, but I didn't care. I had high hopes that its luck would continue to work for me today.

I caught the Red bus and rode it out to the Pit. The Pit was burning so hot that morning that flames were rising with the smoke and lapping at the sky.

The bus curved around the circle of heat-worshipper trees leaning toward the Pit in Purgatorium Park, and as we approached Spoke 9, I could see my destination.

The Hotel Burning Bright is pink on the outside and stands higher than the luxury homes and offices between it and the Pit. When the caldera's burning like this, with flames or glowing clouds rising above the rim, the light it puts out bounces against the hotel's pink facade and makes it look like one of the best sunsets I'd ever seen back home, the kind where there's mostly blue sky around the western sun but there's a few fluffy clouds in the east and the angle of the sun makes the clouds look like lit cotton candy. If my theory held, somewhere in the City someone thought the pink was gaudy, hideous, but, and especially at moments like this, I thought it was beautiful.

I got off at Spoke 9. Walked outward on the spoke for a few blocks and then took a right.

The caldera was popping and crackling today, but as I got closer to the hotel I heard the roar of big equipment punctuated by the pounds of hammers and the cracking of rock.

The construction crew was still working outside the Hotel Burning Bright.

A front loader had scooped up Amlathea with the precision of a choreographed dance. I'd thought at the time that it had to have been a clever getaway driver standing by in a vehicle unrelated to the construction site. But front loaders are big pieces of equipment. What's the likelihood that the foreman of a construction crew isn't going to see it so close by and wonder why it isn't moving, why it's off-site, and why someone unknown to them is sitting in the driver's seat?

I figured if I were the foreman, I would've noticed the front loader, would've noticed something was odd about it, and I would have checked it out. Which would have ruined Victor's pick-up plan.

But Victor's plan had gone off without a hitch.

So as far as I could see, Victor's flawless plan could only mean that someone on the construction crew not only saw something and knew something, but had been in on the plan.

In fact, as I passed the front of the hotel and turned the corner, I saw what I was pretty sure was the exact getaway front loader scooping a pile of debris into a dump truck. It was yellow and had a bunch of stickers on the side of its black scooper.

I crossed the street and walked onto the construction site, pulling the neck of my shirt up over my nose and mouth. A backhoe was digging up the ground, but the disturbed dirt was... not dirt. At least not like any dirt I'd ever seen before. It wasn't even like the gritty black ground covering that carpeted Purgatorium Park.

Bits of what looked like charred black rock and gray flakes of ash mixed with red and orange bits of something I couldn't identify and yellow bits of something I figured was sulfur. Most of what lay under my feet was solid—gritty, chunky, crystalline—but some of it was viscous, and a bit of it shimmery. Every impact the backhoe made against the ground threw up splatters of oily goo and chunks of debris that cracked apart when it landed.

But the most incredible part of all this was the stench. Pungent and invasive. Each time the backhoe slammed into the ground it released a new wave of fumes that irritated my nose hairs and made the back of my throat clamp up.

"Hey!" a man yelled over all the noise, but then a jackhammer started up and I didn't hear what he said next. But he was making his way toward me.

I stood a few feet off the sidewalk, on what was left of a

parking lot. Back home, a cyclone fence would have surrounded such a site, easily keeping out the likes of me. But here? I stayed where I was and waited for the guy who was yelling to approach.

He looked miserable. Sweat-soaked hair, sweat marks stretching from his armpits to the hem of his bright orange T-shirt. His shoes, legs, and cargo shorts were covered in whatever was coming out of the ground.

"Hey," I yelled when I thought he was close enough to hear me. Better to hit him off at the pass. I pointed at the yellow front loader picking up another pile of building debris and loading it into a dump truck. "Two days ago, I saw that front loader head down that street"—I pointed to the street that ran in front of the Hotel Burning Bright—"and scoop up a woman. Do you know…"

The guy had started laughing, keeled right over and was banging his palms on his knees. "Can you believe that? I sent Ed out and around the block. Figured it'd be easier to go around than try to get him to back up. He comes back with a woman in his scoop. Doesn't stop. Leaning out his cab and yelling at me. 'I gotta get her to the hospital,' he says. Woman's standing hunched in the scoop, bumping along, gripping the edge. Didn't look like she needed a hospital, wasn't hollering none, but he took her anyway. Came back with a good-samaritan pin. Said some guy in a hat pushed her into his scooper. You saw that?"

I stood there mute, my jaw dropping open a little wider with every detail. Then, "Yeah, I saw that. Any chance I can talk to him?"

"Ed? Sure." He walked the site's perimeter with me. "What's this about?"

"Management—"

"Ah," the guy said, which I interpreted as *Say no more.* And which I may have done, except I also heard the follow-on *I know all about that.*

"Is this site a Management job?" I asked.

"Everything's a Management job, kid."

I figured the moniker was fair. The guy was probably around the same age as my dad.

"Is it?" I said. "What about the taco truck?"

He frowned at me. Then, "Oh, you mean the one off Spoke 1?"

I nodded. Victor Tamales's taco truck.

"Guess you got me there," he said. "Ed!"

The front loader stopped mid-load, and the driver twisted in his seat to look back at us standing just off the sidewalk. The guy with me waved him over. Instead of opening the door and hopping down, Ed opened his door wide and then jiggled it, making sure it was locked in place. He stood, put his back to us, and climbed down the ladder, maintaining three points of contact.

Seemed a bit incongruous with willingly agreeing to scoop up someone being pushed into his moving front loader. So unless he'd been forced to agree...

"Yeah, boss?" Ed said. He was younger and his hair was less sweaty, but he wore the same orange shirt and he was just as dirty as his boss.

His boss nodded at me. "He wanted to talk to you about the woman you picked up."

Ed smiled sheepishly. "She said I did her a favor."

"How so?"

Ed shrugged. "Didn't say."

"Is she okay?"

"Yeah. Scraped her knee some. I got her to the hospital. She didn't want to go. But the nurse met us outside, said they'd patch her up."

"She didn't want to go?" I asked.

"No. Said she was fine. Said she didn't want to stay."

"Did she stay?"

Ed shrugged. "Nurse got her out of the scoop, I left. Didn't want to get in trouble." He glanced at his boss. He seemed too simple, too pure to be here with the rest of us, let alone to have helped Victor Kane kidnap Amlathea.

"Thanks," I said. "Where's the hospital?"

Ed turned and pointed down the street, away from the Hotel Burning Bright. "Two blocks that way, three blocks out."

"So he wasn't gone long," I said to his boss.

"Nah. Five minutes tops."

I nodded. "Thanks. Thanks, Ed."

"Welcome."

I turned around and headed back to the hotel, leaving Ed pointing at his front loader, asking his boss for permission to get back to work. Definitely too simple and too pure. If Ed fit the reasons to be here, then no wonder I was here.

20

I stepped through the hotel Burning Bright's sliding glass doors and approached the front desk. The man dressed in a gauzy red uniform was the same man who'd checked me out after we both watched Amlathea enter the hotel.

My *Lucky* shirt was on a roll.

"I was in here two days ago," I said to him.

"Yes, Mr. Corbin. Pleasure to see you again." He smiled tightly. His name tag was polished and said his name was Erich. Back home, Erich had probably had impeccable grooming—perfect coif, tailored fit, clean nails—but here, I bet the constant sweat and grit were probably his idea of hell.

"Do you remember seeing that blond woman? Super clean hair, wool skirt, strappy shoes?"

"Yes. Briefly. She wasn't a guest."

"Did you see the guy she met? He had a hat on, one of those neck-flap things."

"Yes. He also wasn't a guest."

"Are you sure?" I remembered Victor walking out from behind the red wingback chair I'd been sitting in. I looked at the chair now, in its little circle of four. The only thing behind the chairs was the elevators. "I'm pretty sure he came down from upstairs."

"I can assure you he didn't."

"How so?"

Erich sighed and tilted his head to one side as he shifted his weight to the same hip, behind the counter. "He must've opened up the wall. I know he opened it when he left. You saw. You followed after him. I saw you, too. You walked right through the wall." He shook his head. "Those so-called trainers said anyone could do it, made me try again and again."

He held up the underside of his forearms. They were covered in scars. Probably from broken glass.

I nodded, not sure what to say. *Sorry* didn't seem right. And even if it was, it didn't seem sufficient.

"Okay," I said eventually. "But how do you know he didn't come from the elevator? Do you have a camera?"

"No, but there's an elevator log. I didn't recall the man checking in, but I saw him come out from behind the chairs. So I checked the log. No one had come down in the last ten minutes, and I would've seen him lurking if he'd been standing back there any longer."

I stepped back from the desk and looked past the circle of red wingbacks. The lobby wall, where the elevators were, was a continuation of the rock wall Victor had opened, the one I had walked through. They were decorated differently—the lobby's wall looked like the same pink marble that covered the floor—but it wasn't the wall material that bugged me. It was the fact that the elevator wall was an exterior wall, same as the rock wall. Victor Kane would have had to have been waiting outside, I don't know, peeking through a gap he made in the wall in order to have come in right as Amlathea was entering the building.

Hat or no hat, anyone walking down the street outside could have seen him. So how long had he been standing out there? Terry had given me a two-hour window. It seemed risky. But I supposed it was plausible.

But it didn't tell me anything new.

I stepped back up to the counter to talk to Erich.

"Yes?" he said.

"How do people pay to stay here?"

"Most don't."

"'Most' meaning they're here on Management business?"

Erich nodded, contempt narrowing his eyes.

Good.

"What about the people who aren't most people?"

Erich raised an eyebrow, then glanced from side to side. But there was no one else around. For such a big hotel, it did minimal business.

Erich leaned on the counter and said, "I've seen a few different things."

"Such as?"

"I don't know. How much is it worth to you?"

I snorted. "I don't know, Erich." Which was part of the problem. I didn't know what was valuable. But more than that, being asked a ransom for hostage information rubbed me the wrong way. I didn't like it, and I wasn't in the mood for it. Not from someone like Erich. I shook my head and stepped away from the counter, toward the sliding glass doors.

But I don't like closing off my options either. So, I called back over my shoulder, annoyed, "Let me think about it and I'll get back to you."

Outside the hotel, I headed left, down the goo-marbled sidewalk, intending to go to the hospital next. I'd ask about Amlathea, and then it would probably be time to walk over to the Management Building for lunch.

Good thing, too. After all that walking last night and this morning, I was hungry.

I stopped at the street corner to let a construction vehicle pass.

And the sidewalk, the ground, opened up in front of me.

Victor Kane smiled out at me.

He grabbed me by the ankles and yanked me down into the hole.

21

I didn't like thinking about back home, about the specifics of back home. Because it just made me sad. Because I just wanted to be back there.

Even though it hadn't been that great.

Don't get me wrong. I'd had a good life.

I'd even gotten to where I thought I wanted to be at twenty-eight. But somewhere along the way I stopped recognizing myself.

I lived in the Pacific Northwest, in Vantucky. It's a suburb of Portland, Oregon, but it's across the river, in Washington state.

I had a nice family.

Not a family of my own, but the one that raised me.

I grew up in a smaller Washington town about forty-five minutes north of Vantucky. My mom and dad still lived there—together, believe it or not, still joint at the hip and happy.

I had a sister. She was okay. We fought a lot as kids, but we were okay now. We'd get together, all of us, once a month or so for dinner at her house. Pizza, usually. She was three years older. Married, with kids. Three of them.

I wasn't married. It's tough finding the right one yourself when you grow up with a great example, because pretty much everyone looks and feels like you're settling for a relationship that's less than what you *know* is possible.

But that doesn't mean I didn't try.

I'd had a fairly steady string of relationships starting from when I was about fifteen. Yeah, I was that guy. Technically, I'd been between girlfriends when I'd suddenly found myself here. I hadn't been happy about being single at the time, but it was probably for the best, all things considered. But I couldn't say I've ever really hurt for companionship. (Until now.)

I'd been spending most of my time working.

I'd had a good job. I was a second-year associate at a big law firm in Portland. Jenkins, Korsak, & Foal. I didn't like it as well as I'd been hoping when I'd applied to law school, but it paid well. Everything that didn't go to rent on my crappy apartment went to paying off my killer student loans. I was just two years shy of shifting my payment plan into a savings plan, and socking away money for...

Well, I didn't know.

Something else.

Something more fun, more life-affirming.

Something less... what I'd been doing.

Which was probably what ended me up here.

But I couldn't complain. Lots of people back home could complain—Earth wasn't doing that great, and my corner was no exception—but I didn't feel that I, Corbin Kohl, could complain.

I had my own place. My hour-plus commute sucked. I took public transit, got on early enough to get a seat (on the way in, anyway), and killed a couple audiobooks a week, but...

I had everything I needed. Most of it was falling apart and in need of repair, but...

I had friends. Some. They were starting to pair up and marry off and pop out kids, so we were drifting apart, having less and less things in common, but...

I wasn't here.

I wasn't clueless.

I'd had some idea of how the world worked and how to get ahead.

Or at least I'd thought I had.

The ways that used to work seemed to be changing faster than I could learn them in the first place.

So much so that I now wondered if I'd ever learned anything useful at all.

Because if I had, how did I end up here?

In the City.

Where I could walk through walls, sure.

But where also some people—like Victor Kane—could open up the ground in front of me and drag me into Hell.

And here I'd thought the City was Hell.

Ha!

Traveling through the ground with Victor Kane was nothing like I'd expected.

And worse than anything I'd ever feared.

It was like walking through a wall. A dirt wall. Worse than glass, not quite as bad as rock.

But the dirt wasn't exactly dirt. And it wasn't exactly a wall.

It looked like dirt, dark and textured, just wet enough to be healthy, not wet enough to be mud. But it roared past my ears like wind.

It had a loamy, pleasant scent, like pulling fresh carrots from the garden. I got to smell it up close and personal as it bombarded me in the face, rushing past me and around me at the speed of light. It felt gritty, like sugar granules in molasses. Scratchy, but not enough to leave marks.

But the dirt wall never ended. It was more like a berm that continuously built itself up and slammed itself down between me and the guy in front of me, dragging me along behind him.

I could see Victor through the dirt, an arm's length away, in this empty bubble of space, but it filled in behind him just before I could stumble into that bubble of space myself.

He kept ahold of me with just one hand, his right hand, his arm stretching back behind him, squeezing my wrist. I didn't fight his grip. I didn't want him to let go and leave me here. I didn't want to be lost in the dirt. We were moving too fast for me to get my footing, let alone my bearings.

"Is this the Illusion?" I asked.

"Smart boy," Victor said. He had a young man's face and

an old man's voice, heavy with the passage of seventy-six years spent in the City. "But only if knowing that helps you. Does it?"

It didn't. The dirt remained, and I still couldn't get my feet under me, couldn't step into the bubble, couldn't widen it around him to include me.

"What am I doing wrong?"

"Everything."

And I suddenly felt dirt in my mouth. I spit it out and tried to pluck the grit from my tongue, but that just exposed my tongue to more grit. "How much longer?"

"Depends on where we're going."

"You're not taking me back to your lair?"

"My *lair*?"

I could hear Victor just fine through the dirt rushing past my ears, but he didn't look back at me as we talked. His dark hair was still cut exactly as it looked in his mug shot. I wondered if that was intentional on his part or a consequence of living in the City. Guess it was a good thing I liked my own haircut.

He was wearing another long-sleeved linen shirt, cream, with light khaki pants. Both clean of dirt. For some reason I'd expected Victor to live in some kind of hidden lair, some hidden cave deep in the ground and filled with contraband.

But maybe he didn't.

I remembered the fourth document in the red file, the picture of Victor's first apartment building in the City.

"Do you live twelve blocks from the Pit," I asked, "off Spoke 5?"

Victor turned his profile toward me, like he hadn't heard me and needed me to say it again. I didn't, but he acted like he was hearing me a second time, maybe repeating the words to himself in his mind.

He laughed.

"Is that a yes?"

"In that old place? Where Management could see me from its tower with nothing but a pair of binoculars?"

"Seriously?"

"Wake up, boy."

"What do you want with Amlathea?"

"You know her name. Did they tell you her name?"

"No."

"So you told *them* her name."

Somewhere during our conversation, the grittiness of the dirt I was still passing through had subsided. I didn't know why. It still looked the same. Like a thick wall I shouldn't be able to see through and a bubble of space around Victor just an arm's length away.

I couldn't remember whether or not I had told them Amlathea's name, whether Terry had known it before I'd mentioned it.

But I remembered the letter in the folder. It had congratulated me for learning her name.

"What does it matter?" I asked, genuinely curious.

"Everything matters, boy."

"So then what do you want with Amlathea?"

"Is that you asking? Is that really what *you* want to know?"

"No," I said. "I want to know how I'm drowning in dirt and you're standing in a bubble, but I don't think you'll tell me."

"Why?" he said, turning his profile to me again. "Because you saw my picture during training's rundown of the City's bad guys? Because Management primed you not to trust me?"

"Well, you did just yank me into a hole without buying me dinner first."

Victor laughed.

He had a laugh that rose up from deep in the gut, like you sometimes see on bigger guys with bigger bellies, except Victor was just as spry and fit as I was, like a guy in his prime.

"Any chance you know who gave Amlathea her tattoo?"

"Her...?" Victor laughed again, but this time with less humor. I could see him shaking his head. "Is your crappy studio really worth it?"

"Could be worse. It's got running water and a pretty rad answering machine."

Victor laughed again, more mirthfully now.

"Where are we going?" I asked. I'd been trying to keep things light and upbeat, but this time my fear filtered the question.

Victor said, still chuckling, "I hadn't decided until now. Hang on. It'll be a couple more minutes. To you, anyway."

"Any chance we can get back by lunch?" After a bit of answering-machine tag, Annie and I had agreed to meet at the cafeteria today. I'd been planning on heading over to the

Management Building after checking out what happened to Amlathea after she'd gone to the hospital. "I'm supposed to meet a friend."

"Not today you're not."

My heartbeat started racing, tightening up my chest. "What about tomorrow?"

My appointment with Cherise Montaire was in two days. She might turn out to be bogus, but I couldn't miss it. And I didn't want to be rushed. I wanted to get a good night's sleep tomorrow night so I could get to the meeting spot early enough to see which color bus line she took, which direction she came from.

"That's up to you," Victor said.

"Up to me." I sighed, sputtering dirt, and used my free hand to rub the crud off my face. It was gritty but not. I can't explain it. I didn't understand it. "What do I have to do?" I said. "I need to get back. I have an appointment. I can't miss it."

All of a sudden, the bubble around Victor stayed put as he pulled me forward. I stumbled into the clear space—

And out into the middle of nowhere.

This was not the City.

This looked like Kansas, with nothing but open fields for as far as the eye could see. Except I didn't see any livestock, no irrigation systems. Nothing but waist-high greenish-gray grass.

The sky was a clear yellow and the air had only the faintest whiff of sulfur.

"Where are we?"

I couldn't see the Pit smoke in front of me or to either side.

I looked behind me.

Way off in the distance the air looked thicker. Grayer, maybe.

Or maybe I just needed it to.

Something at my feet caught my attention.

Grinning up at me, Victor waved from his hole in the ground. There wasn't a speck of dirt on his face or in his dark hair.

"Choose your side, kid," he said, and the dirt closed over the top of him.

22

I jumped a few times on the flattened grass now covering the ground that had closed up over Victor's grin, but the dirt passage didn't open back up for me.

I sighed and looked around, trying not to panic. The air smelled clean and pure, with hardly a hint of sulfur, and I couldn't say for sure that I wasn't imagining, projecting, what little rotten egg scent I did detect. The Pit was nowhere to be smelled, let alone seen. And if the Pit wasn't anywhere nearby, then neither was the City. Nor the Management Building's cafeteria. Nor my studio.

Victor had left me in a field of greenish-gray grass. The field extended in every direction around me, for as far as my eyes could see. But the grass right around me, in a circle maybe ten yards across, had been tamped down in a weave pattern not unlike a crop circle back home. Not that I'd ever seen one of those in person.

Above me, the bright yellow sky also stretched in every direction for as far as I could see, eventually converging with the never-ending field of grass. It looked like it should be hot out, like I should be baking or at least sweating, but the air was cool. Comfortable even. Probably right around seventy-two degrees.

With so much grass, I expected it to rustle. To sway in the wind or at least get knocked around a bit by rodents scurrying about. But there was no wind, and I doubted there was any life out here either. The grass was silent.

Nothing should ever be that silent.

I turned in a circle, slowly, squinting into the distance and looking for something, anything that looked like more than greenish-gray grass and bright yellow sky.

But with every degree of turn, my chest just clenched tighter.

What was this?

Of all the things Victor Kane could have done to me, he left me in the middle of nowhere. No food. No water. No sense of direction.

So why did I have the feeling I should be thankful?

At one point in the sky, as I slowly scanned my surroundings, I thought the horizon looked ever so slightly darker than the more yellow points on either side. It looked gray and promising, and I'd never felt more relieved in my life. I set off walking in that direction, hoping the gray color was Pit smoke and not just random clouds.

Or wishful thinking.

I walked, and I walked. The grass came up to about mid-thigh, and I appreciated the rustling sound it made. Nothing like a little noise to make a person feel a little less alone.

I figured the crop circle I'd been left in for a fluke, a coincidence, until I stepped into another flattened shape, this one with straight edges, like a diamond.

When I got bored looking straight ahead at all the grass and the grayish point on the horizon, I looked straight up at the yellow sky above me.

Back home, I used to lie on the ground outside in the summer and look up at the sky. The blue seemed to stretch on forever, untouchable, especially at night when the stars seemed so far away.

The yellow sky above me now looked touchable.

Not that I could touch it from where I was standing. It was very high above me. But it looked like if I had a high enough ladder or stood on a tall enough building, I could maybe reach out and touch it. Touch something.

I couldn't say what it would feel like or how thick it would be or what lay on the other side. But with the sky that close, the idea of crop circles didn't seem so outlandish.

Not that I imagined an old guy with a waist-long beard dressed in glowing white and sitting on a golden throne on the other side of that sky, looking down at me and either laughing or showing me the way, but...

I don't know.

The things we're taught—and not taught—when we're kids.

The point is, whether it was a crop circle or not, I doubted it was meant for the likes of me. I was pretty sure about that.

Except then I remembered Victor's little grin, his little

wave. Not unlike a frat boy ditching me in the boonies in my underwear.

Was this a hazing?

Should I be investigating these marks in the grass for clues about how to get back to the City?

I had no idea.

But I also had no idea how to go about investigating them even if I were supposed to. They were too big to see all at once from the ground.

So I kept walking.

The grass grew in clumps, and about half of them had a central stalk with a pinecone-shaped head of buds preparing to bloom. The grassy leaves were long and the ends were stiff and sharp. Sharp enough that I didn't immediately notice the grass scratching up my legs. Some of the cuts were deep enough that the blood dripped down to my socks.

Great.

After a few hours, my stomach started growling, and the horizon that might or might not be the edge of the City failed to appear any closer. I was getting nowhere.

I don't know why, but after a few more hours of hoofing it and about a million scrapes on my legs, I dabbed up a dripping red line of blood with my finger and wiped it on one of the pinecone buds. Like a sacrificial offering. Tit for tat. Like maybe the plants were carnivorous and would feed me if I fed them.

I supposed that idea said more about me than it did about any of the scenery.

But lo and behold.

It worked.

A building, greenish gray, the same color as the grass, came into view.

It was small and a single story, probably just a single room. But it was something.

I started running, thrashing through the sharp plants. The long, thin leaves rustled around me.

"Hey!" I yelled. "Hello?"

I didn't see anyone. But if there was someone there, I wanted to find them sooner rather than later. I had to get back to the City. Day never became night here, and although it had felt like hours and hours had passed, I had no idea how long I'd actually been walking. Passing through the dirt had stopped my watch. The face wasn't cracked or anything, but it still said I had a little over an hour before lunch with Annie, but I knew I'd been walking for way longer than that.

"Hello?" I said. "Is anyone here?"

The greenish-gray building had board-and-batten siding and a pitched roof—for a second.

Then it had a flat roof and siding made of old plywood with the knots poked out to make peepholes.

I stumbled and slowed, confused by the building's sudden shift in appearance, but I pushed myself to step closer.

The building shifted to horizontal clapboard siding.

Then to shingle shake.

As I got within touching distance, the greenish-gray building settled into the most rundown version of itself that

I'd seen. The one covered in the old sheets of low-grade plywood with the knots poked out to make peepholes. Grade D, or even X. Two sheets was all it took to cover each side of the building, and there were plenty of knotholes to peep out from.

I could feel someone, something peering out at me.

"Hello?"

Nobody answered.

The wall facing me had no door, and none shifted into place as I got closer. For some reason that felt like a possibility. But it didn't happen.

I walked around the side, brushing my fingers over the rough wood, careful not to let my fingertips poke too far into the open knots.

Illusion or not, the wood felt real, like it could give me splinters.

I turned the corner, expecting to find the door, but again there wasn't one. Only two more sheets of plywood.

The fourth wall was the same. Two sheets of greenish-gray plywood.

Lots of holes.

No door.

"Hello?" I said, and then I stood still and listened.

I didn't hear anything. Didn't see any shifting shadows through the knotholes.

But I did see light inside.

I was too chicken to peek into one of the holes for a closer look, though. Something might gouge my eye. It wasn't worth the risk.

The plywood sat directly on the ground, the sharp grass growing up around it. So I wasn't going to get in from the bottom.

I supposed I could have tried to yank down a plywood wall, but I didn't want to destroy the place if I didn't have to. That wouldn't be very neighborly. Especially when I was hoping for more than a cup of sugar.

Which only left the flat roof.

I could get my fingers into the knotholes and climb up. But did I want to do that? What if there was something inside the wooden box that needed those holes to breathe and hadn't eaten in a while? It wasn't a farfetched thought. I hadn't eaten in a while.

And what about my toes? Could I get the toes of my shoes in one of those knotholes?

I'd been wearing a pair of low-profile hiking sneakers when I'd gotten picked off Earth and added to Management's machine, and I couldn't be more thankful for that. These shoes were great for walking, which the City had me doing plenty of. But the shoes had no traction on the bottom; they'd slip right off the side of this building. So did I want to risk damaging the welt on the toe box of the last pair of shoes I might ever own by trying to shove them into a knothole? Or did I want to take off my shoes and risk my toes along with my fingers?

I took off one shoe and held it up to a few of the bigger knotholes, and, yeah, the toe box wouldn't have fit.

I took off my sock and carefully placed my foot on the ground so as not to cut it on the sharp grass. Then took off my other shoe and sock, shoved the socks into the toes of my shoes, and set my shoes on the ground.

The ground was softer beneath my feet than I'd expected. I'd expected it to be dry. And sharp. The yellow sky looked like it had never seen clouds, let alone rain, or even dew. I'd seen the City have rain before, once, the morning I saw Amlathea meet Victor. But I never saw how the rain happened. The City had smoke, but it didn't have clouds, not any that I'd seen, anyway. And our trainers had told us to stay inside when it rained.

Okay, Kohl. Quit stalling.

I slapped my palms and rubbed them together, then reached up and curled my fingers into a couple knotholes about a foot or so shy of the roof line. I lifted my right knee as high as I could and got my big toe into another knothole, and I pulled myself up.

Just as the roof came into view—two more sheets of knotted plywood—I heard something inside the building move.

"Alright! Alright! I'm here!" someone exasperated said. "Hey, now! Hey, now! Get down from there! What do you think you're doing?"

I let go and jumped back and landed in the sharp grass, cutting my feet, which made me flinch and fall on my butt.

My *Lucky* shirt was so getting retired after this.

23

I inspected the bottoms of my feet for splinters and debris—they looked better than they felt—then reached for my shoes, pulled out my socks, slipped them back on.

"What? What do you want?" said an exasperated voice.

I finished tying my shoes and looked up.

The building was gone. Just gone. And in its place was a grayish-green woman, short and frumpy with wild hair and a fleshy face, dressed in greenish-gray flowing rags. She stood amidst the grass. The greenish-gray pinecone blooms rose higher than her chest. The yellow sky shined behind her like a flat photo backdrop.

"What happened to the building?" I asked as I got to my feet.

"What building?"

"The building you told me to get down from."

The grayish-green woman smiled. "He said you were funny."

"Who? Victor?"

Her smile widened. "He said you were quick."

"Did he say I'd get back to the City by tomorrow? Because that's what I want. I need to get back to the City."

"He said you had an appointment. It won't do any good."

My blood ran cold. I shivered. "My appointment won't? Why not?"

"Cherise Montaire is not an illusion."

I stepped back, shaking my head, not knowing what to say to that.

I hadn't told anyone about my appointment. And I couldn't see Angela or Darryl telling anyone either, let alone someone who would telephone it all the way out here, all the way out to this woman, this grayish-green woman in the middle of nowhere.

Nobody knew me. Why would anyone care?

And if this grayish-green woman couldn't know about the appointment at all, then how could she know who it was with? Especially since Cherise Montaire was supposed to have some magical name everyone found familiar but nobody could remember.

I held out my arms. "Can you see inside me?"

I twisted my torso side to side.

The grayish-green woman intertwined her fingers in front of her, the epitome of patience. "Yes."

"What do you see?"

"Same thing you fear I see. The Twisters weren't lying. But they aren't correct either."

The Twisters. Plural. Angela and Big John.

They weren't correct?

"Does that mean I'm okay or that it's worse than I'd imagined?"

"Both?"

"Both." I shook my head again. "You don't make any sense."

"You don't have the proper context."

I considered that statement and decided it was fair.

I'd been dragged here through the not-dirt. I'd just seen a gray building appear, decide what it wanted to look like, and then disappear, leaving behind this woman. And I, myself, could walk through walls. These three things could hardly be the whole of whatever strange thing was going on here.

"Okay. How do I get it? Context. Can you teach me?"

"You want to learn?" She nodded approvingly. "Most people don't care about context. They only care about how things fit into what they already think they know."

"Is that a yes?"

"No."

"What?"

"I can't teach you."

"Why not?"

"I don't know myself."

"But you just said—"

"What you already believed to be true."

I huffed, feeling exasperated myself.

Around me, the greenish-gray grass rustled, as if a wind had blown through. But there was no wind. There was no weather. There was only the sharp grass with its pinecone buds and the yellow sky and whatever existed beyond it, looking down at me from above me. Most likely laughing.

"Who are you?" I asked.

"Now that is a fair question."

"Then answer it."

"I'm searching for the words."

"Oh, brother," I muttered. "Forget it. Don't worry about it. Sorry to have bothered you."

I looked around me, into the distance, to where the grass met yellow sky. I spotted the section of horizon with the air that looked thicker and grayer than the rest and set off in that direction.

"Where are you going?"

"Back to the City."

"But you made an offering. Don't you want an answer?"

I stopped, turned around.

The woman was waddling after me, arms flailing above the grass. I waited for her to catch up to me.

"What are you talking about?" I said. "I've been asking you questions. You haven't told me a thing."

She flinched at my tone. "I can only tell you what you already know."

"Why? What good is that?"

"Because I'm a figment of your imagination. And because you don't fully know that you know it."

"Come again?"

"Those are the best words I could find. There's nothing here, in this field, but you. I'm your imagination, your inner guidance, whatever you want to call me."

"If you're me, why did I make you look like… like you."

"Because you don't trust me."

"Well, that's the truth."

"It's all the truth."

"What about the part about… about what's inside me?"

"Sorry. Also truth."

"But how do *I* know that. If you only know what I know, then how do I know that?"

"Subtext?"

I considered this, and decided it, too, was fair.

The way Big John had admitted that he and his goggles weren't as good as Angela, but his diagnosis was worse. The way Angela and Darryl had looked at each other and decided not to help me, not maliciously but like I had time or options, and like they didn't know them all.

"Okay, then," I said. "So now what?"

"You made an offering."

"I don't know what that means."

"You wiped your—"

"No, I know what making an offering means. I don't know what making an offering gets me."

"An answer."

"But you haven't answered anything."

"It wouldn't come from me."

"What are you talking about?"

"Bring back the hut."

"I can't—"

"You can. You are the only reason why it was here in the first place. You're the only reason why any of this is here."

"No. This is here and I am here because Victor left me here. Victor decided where he wanted to leave me, and then two minutes later we were here. Or there"—I waved my hand in the direction of all the grass I'd already walked through—"whatever."

"He said it would be two minutes *to you*."

I nodded, because Victor *had* said that.

But I didn't know what it meant.

"Look," I said. "I'm tired. I'm hungry. And I don't want to prattle on about this anymore. I just want to get back to the City. If getting an answer will help me do that, great, let's hear it. But if not, I gotta get going."

"Bring back the hut."

I sighed. "Fine." I looked down at my legs, found a bit of blood to scrape off.

"What are you doing?" the woman, my imagination, asked.

"What do you think I'm doing? The hut showed up after I did my offering."

"And you can't bring it back without taking the action that you think caused it?"

"Nope."

She humphed, disappointed.

I wiped the blood on a pinecone of buds. "Appear mighty hut."

The hut appeared about ten feet in front of me, the rundown plywood version. But it didn't appear solid. I could see through it.

"Is this the Illusion?" I asked.

"I think so," said my imagination. "Don't you?"

But just as Victor had pointed out, knowing that still didn't help me. At least not yet.

"Okay, then. Now what?"

"Add the door."

"There is no door."

"That's because you didn't actually want to go in."

She had me there.

I picked off another flake of blood from my leg and wiped it on another pinecone bud. "Come on, door."

A door appeared. Not unlike the hidden door at the Physical Services Parlor. I had a feeling that wasn't a coincidence.

"What do I do? Go in?"

"That's my guess."

I stepped up to the door and pushed on it.

It didn't open.

I curled my finger into one of the knotholes and pulled.

The door opened.

Inside, the bright yellow sky shined through the holes in the plywood.

On the ground of flattened grass was a piece of parchment.

"Wait," I said, kneeling down. "This looks like the map. The map that was in the envelope, with the letter, in the red folder. I left all that stuff on my coffee table. How did it get here?"

I looked around, but my imagination was gone.

24

It was just me again, me, standing alone under a yellow sky, in a field of greenish-gray grass and pinecone buds that stretched on in every direction for as far as I could see.

No grayish-green woman, no greenish-gray hut.

Just me, and the light-tan parchment map that still lay, inexplicably, at my feet.

I picked it up. It didn't feel like an illusion. It was thick and brittle between my fingers.

This was definitely the map I'd received with the red folder, the one I'd left on my coffee table. I recognized the flowing and squiggly lines, the shaded areas, the patches of upside-down *C*s and *V*s.

Back home, upside-down *C*s and *V*s on a map would have indicated hills and mountains.

I looked around me, just in case there was something I'd missed seeing during my hours-long walk through nothing but grass. I turned in a slow circle, scanning the horizon and everything in between. But in any direction I looked, I did not see anything even remotely resembling a hill. I saw nothing but yellow sky and greenish-gray grass. Flat, flat, grass.

I thought back to where Victor had left me, in a flattened grass circle. I tried to turn the *C*s into those circles. But there were many *C*s on the map, and I'd only seen two crop circles. And anyway, if the *C*s were supposed to be the circles, then why weren't they drawn as *O*s?

Nothing I'd seen in the fields matched anything on this map.

"What am I supposed to do with this?" I asked aloud, waving the parchment, just in case my imagination was listening and still in a talkative mood.

But I got no response.

I folded up the thick parchment and put it in the pocket of my purple basketball shorts, then rested my hands on my hips.

The bottoms of my scraped-up feet were a little tender to stand on, but not as bad as I'd feared. I'd be able to walk without too much problem. That was good.

I also had all the daylight I needed to get back to the City. Night and darkness were not a threat here. That was annoying when I wanted to sleep, but right now it, too, was good.

I was starving, but I'd read somewhere that the brain works better when the belly's been empty for a while. Some kind of survival mechanism that helped cavemen keep functioning to find food. So I decided to chalk up the hunger pangs and stomach growls as good things, too.

Now, if I wasn't mistaken, the horizon I'd been walking towards was beginning to look more and more gray, like the Pit was in that direction, spitting up dark smoke, which meant it would eventually come into view.

And before that, I'd reach the edge of the City.

I started walking again. One foot forward, and then the other. *Just keep going, Kohl.*

With any luck, I'd find a bus right away, hopefully a spoke bus, but even a bus that circled the perimeter of the City and could drop me at a spoke bus would do.

I would take it directly to the Pit.

Purgatorium Park, Spoke 6.

I'd sit there and wait for as long as it took, as long as I could get there on time.

That doesn't make any sense, I know, but I was so hungry, it kind of did.

I hadn't missed my appointment with Cherise Montaire yet. I couldn't have. I was wearing my *Lucky* shirt. No doubt Annie would be mad that I'd stood her up for lunch hours and hours ago, but I had enough sense of time and hysterical optimism to believe that I hadn't yet missed my appointment with Cherise Montaire.

And that was the meeting that mattered. That strange feeling I'd felt in my body this morning, when I'd last woken up in my studio, felt like each cell was wriggling, trying to get away from the cells next to it. Which couldn't be good.

I checked my watch. It still said I had an hour until lunch with Annie. I tapped the face, but not to make it work again. It was like I needed to hear the tap, to know this really was happening. This endless field and me in it, it really was real.

I couldn't see the City, not in the distance. And if the City and whatever all this grass was called wasn't on a round planet, then I couldn't explain how the City would all of a sudden rise into view.

But I couldn't worry about that. I could see smoke. Or something like it. For now, that had to be enough. Maybe instead of rising into view, the City would go from minuscule to life-size. Whatever, I'd take it. I just wanted to see it. I wanted to be heading in the right direction.

All I could do was keep walking.

And play back in my mind what the grayish-green woman had told me.

And look at the map again.

I pulled the parchment out of my pocket and unfolded it. Carefully. Too much folding and unfolding, too much stuffing it into my tight pocket, might cause the creases to tear.

Flowing lines. Squiggly lines. Patches of upside-down *C*s and *V*s. The content of the map in context to the field I was walking in still made no sense to me.

So what about the map itself?

For one thing, how did it get here? To me? At my beck and call, so to speak?

Someone must have put it there, in the hut, right? Maybe not directly. Maybe they used some magical means unknown to me, some means available in this world that wasn't available on Earth. But somebody had to have set the map in motion.

It hadn't been me. I was pretty sure of that. Yeah, I'd offered the grass a sacrifice, but I hadn't been thinking of a map. I *did* want to get home, which may have played a part. But if I was going to give myself a solution, I'd've picked something more obviously helpful. Like a car. Or a teleportation machine.

Someone else had made the decision to leave me the map.

And I was pretty sure it was the same map I had left on my coffee table. It had the same heavy foxing in the upper left-hand corner with lighter foxing speckled around the edges.

Which meant someone had not only decided to leave this map in that hut for me, but they'd taken it from my studio.

I grabbed a handful of grass and yanked it from the ground, scratching up the palm of my hand. But stewing in anger wasn't going to help me.

Ahead of me, the sky along the horizon was looking more gray.

I glanced around me, at the sky's other three hundred and fifty-nine degrees, and they were all bright yellow right up until they met the greenish-gray grass, way in the distance.

So I was making progress.

Towards what, I didn't know. I still couldn't see the edge of the City, or anything else. It was all still grass and sky. But ahead of me, it was grayish-yellow sky. That counted for something.

Okay, so someone had been in my studio. Three options came to mind.

And the *who* mattered because the *who* determined intent.

Was this map for my benefit or for my detriment?

And if the latter, was it just to mess with me, or something worse?

The first and least likely option was Annie. She'd seen the red folder, undoubtedly she had, at the cafeteria. And she knew where I lived; I'd told her myself. But I didn't think she could just waltz into my studio. I didn't know for sure, but I suspected that the same way Management had kept me out of the cafeteria, to punish me when I'd taken a sandwich home, was the same kind of thing they'd use to keep people other than the resident out of an apartment. Unless it suited them to let someone enter.

Let's say, for the sake of argument, that it suited them to let Annie enter.

Even if Annie could get into my studio, I just didn't think she'd know how to get the map to me.

First, she'd have to know where Victor had left me.

Second, she'd have to know how to move the map.

We'd been in the same training, so I figured she'd been here as long as me, probably knew just as much as me and not much more. I didn't know how to do those things, so I didn't think she would either.

Which was a bummer. If it were Annie, I'd know for sure she was trying to help me.

Option number two: Victor Kane.

Victor Kane had the means. He could open walls. I'd seen him do it. He could almost certainly open a hole in the door to my studio and make himself at home on my plaid couch.

He'd also known I was looking for him. I didn't know how he'd known that fact, but he'd obviously learned it from somewhere.

Could he have known about the map? I didn't see how. But given everything else I'd seen him do, I also couldn't see why not.

So assume he did know about the map.

He'd left me here. In the middle of nowhere. But he'd done so after thinking about where to leave me. And he'd done it with a laugh. A humored laugh, not a malicious one. I'd gotten the sense that he liked me. Maybe just a little bit, but, hey, if that was enough to keep me alive, I'd take it.

And as far as bad places to leave me went, these fields were fairly innocuous. Yeah, I could get lost in oblivion. But maybe he'd recognized that and felt sorry for me, and so left me the map.

He knew that I was on assignment, that I was new, that this was nothing personal. He might've taken pity on me.

But if he left me the map, why wasn't it telling me how to get out of here? If he wanted to help me, why wasn't he being more help*ful*?

Which left option number three: Management.

Who in Management?

I had no idea.

But I doubted it was Terry. He was out of the loop. I was pretty sure the assignment envelope's instructions that it was for my eyes only were specifically meant for Terry. Because, really, who else would have access to the folder? Terry and Carl, Terry's assistant, that's it. And I knew Carl hadn't gotten me the map. He'd still be trying to rise out of his office chair.

Which left who?

I could think of one, maybe two people.

But I didn't know who those people were.

I only knew that someone had put the file together and written for my eyes only on the envelope. And I knew that Terry had answered the phone while I was telling him about Victor Kane; then immediately told me to come back later; and then, when I did, he'd had Carl give me the red folder like he, Terry, couldn't be anywhere near it—so who was on that call?

For all I knew, the person who made the call and the person who put the file together were the same person. Unlikely, in my experience on Earth, but possible.

Either way, whoever this person or duo was—Terry's boss, maybe? A colleague?—they obviously knew I had the map. Because they'd given it to me.

They also very likely knew where I lived, because they were part of the machine that assigned me the studio.

But would they know about this place, about these greenish-gray fields? Would they know where Victor had taken me?

I had no doubt they knew *that* Victor had taken me. Probably knew it the moment I'd been taken. I wouldn't be surprised if Management's upper echelon had us all tracked as blinking dots on a map. They'd know the moment my dot blinked out.

But would these grayish-green fields be on the map?

Given how undeveloped the fields were, how isolated I was, how the only thing I'd seen out here had claimed to be a figment of my imagination, I had to think… probably not.

And if Management didn't know the fields were here, then how could they get a map here?

They couldn't.

So there it was: three options for how this parchment map could've gotten here, and none of them truly viable.

Clearly, I was missing something.

25

My feet trudged through the greenish-gray grass. The map dangled in my hand, the parchment sucking dry any moisture I still retained from my fingers. My tongue swirled inside my dry mouth, sandpaper on sandpaper. My stomach had given up growling long ago and was now slowly contracting in on itself.

But all things considered, I figured I was doing great.

If I'd been on Earth right now, day would've become night would've become day at least once, if not twice. I was sure of it. And yet I was still going, still hanging in there.

And straight ahead of me, the yellow sky's horizon was most definitely becoming more thick and gray. More so with every few steps. And the air had more than just a passing whiff of sulfur. I'd never thought I'd be so happy to breathe in that smell. I sucked it in greedily. The Pit was within sensing distance. Which meant the edge of the City couldn't be far. If I leaned into the hunger and the thirst and let the sensation rise to my brain and induce delirium, I might even say I could see the faint outlines of buildings nestled within the gray.

Keep going, Kohl. Keep going.

But I was so tired.

I came across another of those crop circles again. I'd passed through a few of them now, since that first one Victor had left me in. Each time I did, I pulled out my map.

But the map and the circles didn't correlate, at least not to my eyes.

This circle was small, the diameter less than the outstretch of my hands. But it was a better place to sit down for a second than most spots in this never-ending field.

I dropped the map, letting it flutter onto the flattened grass, whatever good it was doing me.

I did a few leg stretches to hopefully keep my legs from cramping, then carefully lowered myself to the ground. I expected the grass to be hard and sharp, to poke me in the butt, but it wasn't so bad. Kinda like sitting in an old wicker chair.

The grass that hadn't been flattened rose around me in a circle higher than my head. Each individual clump of long, sharp grass had a single slender stalk topped with a pinecone bud. I'd been walking so long I wouldn't have been surprised if all these buds had started to bloom. But they hadn't. The would-be petals were all closed up tight still, the bud still dense.

Edible?

I didn't know, but considering where I was and

considering what I'd been told was inside me, how much worse could my situation get, really?

I reached for the nearest stem and pulled it out of the clump.

"Ow!"

I dropped it, and inspected the side of my hand. It was bleeding. Apparently the sharpest part of the grass was nearest the ground. So sharp, I could see blood clinging to the remaining blades.

I held my hand to my mouth, my tongue to the cut, staunching the sting of pain. If I'd been feeling tired before, I was awake now. Might as well just get up and keep going. Stupid grass.

I got one knee under me and was about to pick up the map and start walking again when something caught my eye. Maybe I was in such a state of delirium that my mind was committing that fallacy, the one where you see connections between unrelated things, connections that aren't really there.

Then again, maybe I'd already made that fallacy when I'd first unfolded the parchment and assumed it was a map.

I hoped it was this second option.

Because I saw something now.

Something new.

I picked up the map and the pinecone-shaped bud and sat my butt back down on the flattened grass, spreading the map out on my lap.

I'd thought it was a map, and still did. But what if it wasn't a map in the macro sense, a land map?

What if it was a map of something smaller? A micro map.

What if this map was to scale?

I set the pinecone bud on top of the parchment.

I'd thought all those upside-down *C*s represented hills. But next to the pinecone bud, they looked an awful lot like its closed-up, scale-like petals. Did that mean something?

That had to mean something.

This map had been taken from my coffee table and left with my imagination. Whether someone had done that to help me or trick me didn't matter; they'd only succeed, either way, if something about this map was actionable. Right here, right now, in this field.

In this field of nothing but endless clumps of greenish-gray grass and pinecone buds.

But what did the rest of the map mean?

I didn't know yet, but another thought struck me.

Management had given me the map, the assignment, but Victor had brought me here. And now the map was here. Management's map.

Had Management known Victor would bring me here? Had they expected it? *Wanted* it? Not because they knew about these fields and where they were, but because they *didn't* know.

Was I not so much their investigator, but their bait?

Here, kid, take this red file. Go looking for Victor Kane. He'll catch wind of your search—somehow, who knows how—and he'll take you somewhere. Could be somewhere bad, sure, but you're a genial kid. You're personable, persuasive, resourceful. We think he'll take a shine to you, leave you in a place where you could make it back. Maybe. Yeah, you might get stuck there for eternity, but it's a risk we're willing to take. And we're patient. Because, hey, we have eternity, too. And we have a theory. It only took us seventy-six years to come up with it, but we have it now, and it involves this old map. What about the map? No idea. No idea where all Victor might leave you, either. But that's exactly where you come in.

I laughed out loud at how ridiculous it all sounded, how loopy my hungry, delirious brain was being.

But what other lead did I have?

The map and its strange arrival. The upside-down *C*s that kind of looked like bloom scales. Even the hand-drawn patch of *C*s, un-outlined as they were, kind of looked like the shape of a pinecone bud.

So what did the other map markings mean?

Maybe the upside-down *V*s I'd thought were mountains actually referenced the sharpness of the grass. They weren't all drawn together in a patch, but more randomly, spaced out around the parchment.

And the lines? Flowing and squiggly? Not unlike all the lines of blood dripping down my leg.

I wiped my freshly bleeding hand on the nearest standing pinecone bud. "Come on, Imagination."

She appeared sitting in front of me, knee to knee, barely fitting inside the circle. Her face was still fleshy, but her hair was less wild, her clothes less tattered. She smiled at me, almost pretty.

She said, "Did you figure it out?"

26

There was no wind, but if there had been, I would have said that it shifted.

The smell of sulfur rushed up my nose, sudden and strong, like I'd been standing upwind of it but now stood right in its path. I slapped the back of my hand to my nostrils and instinctively leaned back to avoid the smell.

But it was everywhere.

I could hear bubbling and popping. The sounds of the caldera. I could hear it. I could hear it, but I couldn't see it. I couldn't see anything but the grayish-green woman who claimed to be my imagination, the yellow sky above us, and the grayish-green grass that stood tall all around us—but I could hear it, I could hear the Pit. Never thought I'd be so happy to sense it so close, but I was. I was.

I couldn't feel its heat, though, not yet. I wasn't sweating just yet.

But I was close.

Not physically, no. But I was close. I knew I was close.

"I don't know what this means," I said, waving the parchment map. "I don't know how it got here. But I think I know *why* it's here."

"Why is it here?" asked the woman. She sat cross-legged in front of me, her knees kissing mine, her hands folded patiently in her lap.

But I felt no similar patience. I wanted out of this field.

"Victor gave it to me."

"Why?"

"Not to get me out of here. It's not for that. I don't know what it's for. But it's not going to lead me out of here. There's no way out of these fields, not by walking, no matter how gray that part of the horizon gets."

I'd had only an inkling of that fact before, but the smell of sulfur, the sounds of the caldera, I was almost certain of it now.

My imagination nodded. "Then why'd he give it to you?"

"To get me thinking about the folder, about who gave it to me, about why I'd been given this assignment."

"Why?"

Victor's opening-the-ground skill hadn't been mentioned in training. His wall-opening skill had been, but not his ground-opening skill. The main story I'd learned about Victor Kane was the one that led to his name, the one about him storming the Management Building (Why? For what?) with a cane (What cane?). I had to think that was because that story was the only real set of details Management had on Victor.

"Because Victor's winning," I said.

"What's the game?"

"I don't know. Something to do with control? The guys at the construction site, digging up the ground with their front loaders, seemed resigned to their fate."

Everything's a Management job, kid. Say no more.

"The front-desk guy at the hotel, he seemed the same," I continued, "albeit from a different angle. He'd been willing to notice information, to sell me information, but he wasn't willing to do anything real with it to get ahead."

He still hadn't figured out how to walk through glass doors, let alone walls.

"But Victor," I said, "Victor can do things Management seems to be unable to do, things they don't even know about."

The woman nodded, her brows rising, like I was on the right trail.

"And?" she said. "So?"

"So, then I come along. Willing to look up information I don't have. Willing to chase after Victor when he makes an escape. Willing to walk through walls I've never tested before."

And be punished for it in the form of something inside me eating away at me.

But I tamped that scary thought down again. I couldn't let it distract me now, not now, not when I was so close to getting out of this field.

"As soon as Management realizes that about me, that I'm a doer, they give me this assignment. Victor already knows who I am, what I look like, at any rate. And he has abilities no one can list. He probably kept tabs on me, maybe saw me reading the red file outside the Physical Services Parlor, saw his own mug shot looking back at him. He doesn't want me following him, spying on him for Management. I wouldn't either. So he decides to get rid of me."

My imagination grabbed my hands, encouraging me, and the words came faster.

"As soon as he heard me asking about him, he grabbed me. But management was right. They'd said in that letter that I'd have to be personable, persuasive. Victor came to meet Amlathea himself. He brought me here himself, too. He might have people, but I doubt he has many."

"He wants to recruit you."

The idea sent a shiver up my spine. But I couldn't tell if that was from fear or excitement.

Or maybe a bit of both.

I nodded. "So this is a test. Victor's test. If I can pass his test"—and I was getting close, I knew I was getting close. The sulfur smell, the caldera's crackle. Even the temperature was rising now, the heat starting to make me sweat—"he'll let me out of here."

I knew it was true. If I could just pass his test.

"But if you get out of here..."

"Yeah. If I get out of here, then I pass Management's test as well."

"They'll want answers."

"They will. They'll want to know where Victor took me, how he got me there. How I got out. Why he let me leave."

"Will you tell them?"

That was the question, wasn't it?

But I knew the answer.

So then why was I still here, sitting in this field? Why was the sulfur smell still strong, the heat rising, the caldera boiling hot—but not where I could see it?

"How do I tell him?"

"Tell who?"

"Victor. How do I tell him that I won't tell? I'll talk to Management, I'll have to. But I'll lie. I'll say I don't know. That he kept me drugged and stupid, to throw them off."

"I think you just did tell him," said my imagination. "Don't you?"

I did.

So then why was I still sitting in this flattened circle of grass in the greenish-gray field?

"So what, then?" I said. "Is keeping his secrets not enough? What else does he want?"

"I think you know."

27

I feared my imagination was right.

And when the sulfur smell subsided, the heat cooled, and the crackling quieted, seemingly in response to my hesitation, I had no doubt I knew what Victor Kane wanted from me.

"He wants me to work for him."

The sulfur smell returned. The air crackled. The heat blazed against my face, making my skin drip sweat like a heat-worshipper tree, as if the fiery inferno of myth bubbled just below my ass.

For now, the greenish-gray grass and its pinecone buds still surrounded me and my imagination. But I had the sinking feeling that if I stood up I would find myself on a tiny grass island floating in a flaming pit of hellfire, that there was no going back to the seventy-two degrees and the fresh air of the endless quiet fields, that I would remain here, imprisoned in this tight circle of grass, until I made my answer.

Was Victor Kane *that* powerful?

If he was, no wonder Management had been willing to risk me in order to learn any amount of information they could about him.

Victor Kane, though, he'd left me alone. Until I'd been put on his case, he'd been perfectly happy to let me go about my business while he went about his.

But Management? Management had given neither of us that choice.

"Okay," I said on a sigh.

But before I could add more clarifying words—*Okay, I'll do it, I'll work for you*—the wicker-like grass I'd been sitting on became sticky red vinyl.

The backs of my legs started sweating immediately.

I was sitting on the bus. The Red bus, judging by the red vinyl seat.

My imagination was gone.

So was the parchment map. I patted the pockets of my purple basketball shorts, but, yeah, it was gone.

I was sitting in my usual bus seat, behind the driver. The colorful map on the plexiglass wall that separated us showed the spoke-wheel map of all the different bus lines.

A few other passengers were riding in the back of the bus, but none of them were staring at me, surprised to see me suddenly sitting here. They were all staring out their respective windows.

The open window behind me offered the tiniest bit of breeze. It ruffled the back of my hair. The sky was grayish yellow, and the air smelled of sulfur. Not as strong as before, during my last moments in the grass with my imagination. Not as strong as when I visited Purgatorium Park, either. Maybe about as strong as when I walked around the neighborhood near my studio.

I turned and looked out the bus's window.

We passed the thirty-fourth block, and then the thirty-third.

In the far distance, towering over the City, I could just make out the digital clock, clicking down the years, months, days, hours, minutes, seconds, at the top of the Management Building.

"No way," I said.

But I checked my watch.

It still said I had an hour until lunch with Annie.

Except now the second hand was ticking again.

So not only could Victor Kane open walls and travel through the ground, but apparently he could stop time.

I wondered if Management knew about that. I wondered if Management could do it. I smiled, liking the odds.

I rode the bus to Purgatorium Park and got off at Spoke 6. The ride was about forty-five minutes, and the walk to the Management Building cafeteria added another five. I got to my lunch date with Annie with a few minutes to spare.

Which was just crazy.

The first thing I did was hit the drink dispenser and guzzle a couple gallons of water. The water at Management's cafeteria tastes a lot fresher, less like rotten eggs, than the water at my studio, even after I run it through the water filter that's in my fridge. I was so thirsty that even after the third refill, my mouth still had that dry, parched feeling.

Stopping time didn't also stop thirst, that was for sure.

The cafeteria was mostly empty. Maybe a dozen or so people sat alone, spaced out among the forty or so tables, but mostly concentrated at the tables that stood at the three edges of the room, next to the floor-to-ceiling windows that looked out onto the buildings next door and the streets below. None of the people had Annie's purple-tinted hair, nor were any of them standing on their chairs and waving to get my attention.

I'd beat her here. Too crazy.

I grabbed a tray and waltzed up to the start of the buffet counter at the back of the room. There was no line. And no wonder. All the heat lamps were off. No steam fogged up the sneeze guards. The digital menu on the wall behind the food counter said they were serving sandwiches.

Bologna.

Not my fave, but I was as starving as I'd been thirsty, so I asked for four sandwiches, topped with lettuce, tomato, onion.

"Actually, just add all the veggies," I said. "Yup, even the pepperoncinis. Why not?"

I squeezed half a bottle of mayo on top, a little mustard. I was so hungry, it looked delicious.

I grabbed my tray and took it to the same table Annie had been sitting at the day before.

Had it only been the day before?

So crazy.

I sat in my same seat with my back to the window and dug in to my first sandwich. Not bad. Most of the veggies, especially the pepperoncini, masked the bleh of the bologna. I'd finished the first two sandwiches when I spotted Annie.

Her short, purple-tinted hair was mussed, like she'd been rubbing her hand through it all morning. She wore denim overall shorts with a fitted T-shirt and purple Doc Martens high-tops with frilly white socks sticking out the top.

She had a spry step, light and energetic, even in those heavy shoes. I hadn't known her long enough to know if she always walked like that or if she was having a particularly good day. Though my guess was that she probably always walked like that. Animated. Always animated.

She grabbed a tray and scanned the tables on her way up to the buffet counter. I took one hand off my sandwich long enough to raise it to shoulder level and wave, then grabbed the bread again, pinching it closed to keep all the veggies from falling out.

Annie waved back. Big and animated.

I had one sandwich left, but I saved eating it until after she joined me.

"What a day," she said as she set her tray on the table and flopped into the chair next to me. She had dark circles under her eyes. Instead of a sandwich on her plate, she had a pile of veggies on a bed of lettuce and two pieces of bread on the side. "How's it going for you?" she asked, forking up pieces of salad. "How's that red folder treating you?"

"Like a tool." I hadn't been expecting to talk about it, about any of it. I figured the Management Building had ears, that Victor Kane didn't want me talking about him, that saying anything could get me in trouble.

But talking to my imagination had helped me make progress, and I figured if I was going to learn some things, I'd have to share some things.

Annie raised an eyebrow, her mouth full. "Do tell."

"You want to tell me about your day first?"

"Nope. Nothing juicy there, just a lot of menial tasks for a thankless woman. So let's hear it. What did you do to get a red folder?"

"What do you know about the folder?"

"Uh-uh," she said. "You first. If I go first, you won't go at all."

"That's fair." So I told her about my assignment at the Hotel Burning Bright, to watch for a meeting between a woman with a tattoo—

"A Capricorn tattoo?"

I stopped talking and stared at Annie. She took another bite and chewed, smiling at me with big faux-innocent eyes.

The assignment had been to look for a *sea-goat* tattoo. But after I'd reported in about what I'd seen—"Yeah, that's what Terry called it," I said. "A Capricorn."

"Terry's your boss?"

"Yeah."

"You know my boss is named Sherry? And the boss on the floor below me is named Mary? And a couple more I've heard mentioned are named Kerri with a *K* and Cary with a *C*?"

"Is that a coincidence?"

"Is anything, in this place?" She let me think about that for a split-second, then said, "Anyway, you were saying."

"No, what do you know about the Capricorn tattoo?"

"About the tattoo? Nothing, really. I just overheard Sherry talking to someone on the phone about someone seeing the woman who has it."

"*The* woman?"

Annie paused her fork and looked up, then shrugged. "I think so."

"She say why that matters?"

"No, but I can imagine."

"What do you mean?"

"Capricorn? The sea-goat? Tail of a fish, head of a goat. Half heaven, half hell."

"Wait, half heaven?" I said. "Really?"

"Goat's a common symbol for the D-man. Fish is a common symbol for the other side."

Common enough that both symbols appeared in my mind.

Specifically, the goat's head as I'd seen it depicted inside an upside-down pentacle, with the goat's ears in the top points of the upside-down star and the beard in the bottom point.

And the fish symbol, I'd seen that before, too, back on Earth, on the backs of cars. It was a simple symbol made with two curved lines, one set of ends meeting to form the fish's head, the other set crossing to form its tail.

Interesting. Very interesting.

I said, "And you're not saying the D-man's name because..."

"Names have power?"

"Do they?"

"Well, if they do, I don't want to be on the triggering end of it. I say the guy's name and suddenly he hears me and I'm smoted or whatever. No thank you."

"Don't you think we're already smoted?"

"Semantics. Things can always get worse. Just like they can always get better. I prefer they get better."

I did too. Guess we had that in common.

"So who's the woman with the tattoo?" Annie asked.

"All I know is what I read in the library."

"They didn't tell you when they gave you the assignment?"

"Nope. I found her name in this book about the City's prominent residents. But it just said the person with a sea-goat tattoo is Amlathea. Like a cross-reference."

"You found that book at the library you mentioned in your phone message."

"Yeah."

"Huh."

"What?"

"That's pretty cool."

"Is it? I guess it is. And to answer your first question, that's what I did that got me a red folder. I found out her name."

"Really."

I shrugged. "That's what it said in the letter in the folder."

"In an envelope? For your eyes only?"

"Yeah. Why? What do you know about it?"

"Not much. Came to work one day and there was a red folder on my desk with a note to print off some documents. Went to put the documents in the folder and found an envelope."

"Was it thick?"

"What do you mean?"

"The envelope, was it stuffed?"

"No. Why? Was yours?"

"Yeah. Who got the folder?"

"I don't remember. It was one of my first tasks on the job and I hadn't sussed out what to pay attention to yet. I do remember I tried to give the folder to Sherry, but she told me to leave it on my desk. Later I went to lunch, and when I came back it was gone."

"Did she tell you to leave it on your desk like she didn't want it anywhere near her?"

"Exactly like."

"Terry, too. What do you think that means?"

"No idea. But it's gotta mean something. I'll keep an eye out."

I nodded, took another bite of sandwich.

"What did yours say?" Annie asked. "Your letter?"

But her tone was different now, hesitant, like she didn't expect me to answer, or at least didn't expect me to tell the truth.

I wasn't sure if I was going to, either.

Victor Kane didn't want me telling his secrets.

Management didn't want me telling theirs either, and that was for certain. The envelope had said *For Corbin Kohl's eyes only*. Even Terry had obeyed.

But if I was going to figure this out, if I expected to get any more information out of Annie, if I was going to be better than that front-desk clerk at the Hotel Burning Bright who was only willing to exchange information for money—if I was going to have any kind of real friends here at all—then I had to share.

And I had to do it first.

28

But not here. Not in Management's cafeteria, where there were too few people to drown out our voices.

Annie had finished her salad and was now pulling chunks off of her bread slice.

"Can we go somewhere else, or do you need to get back upstairs?" I asked.

"I'm supposed to go back, but Sherry's out for the day. I can probably leave."

"Okay. Finish up. Let's go."

I stuffed the rest of my sandwich into my mouth. Annie dropped her uneaten bread onto her plate. We bussed our trays and took the escalator downstairs.

As we rode, I stretched one of my legs out on the steps.

Annie pointed at it. "What did you do to your legs?"

My shins were covered in scratch marks, some old, some newer, a couple still showing dried beaded blood. I rubbed at them, as if that might make the marks go away.

I said, "I'll tell you..." and I nodded toward the exit doors.

Outside, the scent of sulfur hit strong. The sky above was grayish-yellow still. The traffic was relatively heavy for the City, but still much lighter than a major Earth city's rush hour.

"Purgatorium Park?" I asked. "You've convinced me that I should avoid being heard. I'm not supposed to be sharing anything I'm going to tell you."

"Sure," Annie said, looking up at me. The top of her head barely reached my shoulder. Her big brown eyes looked more concerned than excited, and I found that comforting. Hopefully it meant she would keep my secrets, even if I wasn't keeping them myself.

We crossed the street, dodging between cars, and headed for the park.

"Have you been on the rim yet?" Annie asked.

"No. Have you?"

"No. But I think the noise level up there might be worth the trek."

"Do you have time?"

"Go all in or go back to the office," she said.

So we followed Spoke 6 all the way to the edge of the park, where the road stopped at a curb and became a paved walkway that passed between two big heat-worshipper trees and led all the way to the base of the caldera's rim.

From there, the path took a sharp right up a slow incline.

After the first few steps, I was certain that this was a bad idea, huffing and puffing, my legs burning, still tired from walking in the fields.

Beside me, Annie still had that spry step, like the hill meant nothing.

The rim was six or seven stories high, and we'd be closer to Spoke 3 than Spoke 6 once we finally got there. But now that I thought about it, that wasn't such a bad thing. It would put us even further away from the Management Building.

By the time we made it, my *Lucky* shirt was a dark, wet green, and I had hot spots on my heels that would most certainly become blisters by the time I walked back down.

The heat was so hot, I had to blink continuously to keep my eyeballs from drying out.

But the view.

Spectacular.

I'd known the caldera was big, almost a mile across, but that hadn't computed in my brain in the same way seeing it in person did. The lava or hellfire or whatever it was called, the liquid fire, was low in the pit, maybe three or four stories down, bubbling and crackling, but not throwing up flames.

Thank goodness.

The gray smoke that was darkening the yellow sky looked to be coming from something floating—and burning—in the Pit.

Something the size of a human.

But maybe it was just a big branch... that weighed a couple hundred pounds... that someone dragged up the side of the rim... the rim I'd barely been able to drag myself up...

Yeah… probably not.

Man, I hoped no one had climbed all the way up here only to fall in.

(Or worse.)

A packed-dirt walkway, maybe four feet across, went all the way around the rim, and I stepped back a few paces, to its outer edge, lest the same fate of the person burning in the caldera befall me.

"Over here," Annie yelled. She stood barely an arm's length away, but she'd been right about the caldera's conversation-shielding abilities. The bubbling and crackling was not only loud in itself, but it echoed off the sides of the rim. Continuously.

Annie was pointing at an empty bench about twenty feet further to the right, along the path.

The bench sounded good to me. A total relief, really. Sitting is always safer than standing.

I sat on the right, Annie on the left. There were other people milling about along the rim, a couple dozen or so, but they were basically dots in the distance. None stood anywhere near us, let alone within earshot.

"So?" Annie said, raising her voice to be heard. "What did your red folder say?"

Caldera noise-shield or no, I didn't feel comfortable yelling my secrets, so I leaned closer and spoke into Annie's ear. She had a lot of piercings.

I told her the envelope had contained an assignment letter and a piece of parchment I thought was a map.

"A map to what?"

I blew out a breath, recalling all the deliberating I'd done over the map while I'd been stranded in the field.

"I don't know. And I don't know if I can show it to you. I'm thinking not. The envelope said for my eyes only. But it said nothing about *telling* anyone. So right now I feel like I'm operating in safe territory. Technicalities and loopholes and whatnot." Witness my legal experience at work. "But if I were to *show* any of it to you..."

"Okay. I get that. What did it look like?"

"Like a map? Sparse, though. With upside-down *C*s I thought were hills, upside-down *V*s I thought were mountains."

"But you don't think they are anymore?"

I inhaled a deep breath and held it for a second, wondering how much I should share. But as Annie might say, go all in or go it alone. I blew out the air.

"Do you remember in training when they showed us all those mug shots?"

"Of Victors? Yeah. Is one of them your assignment? 'Cause that tracks. That's what I was told to print out and add to that red folder left on my desk, Victor documents."

"Which Victor?"

"Victor Mercedes."

"Huh." I didn't remember hearing about that Victor, but the name was usually a giveaway. "As in the car?"

"Yup. The documents were just an intake sheet, his mug shot, and a report about how he became a Victor."

"Let me guess. Somehow he got a car?"

Annie tapped her nose.

"How'd he get it?"

"Didn't say. Just said he had one. The first one."

"The first... car? How long's he been here?"

"Since before cars were a thing back on Earth."

"Seriously?"

"Yup."

"How does that work?"

"Don't know. But the thing that makes me happy? I don't think Management knows either."

"But the envelope inside the folder, you said it was thin, not thick?"

"Yup. One sheet is my guess. The assignment letter."

"Huh."

"What?"

"Makes me think the map I got must be specifically about Victor Kane."

"*That's* your assignment?" Annie reared back and turned to face me, on the bench. "You've gotta be kidding me. Victor *Kane* is your assignment? The guy who can open walls and who knows what else? D'you know he stormed the Management Building and got away with it? I hear he's Management's most wanted. *He's* your assignment?"

I stared at her, taken off guard by her surprise and her level of animation. But until now, I'd kept the details of my assignment to myself. I hadn't mentioned Victor's name.

I guess now I knew why that instinct had been so strong. People talk about Victor Kane.

I didn't know what to say. I wanted to tell her everything. There were no greenish-gray plants in the City, nowhere I could make a blood offering and summon my imagination to come talk to me about this. If I was going to have a confidante in the City, Annie was my only option. But I didn't know where to start.

But Annie made it easy.

"Did you find him?" she asked.

"Not exactly," I said. "He found me."

I told her about being pulled into a hole, traveling through the dirt, being left alone in the greenish-gray field.

"That's how I got the scratches."

By the time I'd finished, Annie's eyes were bugging out of her head. "How'd you get out?"

I told her about walking forever, about seeing just enough yellow sky turn just enough gray to maintain my motivation to keep walking in that direction, but that the walking was all for nothing. That I didn't get out of the field until after I realized Victor wanted me to work for him, and had agreed to do so.

"What does he want you to do?"

"I don't know. I got back about"—I checked my watch—"three hours ago."

"Wait, all this happened this morning?"

"It happened in a split second. He took me an hour before I had to meet you for lunch, and I was back in the City at the exact same time. But it felt like I was gone for days. Maybe weeks."

"And Management gave you a map," Annie said, her tone pensive. "*In* the envelope, secreted away from the menial assistant."

I thought of Carl, slowly rising from his chair, but couldn't imagine him printing off documents.

Or maybe that's why they'd needed twenty-four hours.

"They didn't say what the map was for?" Annie asked. "Or where to get started?"

"No—wait. You said the Victor Mercedes folder had three documents. Was there an address for his first apartment?"

"No. Why? Was there one for Victor?"

"Yeah. But here's the thing that's still bugging me about all this. The folder documents were about Victor, but the assignment letter was more about Amlathea. *What does Victor want with Amlathea? Where did Amlathea get her tattoo?* That kind of thing."

"They want to know about her tattoo?"

I shrugged.

"Huh."

"Yeah." I leaned back against the bench and rubbed my neck. My throat was sore from having to find the right pitch and volume to be heard above the caldera noise but not by anyone other than Annie.

Annie leaned back, too, but almost immediately she sat up again. "I should probably get back."

"Sure," I said, standing. "I should probably get back to my assignment."

"What are you going to do?" she asked as we headed back down the path circling the side of the rim.

Going down was way easier. Thank goodness. I'd thought the strained sensation in my body was from the exertion of climbing the Pit, but the sensation was still there, tingling in my body. Not quite painful, but not quite comfortable either. Not unlike the pins-and-needles feeling of a foot that's fallen asleep and was now waking back up again.

My appointment with Cherise Montaire was two days away. I hadn't missed it. And we would meet right down there, at Spoke 6. It couldn't happen soon enough.

I'd be really happy if I could have this assignment done before then.

But as for what I was going to do next?

"I don't know yet," I said. But whatever I did, it needed to be something good. Something neither Management nor Victor Kane was expecting. Something that might clue me in to this assignment's endgame.

Good thing I had the whole way down the side of the caldera to think about it.

29

I walked with Annie the five blocks up Spoke 6 to the Management Building.

It was coming on three o'clock. Not that time really matters around here with night never showing up and most everyone being on something akin to island time. But I figured everywhere I might want to go this afternoon and evening would probably be open to me.

So where to go, what to do next?

I figured I had five options.

For one, I could satisfy my curiosity. Annie had said she'd printed out only three documents for the red folder that she'd prepared for someone. I'd gotten four documents. Why?

For two, my body felt weird. Just... not comfortable. It could be the onset of the thing inside me, or it could just be the fixable result of having traveled through the dirt with Victor. If I could get my body feeling better, that would be awesome.

Three, I'd been in the middle of something when Victor grabbed me off the sidewalk. Call me OCD if you want, but that unfinished investigation was gonna bug me until I got it done.

Four, Victor's apartment. Out of all my options for what to do next, this one gave me the most anxiety. Which probably meant it was the thing to do. But... ehhhh...

Five, love me a good research trip to the library. I had things to look up. Okay, maybe not *had* to look up, but, well... it might be a nice way to procrastinate option number four.

I told myself I was ordering my to-do list by way of what was most convenient to where I now stood, near the Management Building, but that was a lie.

Victor's first apartment was close to the Management Building. I remembered him complaining about it being close enough that they could spy on him with binoculars. It was definitely closer to where I was now than the hospital. But... ehhhh...

You know what the problem was? Why I didn't want to go to Victor's old apartment?

I didn't fully know what Victor wanted from me.

I'd told him I wouldn't tell on him to Management, but that hadn't been enough to get me out of the fields. It was only after I'd promised to work for him that I'd gotten out.

But what did *work for him* mean?

Where was his assignment for me?

I mean, don't get me wrong. I was happy to not be

ordered around simultaneously by two different bosses, but when was the Victor job gonna drop?

And what would it be?

I had no idea.

I needed to figure out what Victor wanted from me. But so far I had no idea how.

All I knew was that I didn't feel comfortable going to any place related to Victor until I knew more about what was going on.

On both sides.

I figured Management's interest in Victor was because he had so many crazy skills. I figured they wanted to know how he'd come to learn all those crazy skills.

But I also figured that I could be completely wrong about that, because, really, Management hadn't asked about any of Victor's skills in my assignment.

They'd asked about his relationship with Amlathea.

I whispered to Annie, "Do you know anywhere to get a tattoo around here?"

I was riding back up to work with her on the elevator, figuring I'd start my task list by ticking off item number one.

It was pretty big, the elevator was, and shaped like an octagon, with doors on seven sides. It could hold maybe thirty, forty people. But the Management Building only had the one elevator, and it always exceeded capacity. I was sandwiched on all four sides by Annie, two people in shorts and suit jackets, and one of the eight walls—thankfully, because at least it didn't sweat.

The elevator always smelled like rotten eggs. I never knew if that was *just* the sulfur, but I had my doubts.

"No, not yet," Annie said, answering my question about where to get a tattoo, "but I'll keep an eye out, ask around."

I rode with her all the way up to her floor, then walked the stairs back down to Terry's floor. I didn't know why, but I felt I needed to talk to Carl without Terry knowing, and I didn't want the elevator ding announcing my visit.

The lights in the red, windowless room outside Terry's office were set to dim. It made it feel slightly cooler in here. I found Carl sitting behind his dark wood desk. To the right, Terry's door was shut and light shone beneath the crack.

Good. I'd be able to see Terry's shadow if he decided to come out.

Seemed the *Lucky s*hirt was doing its best to redeem itself.

Carl was slouched in his office chair, chin resting against his chest. He had his arthritic fingers interlaced over his stomach and his eyes closed. He exhaled in soft, rhythmic bursts that made his lips puff out as the air escaped.

Seeing him made me smile. You had to love the old, wizened guy.

I nudged his forearm. Up close and when he wasn't eating peppermint candy, he smelled faintly of pipe tobacco. There'd been an old partner at my law firm, probably as old as Carl, who'd smoked a pipe. I hadn't minded the smell. Kinda liked it. "Hey, Carl?"

He opened one eye. "Yes."

He had a droll and groaning tenor that said the word like it had at least two syllables.

"Sorry to bug you. I was wondering if you could tell me anything about my red folder. Did you print out the documents?"

"Yes."

"Are there always the four documents?"

One corner of his mouth rose in a smile, and he stretched another tiny word into two syllables. "No."

I'd been planning to ask a different question—*why* I'd gotten the fourth document—but that half-smirking smile...

"Were you supposed to give me that fourth document?"

The other corner rose, full smile. "No."

"How long have you been here, Carl? In the City?"

"Longer than most."

He didn't sound happy about it.

And I had a feeling it was an understatement, that maybe Carl had been here so long he'd actually had time to age. But I'd have to satisfy that curiosity another time. I could hear Terry rustling around in his office, and I wanted to get out of here before he caught me.

"Do you know Victor Kane?"

"Not personally. He's a baby."

Guess that partially satisfied my curiosity about Carl. Victor Kane had been in the City seventy-six years.

"Why'd you give me Victor Kane's first apartment? I don't see how that could be helpful. The guy can travel through dirt. As far as I know, the City doesn't even have dirt. It's got rock, sulfur… no dirt. So it seems to me Kane's moved up in the world. So why would he still be living in his old apartment?"

"Never said he did."

"Then why would you tell me to go there?"

Carl shrugged. "Just a hunch."

I frowned at him. "Are you helping me? I want to believe that you're helping me."

The corner of his mouth rose in a smile again, just the one corner. "I do what I can."

I sighed, wishing he would do more, and glanced at Terry's office door. I could hear him moving around in there. *Come on,* Lucky *shirt. Just a few more minutes.*

"Do you know what Management wants with Victor Kane?"

The smile dropped again. "Make him into someone like me."

"What does that mean?"

Carl sighed, like he'd have to think about it. I waited a beat, but I had a feeling that even if he had an answer it might take him as long to tell it to me as it took him to rise out of his chair.

The sounds in Terry's office—drawers opening, chair wheels rolling—I didn't think I had that kind of time.

"Did you see what was in the envelope you gave me, in the file?"

"No."

Short, clipped.

Angry.

I hadn't thought so, but I hadn't expected the anger. Interesting.

"How'd you get it? The folder?"

"They appear on the desk from time to time."

That's what Annie had said.

Footsteps in Terry's office.

I needed to go, but I still felt like I knew nothing.

"Quick, Carl. I don't know what I'm doing and I'm getting nowhere. What's the one question you wish I would ask you? What do you want me to—?"

Shadows appeared under Terry's door. The knob rattled.

I gave Carl a thankful smile and escaped down the stairwell.

30

I didn't know what to think about my conversation with Carl. It was the most I'd ever heard the man say. But there were questions I just hadn't thought to ask him until I was already in the cool, dusty stairwell, clomp-clomping down the twenty-one stories.

Like, why did he give me the fourth document?

And was there anything else he could have given me?

Although I sort of knew the answer to both. He'd said he'd done what he could.

But to what end?

I was pretty sure he meant to help me.

But help me do what?

Succeed with Management's task?

Stay safe from Victor?

Something else?

Carl didn't know what Management's task for me was. I was pretty sure about that. He'd seemed unusually angry about not knowing what was in my assignment envelope. So

I didn't think he meant for the apartment printout to help me with the task directly.

How could it if he didn't know what the task was?

But he had said he was playing a hunch.

He could have said that when he went to print off the three documents he found four and just printed them all. But he didn't. He'd said he'd had a hunch.

Hunches come from the brain constantly taking in information and drawing connections on a subconscious level.

As far as I knew, Carl only worked in that windowless red room and his desk was always clear. What information was there to learn?

I supposed he could've overheard a few things, if Terry left his door open and talked loud enough. But Terry wasn't privy to my assignment's specifics either.

But this was only what I knew of Carl *now*. It sounded like Carl had been in the City for... jeez, by the looks of him, who knew how long? This side of forever. Carl's brain had probably been gathering information about red folders and the City and whatever else for a very, very long time.

But ruminating about the origins of Carl's hunch probably wasn't going to get me off the hook about visiting Victor's old digs.

The only way to know for sure how Victor's old apartment could help me with my assignment or anything at all was to go there and see what was what.

Knowing Carl, and not some faceless Management head, had given me the printout did help with my anxiety about going. But not enough to prioritize it any higher on my task list.

I exited the Management Building and headed across the street. Next stop was the Physical Services Parlor.

I reached the glass front door, but hesitated about pushing inside. I hadn't exactly left on the best terms last time. Which had been just yesterday.

It felt like forever ago to me.

I'd had time to set aside my anger about Angela and Darryl choosing not to help me and to see instead that they had helped me. They didn't have to give me Cherise Montaire's name. They didn't have to make me an appointment. Angela had even offered to take another look at me before I'd stormed out of there.

That look they'd shared, the one I'd interpreted as them deciding not to help me... I figured I'd read it correctly. On the surface. They'd chosen not to do something. But not because they weren't willing to help me or be my friend.

They'd seen the red folder.

They'd known what it was.

And, unlike Carl, they'd chosen not to get involved.

I couldn't blame them.

But I wasn't carrying the red folder today.

I opened the glass door and let it close behind me. The welcome bell ding-donged over an electronic buzzing sound deep inside the store, then silence. The green and bare anteroom was even cooler than it had been in the Management Building's stairwell and somehow smelled even less like sulfur. I stepped up to the hidden door in the pressboard and knocked.

Waited.

I heard footsteps beyond the door. Slow and heavy.

Darryl.

The hidden door pushed open towards me just enough for him to peek his big, meaty head out.

"You know, I think you're the first person to ever knock on this door. Come on back."

He gave the door a push, swinging it open toward me, then headed back down the hallway. Today's tank top was purple, and the back of it was slender enough to settle between his massive rhomboids.

I caught the door, stepped through, and let it close behind me. "Is Angela here?"

"They got you walking through walls again?"

"Something like that?"

"Angela's not here, but I can give you a Twister. Head into that first room, there, and I'll be right in."

I pushed through the saloon door into the same unfinished room where Angela had given me a Twister. Concrete floor, exposed two-by-fours. There'd been just barely enough room for Angela and me to walk around the waist-high, sheet-draped table. There would be even less room for me and Darryl.

I hopped up onto the edge of the table and let my legs dangle.

"Wasn't expecting you back so soon," Darryl said while he was still out in the hallway.

But he didn't elaborate, and I didn't know what to say about our last encounter, since I wasn't sorry for feeling mad about them holding out on me at the time. So I just grunted, "Yeah."

Darryl pushed open the saloon door and came in with a set of goggles on his head, like the steampunkish ones the Training Facilities service techs used.

I must've frowned or scowled or something as I was looking at them, because Darryl said, "I can't see through the Illusion like Angela can. If you want to wait for her…"

To be honest, I did kinda want to wait for her. But I didn't want to be rude to Darryl. And I figured if the goggles worked well enough for Training Facilities—and they had, the pain of walking through walls went away after I visited a goggle-wearing service tech—then there was no point in me complaining now.

"I'm good."

"Then lie back."

I did so, but I still had questions.

Darryl pulled up the sheet and dug the Cellular Twister out from the shelves underneath me.

"What is the Illusion?" I asked.

"What is the Illusion," he said, as he unknotted the cord and plugged in the Twister. "That's kind of like asking a fish what is water."

"So only someone outside the world of water—the Illusion—can see it?" I thought about that, then shook my head. "Doesn't make sense. Angela's a fish, and she can see water. You put those goggles on, and you can see it, too."

"These?" he said, touching the goggles on his forehead. "These don't let me see through the Illusion. These are more like tiny X-ray machines. I can see the alignment of your cells, but I can't see the Illusion."

He pulled his goggles down over his eyes.

Then frowned.

"What do you see?"

"Uh... well, I'm seeing why you're seeing Cherise Montaire in a couple days."

"How bad is it?"

"Not great. The appointment's not tomorrow but the next day, right?"

"Yeah."

"That's good."

"Then why are you still frowning? What do you see?"

"Here." He took off the goggles and handed them to me. "Put 'em on."

I sat up and took them eagerly, settling the goggles down tight over my eyes. They sealed out all of the room's light.

The lenses were like looking at the black and white speckled static on an old analog TV. Only the speckling I was seeing on the lenses was tiny tiny tiny.

I saw the individualized cells or atoms or whatever of the two-by-fours and the pressboard that framed the room in front of me. Lines, like an analog TV's interference lines, delineated the edges of the boards, but the knots in the wood showed up as dark sections, less uniform than the black and white speckling.

I looked where Darryl had been standing, and saw the

outlines of his head, shoulders, and arms, and the outline of his tank top, like a flat image. Inside the outlines—and outside his outlines, for that matter—the speckling was uniform.

"Look at yourself," he said.

And my heart started pounding. I closed my eyes behind the goggles as I looked down at my lap, then let out a breath and opened them.

"Wha—?"

My legs were outlined. Outside of them, the screen was uniformly speckled. But inside the lines of my legs...

Zigzags.

Dark areas.

Light patches.

Scribbled lines, like stretch marks.

Blinks.

I checked my hands, front and back, my palms and knuckles, my forearms, biceps.

They were the same. Worse in some places, like my right arm. All the uniform speckling was interrupted by marks of disturbance and interference.

"What the hell is all that?" I asked.

Darryl said, "The serpentine pattern—"

"The zigzag?"

"Yeah. That's from walking through walls. And the dark and light areas are probably just dust?"

"Probably?"

"Most likely. I'll dig out the Duster."

"So the blinks are the problem?"

"That, and the striations."

"The scribbled-looking lines? Like stretch marks?"

"Actually, yeah, maybe. I don't know what they are. But they might be something like stretch marks."

"Is that good or bad?"

"I don't know. But the blinking? That's the weird part."

"The tech services guy I saw at Training Facilities said it looked like a cancer without the tumor."

"Well, keep watching and you'll see what he means."

I stared down at my hands, at the blinks, the zigzags, the striations—

"They're growing. Are they spreading? What the hell are they doing?"

"Just what you said. I don't know why. I don't know what they are."

I shook my hands hard, but it didn't make it stop. My next exhale came out like a whimper. "I need to see Cherise now." I took off the goggles. I couldn't look at it anymore. "Now. Today. Can you get me in today?"

Darryl shook his head, took the goggles, put them back on.

"What about Angela?" I said. But her name wasn't more than a whisper. I was grasping at straws, and I knew it. Angela had already seen me. She'd already done what she could do. She'd gotten me my appointment with Cherise Montaire. The only thing left for me was to wait for it.

Darryl pulled up the sheet again, probably looking for the Duster.

I lay back down, my heart pounding, my body abuzz. I needed to think about something else.

"How does Angela see through it? The illusion? She's a fish, but she can still see the water," I said. "How?"

Darryl came up with the Duster. "Some fish get caught and pulled up out of the water, then thrown back in. Now they know there's something there. They don't know what it is. They still can't see it, can't feel it, can't explain it to the other fish. But they have felt its absence."

"Its absence," I said. For some reason that idea gave me the willies. "So was Angela pulled out of the Illusion? Why? How would that even work?"

"I couldn't tell you her story even if it was mine to tell," he said, not unkindly. "I wouldn't get the details right."

"Will she tell me?"

He shrugged those massive shoulders. "Timing's everything. You ready for this?"

He shook the Twister. I nodded, and he plugged it in. Turned it on.

It roared like a hair dryer. I tried to focus on the sensation of my cells twisting back into place, on the image of those zigzags speckling back out.

But all I could think about were those blinks and striations.

And the new ones still being formed.

31

When Darryl finished with me, I headed back over to the Management Building. It wasn't quite dinner time yet, and I wasn't quite hungry after my four sandwiches at lunch, but I figured after the very long and mostly starved day I'd had, I might as well eat while I could.

Even if all the guy behind the sneeze guard could serve me today was bologna sandwiches.

It was so quiet in the cafeteria at this time of day and with this kind of menu that the clatter of setting my own tray down on the table startled me. I looked around, embarrassed that I'd disturbed people, but the scatter of other odd-houred, shorts-wearing bologna eaters were off in their own worlds.

Darryl hadn't asked me what I'd walked through. It probably didn't matter to him, given the goggles. On the speckled lenses, twisting looked like twisting and dust looked like dust, whatever the kind or cause.

I wondered if Angela would have asked me.

And I wondered if I would have told her the truth if she had.

I shoved the last bit of sandwich into my mouth and bussed my tray, pretty sure I'd be tasting that bologna for the rest of the night, then headed back outside.

Sulfur is not the best scent to smell after eating a grand total of seven bologna sandwiches, but the Pit was pumping out the stench like it was a contest. Pumping out the heat, too, which felt like it was hindering my stomach's ability to finish its job.

After weeks of constant heat, you do start to get used to it, start to sweat a little less. But sweat was dripping off me now. I should've grabbed a few napkins on my way out of the cafeteria. But it was probably better that I hadn't. Probably would've gotten me banned again.

I figured I'd eaten too many sandwiches—please, let it be the sandwiches—but a part of me worried that the striations, the blinks that I'd seen in the goggle lenses, might be reaching a critical mass and starting to cause more symptoms than just the strange tingling and poking sensations I felt in my body.

I just had to make it two more days.

That same part of me that worried it was more than bologna sandwiches worried that Cherise Montaire would take one look at me and shake her head, but I shut that worry down immediately.

I just had to make it two more days. And that's all there was to it.

I headed over to Spoke 9.

The Hotel Burning Bright's glowing pink facade rose above most of the surrounding buildings. I used it as my beacon, then continued past it, toward the construction site.

Ed had said the hospital was two blocks over and three blocks further out, away from the Pit. I was expecting a big white building with a large red sign that read *EMERGENCY*.

I followed Ed's directions and found something more akin to a doctor's office. It was a single-story, brown. And the slender windows in the front of the building, facing the Pit, were textured stained glass in seventies pea green and gold.

With windows that small, the building had to predate the Pit Mandate.

It also had a circular driveway, a sort of drop-off zone. It was the first driveway I'd seen since I'd arrived in the City. The brown building was set back from the sidewalk to make room for it, and part of the building's roof extended over the driveway's apex, providing its arriving patients with shade.

Shade!

As soon as I veered off the sidewalk and into the walkway that followed the driveway, a woman came out to greet me. She wore a messy bun and magenta scrubs patterned with cats riding bicycles.

"You poor thing. Come in. We'll get you some fluids and electrolytes. The Pit heat has been excruciating lately."

"I'm fine," I said, wiping the sweat from my forehead and into my hair. It was like a rain forest up there. "I just—"

"Nonsense. Come in, come in."

By now, I'd reached the shade, and it was at least ten degrees cooler under there, so she had me. I was hers.

With a huge sigh of relief, I let her pull open the door and usher me into the waiting room.

The room was white with dark wood wainscoting that looked like it might give you splinters if you leaned on it. A big, colorful wire bead maze sat in the corner with a shelf of picture books. I didn't like the looks of that. I hadn't seen any kids in the City, and I'd taken comfort in that fact. Maybe even took it for granted.

No other patients were in the room. Nobody sat behind the check-in desk, even though the sliding glass window was open.

The woman with the cat scrubs escorted me to the side of the room opposite the entrance and sat me in a chair between the bead maze and a door with a thin window above the doorknob that I assumed led to the exam rooms.

"You just wait right here."

She smiled at me with bright eyes, then opened the door.

They had music playing.

It was kids' music. The vocals sounded like some cartoon character that would've annoyed me in under two minutes back home. But I hadn't heard music since I'd gotten here. I got the gist of the lyrics pretty quickly and started quietly singing along.

Shade. Music. This place was like—

"Heavy, *oof.*" The woman with the cat scrubs came back with a pink plastic tray of things. She set the tray on the chair next to me and took from it a juice box. She detached the straw and poked it into the box before handing it to me.

It was grape.

Back home, I would've chosen apple or orange over grape, but I was not complaining. In fact, this juice was so good I might become a convert. I sucked it down, and she gave me another. Then aimed a blue and white plastic gun at my head.

"I actually don't feel that bad," I said, "just had a lot of bologna sandwiches, and then the smell and the walk here."

"You're here, but not because you're sick?"

She gave me a confused look, and I couldn't blame her. Why would anyone go near a hospital if they didn't have to? The smell alone could turn you into a patient.

This doctor's office smelled more like fruit juice now that I'd had some. I didn't mind it.

But it wasn't why I'd come.

The gun beeped. "A hundred and eight degrees," she said. "You're fine. Probably just dehydrated. I'll get you some more juice boxes for the road."

"There was a woman who came by here"—I tried to count the days, but my time in the gray fields made it difficult—"couple days back. She rode here in the scoop of a construction front loader?"

"Oh! Am—" She'd been about to say Amlathea's name, I just knew it—she knew Amlathea—but she caught herself and her eyes locked on mine. She feigned an expression of innocence. "Was there?"

"You know there was. White sweater, wool skirt, strappy heels. Blond hair with the roots still dry."

Somehow I suspected that even after the ride in the front loader, her hair had remained free of sweat.

The woman shook her head, but she was a bad actress and a bad liar. "Doesn't ring a bell."

"You were about to say her name. Amlathea."

The woman blanched and looked around like someone might've overheard me. But there was still no one in the waiting room.

"Amlathea," I said again, and she waved at the air like she could swat away the word, the name.

"Shhh," she said.

"Amlathea, Amlathea."

"Quit saying that."

"Why? Are you afraid of her?"

"Of Am—?" She caught herself again and shook her head, angry at herself.

But not afraid of Amlathea.

"Why don't you want me to know about her?"

She stood and grabbed her tray. "Let me get you some juice boxes so you can be on your way."

She fumbled to balance her tray and open the door.

I jumped out of my chair and opened it for her. She wanted to say thank you, but huffed instead. I followed her inside.

"You can't be in here," she said.

"But you're not going to throw me out. You don't have it in you."

"So you see, and yet you don't see."

"What's that supposed to mean?"

I followed her to the end of the hall, passing a handful of exam rooms on either side. All empty as far as I could tell.

The hall ended at a break room with four chairs, a small round table, and a fridge. She set the tray on the table and opened the fridge. Unlike the empty fridge in my studio, hers was stocked with juice boxes. She gathered a bunch in her arms and passed them off to me. I struggled to keep them all from falling, wanted to ask her for a bag but figured that might be asking to much, and ended up cradling all the boxes in the upturned bottom of my *Lucky Shirt*.

Fitting, I supposed.

"I hope you feel better," she said, shooing me out.

"Do you know Victor Kane?"

She gasped. "You need to leave."

"So you do?"

She nudged me, gently, down the hall.

"Look," I said, "I'm new here. I've been asked to find out what Victor Kane wants with Amlathea."

"No. Absolutely not. You need to leave."

"Is that because it has something to do with this place?"

"No, no, no. Go, go, go."

"I'll go," I said. "I won't tell. But I do need to tell them something."

"It doesn't matter what you tell them."

We reached the door to the waiting room. I was holding the hem of my shirt up to keep the juice boxes contained, so she opened the door for me and all but brought a foot up to my ass in her effort to kick me out.

"What does that mean? You don't care if I tell them that whatever Victor wants with Amlathea, it has to do with this hospital?"

She flinched at the words *them*, *Victor*, *Amlathea*, and *hospital*.

But she said, "They've been looking for her for so long they can't remember why. Nothing you tell them will help them."

I thought she'd shut the door behind me, but she came with me, ushering me toward the exit.

"Then why are you so eager for me to leave?"

She didn't answer, just nudged me along, having more success with it than she would have had I not been intent on taking home every juice box I'd been given.

I suddenly thought of Ed.

"The guy driving the front loader said she didn't want to stay. But he didn't stick around to see if she did. Someone helped her out of the scoop."

The woman in the cat scrubs made a face. She was terrible at hiding her feelings.

"*You* helped her out of the scoop," I said, as she nudged me through the entrance doors, and into the bright. "She didn't mean it, did she? She only said she didn't want to go to the hospital."

She didn't answer, had stopped pushing me along.

I looked back at her, but she was gone.

So was the building.

I mean, there was still a building on the lot, but it was different now. A typical post-Pit Mandate glass building.

I stood one step outside its entrance doors—glass sliders still, but now stretching floor to ceiling, like the windows on either side—but the shade and the roof that had provided it were gone.

So was the driveway.

I stood on the sidewalk, next to the road, the bright yellow sky overhead beating down on me.

32

I managed to get most of my juice boxes back to my studio and into the fridge, only losing a couple to the Red bus driver and another passenger who'd asked for one.

I'd almost lost the whole bundle when I tripped on the sidewalk and all the boxes went flying. I'd been walking along smooth pavement, away from the doctor's office, or whatever it had morphed into, and toward the spoke to catch a bus, when I caught my foot on something. I stumbled forward, spilling the juice boxes everywhere, and when I looked back to see what I'd tripped over, I swear I saw a hand poking out of the sidewalk, wagging its index finger at me, *tsk-tsk-tsk*, before the sidewalk closed back up again.

Victor was letting me know he was watching me.

And probably that he didn't like what he was seeing me do, where he was seeing me go.

But he still wasn't telling me what he wanted from me.

I figured him saying hi was just one more piece of evidence that the hospital couldn't be just my imagination.

Another piece: Ed had mentioned the hospital first. He'd told me where to find it.

But if the hospital wasn't my imagination, then how did it morph into something else? How had it changed from an old, funky, seventies-style, single-story pre-mandate building into an all-glass building with the exact amount of floors allotted to it by its position relative to the Pit, no more and no less?

Was the glass building I'd left even still a hospital?

I couldn't shake the thought, the worry, the depressing idea that I'd lost the ability to see the doctor's office.

Its shade. Its music. Its juice boxes.

Could I get back there if I actually did get sick?

Hurt?

Come to think of it, should I have asked the nurse to take a look at the blinks and striations in my body?

Had I missed my chance to be seen by a real physician instead of some charlatan witch doctor named Cherise Montaire?

Had no one mentioned going to the hospital about what ailed me in the first place because most people couldn't see the hospital and didn't know it was there?

Ed had been able to see it. Ed had dropped off Amlathea and been on his way. The kindest, gentlest of souls I'd seen in the City so far. No one else even came close. And still, the nurse, Amlathea, it sounded like they had tried to keep it secret from him.

Something else, though. Ed had called it a hospital. Ed seemed like a simple guy, but I had a feeling his idea and my idea of a hospital were probably close to the same. Had the building Ed seen looked like a big hospital to him?

Had I been lucky to see it as an old seventies pediatrics office?

And in I'd gone, determined to learn what I wanted to know, invited so generously, then booted out the moment I mentioned Amlathea.

And Victor? Forget about it.

I'd sensed fear in the woman when I'd mentioned Victor.

But had that been fear of Victor?

Or had it been fear that Management had learned another detail about the hospital? Or something about Amlathea? Something that the woman had told herself Management could never learn?

I had a feeling it was that one.

I sat on my plaid couch and put my feet up on the coffee table, ready to call it a day.

The answering machine light was blinking.

Blink-blink, pause. Blink-blink, pause. Did two blinks mean two messages?

I pulled the machine into my lap and hit the *PLAY* button.

The machine told me I had two new messages.

The first was from Terry, my boss.

"Corbin Kohl. Terry Peaches, here. Management wants a progress update. You can leave your report in the mail slot on the first floor. There should be pen and paper there as well, if you need some."

He clicked off without giving me a deadline. I assumed that meant my report was expected immediately.

I didn't have much to tell them. Just a handful of suspicions and people I didn't want to get in trouble.

The next caller didn't give his name. But I could tell who he was by his droll, groaning tenor and slow delivery of words.

"Hello?... Hello?... Corbin?... Bugger all."

Different beep tones came through the phone at slow intervals. Carl must've pushed some buttons on the phone. I could just picture him sitting at his desk, the action of pushing with a finger requiring the stiff movement of his entire arm.

"Hello?" Carl said again, and then he sighed. I thought he might hang up. Then, *"Corbin? You asked me what I wished you would ask, what I wanted you to know. You never asked me about my hunch.*

"The man we discussed, his old place is down the street from me. I pass it on my way to the bus stop when I come to work. It used to be an old apartment house, like mine, probably like yours. Used to be. And I'm sure to some people, maybe even most people, it still is. Maybe you haven't been here long enough to catch my meaning, but that's about all I'm comfortable saying into this here pho—"

The machine beeped, having reached its message time limit, and cut Carl off.

I played Carl's message again. Then went to take a shower. The water came out hot and stinky, but I was grateful. I imagined clumps of dirt and dross dripping off me and circling down the drain, along with all the soot.

Victor Kane's old place used to be an apartment complex.

But to some people, or to Carl at least, it wasn't an apartment complex anymore.

So, then, what was it?

I washed my shorts and my *Lucky* shirt in the sink and laid them out on the kitchenette counter.

Maybe it was because I'd just witnessed an old doctor's office become a glass building less than a couple hours ago, but I had a feeling I might've caught Carl's meaning exactly.

Victor's building had morphed into something else.

But was it something better or something worse?

And how much of that answer was based on the person doing the looking?

I still had the disappointing suspicion that my no longer being able to see the doctor's office was a bad thing. That when I could see it, I'd been more like Ed. Purer of heart or spirit or something.

Was Carl like Ed?

Would Carl see a doctor's office, a hospital, a generic glass building? Or would he see something else?

And what would Victor see?

I closed the curtains and climbed into bed.

I had a feeling Amlathea was on the Ed side of things. The nurse at the doctor's office had kicked me out like she'd been protecting her.

And maybe she'd been right to do so. Maybe the morphed building proved it.

I flipped onto my side and pulled the blanket over my head. It was hot under here, but I had no other comfort.

Had I fallen? Here I'd been wondering how to move up in this world. But what if I'd fallen?

What would I see if I went to Victor's apartment?

What would I be able to see?

If Carl was trying to pique my curiosity to go down there tomorrow, he was doing a good job.

33

I put on my panel board shorts today. They were pale blue on top and orange with blue palm trees on the bottom. They had a back pocket and, most importantly, an inside pocket that just barely fit the parchment map. It bulged a little against my left leg, making the shorts stick out some, but I figured anyone who noticed would chalk it up to a bad fit, and no wonder. I mean, I did find these shorts in a big pile of clothes at the free-for-all wardrobe builder that training had held for us.

I gave my *Lucky* shirt a rest and instead put on another score I'd found in the free-for-all pile. A blue Fearless T-shirt with white lettering on the back that said, in two lines, *NOW YOU SEE ME NOW YOU DON'T*, with the "NOW YOU DON'T" blurred out.

I thought it was apropos for the day. Or maybe just wishful thinking.

I got to the Management Building well before nine o'clock in order to take my time scoping out the mail slot

Terry had mentioned in his message, where I was supposed to deposit my assignment report.

I wanted company on my adventure today, but I didn't know if I should ask for it. So instead of calling Annie and asking her to meet me in the lobby, I figured I'd leave it to fate to decide.

I stood just inside the Management Building's entrance. The first-floor lobby had gray slate floors, high ceilings, and wall-to-wall windows on three sides. Straight ahead, upon entering, was the elevator. The escalator down from the cafeteria stood off to the right, and the fire-stairs door found between them blended into the cream paneled back wall.

Aside from a few fake, potted heat-worshipper trees, a couple benches, and a handful of people in shorts coming and going, that's about all there was to see in the lobby.

Finding the mail slot took some searching.

I supposed it had to be along the back wall, but I found it nestled into the wall under the escalator. Either way, same result. Someone entering through the back of the building could pick up my report without being seen by the likes of us peons.

When Terry mentioned paper and pen in his message, I'd imagined something like the paper strips in the library. What I found was a form. It looked like one page, but it felt thick. It opened like a book into two pages and had questions front and back.

Some of the questions were easy. *Who is your target? Where did you see them?* But some of the questions were just... weird.

Was the Pit smoking?

How long has it been since it rained?

Weird or easy, I had no answers yet for most of these questions. I folded up the form and slid it into my back pocket, another tight and bulky fit.

I looked around. Still no Annie. I thought about riding the elevator up to her floor and seeing if she was here yet, but... I don't know. That felt like pushing my luck. If she was already at her desk, that was fate telling me no.

I took the stairs to the cafeteria, two at a time and as fast as I could, so as not to miss Annie coming into the lobby. I ran to the escalator and peeked down, but I didn't see her. Fate was still saying no.

Breakfast was oatmeal. Plain. I got a big bowl of it anyway and took it to what I was starting to think of as my usual table, the one at the front right corner of the dining hall. I sat with my back to the table, facing the windows. I figured if I saw her outside, I could pound on them to get her attention.

But I didn't see her. I ate slowly, too.

I bussed my bowl and headed down the escalator. Still no Annie.

Fate had decided. Guess I was going to Victor Kane's all by myself.

That's okay. It was probably better this way.

I headed outside and hung a right. The sky was dull yellow today, the air full of ash, making it smell more like soot than sulfur.

Yeah, this was better. It was definitely better to go it

alone. I didn't know what to expect at Victor Kane's old place. It could be dangerous. I didn't want to put Annie in danger. This was my assignment, not hers.

Victor Kane's old apartment was twelve blocks from the Pit, off Spoke 5. Building numbers weren't really a thing in the City. You either knew where you were going or you figured it out by how the building looked. So, even though it would probably be faster to cut over to Spoke 5 right now, then up seven blocks and work my way back, I figured I'd walk up Spoke 6 and then hang a left. That would let me see and scrutinize every single building between Spoke 6 and Spoke 5 for the one apartment that used to be Victor's.

Give me time to muster courage, too.

So instead of crossing the street, I took another right and headed up Spoke 6.

The Indigo bus passed me and farted to a stop at the corner up the street.

Annie stepped off it, onto the sidewalk. Her purple-tinted pixie hair was sleeked in place. She wore the denim overall shorts and purple Docs again, paired with a pink fitted T. I waved as she turned toward me.

"Corbin. What are you doing?" She pointed at the glass building next to us. Inside, I could see the mail slot from this angle. I'd never come this far up Spoke 6 before. "Work's that way."

"You want to go with me to… look at something? Can you?" I added, since she probably had to work.

"What is it?"

I shrugged, not wanting to say anything of detail so close

to the Management Building, let alone yell it. I waited until we walked close enough to each other, then said, hoping she'd get it, "Something... red?"

Her brow puzzled, but then shot up. "*Oh*. Really? You're going to share?"

"Technically, where we're going was in the..." I didn't want to say *folder*.

Annie supplied, "thingie."

"Right. This place was in there, but it was added, not... ordered." I made a face, not sure if I'd made myself clear.

But Annie said, "Heck, yeah, I want to go. Now?"

"Yeah. I have to..."

Not wanting to say *report in*, I pulled the form from my back pocket and showed it to her. For all I knew, Management had omnipresent eyes as well as ears and was watching me and Annie, totally understanding what I was up to, but... whatever. If chastised, I would stick by my technicalities: I technically hadn't shown anyone the my-eyes-only envelope's contents; the address I was going to now had been supplied by Carl, so I could technically claim it wasn't related to the assignment; and, technically, no one said I couldn't ask for help.

Annie took the form and unfolded it into its two-page spread. "What is this?"

"Let's walk, huh?"

She about-faced, still studying the form, and headed up Spoke 6 with me, away from the Management Building. I decided right then and there that I really liked this person. Here she'd been on her way to the office only to completely blow off work because I'd asked. And, sure, because she was curious about red folders and Victors and whatnot, and probably because she liked adventure—she had mentioned wanting to take the bus out to the end of the line—but she was coming with me, because I'd asked.

I had a friend.

"Is this how you report in about your red-folder assignment?" she said, speaking the last three words at barely a whisper.

"Yup. I got a call last night. No deadline given, so I figure they want it ASAP."

"Oh yeah. If they asked yesterday, you're already late."

"Thanks."

"Keepin' it real." She refolded the form and handed it back to me. "So where we headed?"

"Vic's old apartment."

"Are we not saying his name?"

"Not while we're on the sidewalk, no. Names may or may not have power, but Vic's got ears, and I'm pretty sure he tripped me yesterday after I said his name a few times."

"And you don't think he can figure out you're talking about him right now?"

She had a point. I looked down at the goo-marbled sidewalk, just in case. But it seemed he either wasn't listening or was playing a game of wait-and-see.

Annie said, "So how'd you get the address?"

"Carl gave it to me. Terry's assistant. He printed it out with the other three documents. He said he had a hunch."

"Huh. How did he find it?"

"What do you mean?"

Annie said, "So I've only gotten the one red folder, right? But the note said to print out the documents. I was all irritated because, like, with what computer? I have a phone and Sherry's printer, that's it. But the documents were all in a single file already sent to the printer. I just had to click it, and it printed. There were no extra documents."

"So Carl shouldn't have been able to give me a fourth?"

"Not unless he knows something I don't."

"I'm sure he does. The guy's old enough to be ancient and has been here even longer." I chuckled. "Probably since before they had printers."

"What did they do before printers?"

Her tone was oddly quizzical. I glanced at her, wondering if that was a question just about how things used to work in the City or whether it included how things worked back in the day on Earth as well. I wondered how old she was. I'd figured she was my age, late twenties. But I'm bad with ages. Unless someone's as old-looking as Carl or obviously a child, I tended to think everyone was my age.

But I didn't ask. I didn't want to offend.

My old law firm had analog files. The partners kept them in banker boxes stored away in their attics and basements, but mostly in a building off-site.

"Maybe they have a filing room," I said, trying to imagine Carl poking around in one.

"What's that face mean?" Annie asked.

"I'm just trying to imagine Carl going to the storage room, looking for the right filing cabinet, finding the right drawer, flipping through the files and then through the documents, making a copy. That's a lot of work for anyone, but Carl's a guy who takes ten minutes to get out of his chair. If he went through that much trouble to get me Victor's old home address—"

"It must be important."

"Yeah."

Maybe even very important. Like so important it verged on life and death. Or whatever the equivalent was around here.

Annie said, "So what was his hunch?"

"He said that the building used to be an old apartment house."

"Okay. What is it now?"

The way she said it—like *Sure, things change. And?*—I got the feeling she hadn't had any strange instances of seeing something one minute and seeing something different the next. No walls that suddenly had holes and then closed up again, no sidewalks that became tripping hazards, no old, pre-mandate doctor's offices that became post-mandate glass buildings.

I sighed, feeling like I was about to enter chosen-one territory—not that I was a chosen one, just that I might sound to her like I thought of myself as one.

But she'd come with me on this adventure into the unknown. She deserved to know as much as I could tell her.

"I don't know what it is now. But I think it might depend on who's looking?"

She looked up at me, gaze skimming over my shoulder to

meet my eyes. Her brow wrinkled. "So you brought me to see if I see what you see?"

"That's part of it."

"Is the other part that you're scaaared?"

I blew out a cheek-puffing breath. "I do feel better having you here, yeah."

She shrugged—"You're welcome"—then shoulder-bumped my elbow. "Let's go catch us a Vic."

34

We'd passed half a dozen buildings so far as Annie and I walked the twelfth block, headed toward Spoke 5. The architecture was a mix of old apartment buildings and old Victorian homes converted to rooming houses. Heavy on the *old*. They were all pre-mandate. None of the buildings on the right side of the street, facing the Pit, had floor-to-ceiling windows.

I didn't pay any attention to the backs of the buildings on the left side of the street.

I did the math, and at twelve blocks from the Pit, the street was a little over .8 miles between spokes. Victor's old apartment was off Spoke 5, so I figured we had about a thousand steps to go before I really had to start looking for the place.

At one point the air became almost unbearable with dark soot and ash. It brought to mind my and Annie's trip to the Pit and the image of something charred floating in its lake of fire. Man, I hoped nobody had fallen into the Pit. But it smelled like that hope was in vain. I pulled the neckline of my T-shirt up over my nose, happy (for the moment) that it was a thick black cotton material.

"Lucky," Annie said when she saw me do it, and that made me feel pretty good, considering I'd left my *Lucky* shirt at home. It was nice to know its magic was still with me. Annie's pink fitted T was a scoop neck, so she buried her nose and mouth in the crook of her elbow.

"Are we there yet?" she said with mock whine and flashing me a grin.

"I don't know. I got the impression from Carl that I'd know it when I saw it."

And not just because the printout he'd given me on Victor's old apartment building had included a picture. I'd thought all that information would be out of date, given that the building was at least seventy-six years old and near the Management Building. Most every other construction I'd seen around the Management Building was newer. But by the looks of this old street, maybe Victor's place hadn't been upgraded.

Or was I only seeing what I was able to see?

I pointed at the building next to us. It was a pale blue Victorian with scallop trim.

"What do you see?" I asked.

"What, you mean the ugly blue Victorian?"

"Okay."

"Is that what you see?"

"Yeah. How about this next one?"

"Two-story apartment complex I'd hate to live in. Those

windows are tiny. I know people complain about the big floor-to-ceilings facing the Pit and sucking in all the heat, but I'd take those over tiny windows any day."

"Is your apartment pre-mandate?"

"Yup. I've got tiny windows. Not *that* tiny, but I'd rather have the big ones. I mean, you can make curtains. You?"

"They're not floor-t0-ceiling, but they are pretty much wall-to-wall."

"Lucky."

I smiled, both because I loved hearing the word again and because I was: I was lucky. All things considered. I was out and about making my own agenda. Sure, I was stuck here in the City and I didn't know why. And, yeah, I had a looming health issue. But I had an appointment tomorrow with someone who might be able to give me answers to both questions, and getting an appointment with her at all, let alone so soon, was lucky.

I slowed my pace, taking my time as I inspected each building we passed. I figured we were getting close, and when I saw the blue line bus cross the intersection down the street, driving up Spoke 5, I started getting nervous.

Annie announced what she saw.

"Pink Victorian ... white Victorian ... four-story apartments ..."

I tried to recall the picture on the printout. But all I remembered about it was that the print job was black and white and didn't have much contrast. It had been hard to see any of the building's features.

Still, Victorians are pretty distinct. Especially the

roofline. But maybe it had been cut off in the photo. I couldn't remember.

"Three-story apartments ... gray Victorian. We're starting to run out of buildings, Corbin. Do you see anything? What should I be looking for?"

"I don't know. Maybe this is a bust. Maybe Carl doesn't know what he's talking about."

Maybe he'd been having a senior moment... when he went out of his way to copy the document for me... and then went out of his way again to call me and tell me about his hunch...

"No, it's gotta be here. There's gotta be something."

"Blue Victorian ... pink Vic—"

"What?"

"Pink Victorian?"

Annie pointed at the building next to us. We were six buildings from Spoke 5. I could see the last five from here. Four apartment complexes and another Victorian.

But the one we were standing in front of...

"What do you see?" I asked.

"A pink Victorian. Why? What do you—"

"Where's the front door?" I asked.

She pointed. "Right there."

"Go stand in front of it."

She made a face—"Okay"—and walked a few paces further up the sidewalk. The buildings didn't have yards or landscaping or anything like that, and Annie stayed on the marbled goo, hugging the sidewalk's inner edge. Soot and ash drizzled down on her.

"Touch the doorknob."

"It's not a knob," she said, looking at me strangely. "It's an ornate handle, with a thumb-press. You can't see it?"

I shook my head.

"What do you see?"

"Uh, I think it was an old apartment complex. Narrow, like the Victorians, but not ornate. At all. It's just a brown box with slender windows."

"What do you mean *was*?"

"You said it was a pink Victorian and now it's, I don't know, flickering, like it's trying to look to me like a pink Victorian."

"Flickering?"

"I see a brown building. But I can kinda, sometimes, see your Victorian."

"Is the front door right here?"

"On the brown building? Yeah. It's green, with a silver knob."

"What do you want to do?" Annie asked. "You want to go in?"

I definitely did not want to go in.

"Let's go around back," I said.

"Okay." She rounded the corner of the building.

"What are you doing?"

"Cutting through." She pointed down a narrow alley between the buildings.

Shivers ran up my arms, and not the good kind. I shook my head.

"What?" she said. "You want to go around?"

I nodded.

"Okay. I'll meet you there." Before I could protest, she headed down the alley.

I didn't run, but I walked a pretty fast clip to the end of the street, up Spoke 5 and back down Thirteenth. Up ahead, six buildings away, the sidewalk was empty.

Annie was not waiting for me.

"Annie," I hissed. I got to the alley and looked down the length of it. The passage was narrow, but light shines down from the yellow sky like it's high noon all the time, so even with all the soot and ash raining down, the alley was lit well enough to see.

No Annie.

"Annie," I said anyway. But there was nowhere for her to hide. The building was decidedly a three-story brown box. The wall abutting the alley was straight all the way down, from sidewalk to sidewalk. I kicked myself for not having taken a better look down the alley when I could see the Victorian. Did the Victorian have alcoves Annie could hide in?

Or had Victor Kane stolen her?

"Annie!"

"What?"

I jumped.

Annie, with her purple-tinted pixie hair and her denim overall shorts and her purple Docs, came bouncing up the sidewalk.

"What did you find?" she asked.

"Nothing," I said, still catching my breath and reeling in my annoyance that she hadn't been where she'd said she'd be.

"Well, you'll never guess what I found."

<h1 style="text-align:center">35</h1>

Annie grabbed me by the wrist and pulled me down the sidewalk behind the back of Victor Kane's old apartment building.

It was the strangest building I'd seen yet in the City, and Annie was running past it like it was same-old.

I pointed at it. "Is this still a pink Victorian to you?" I asked her.

"Yup."

It was not a pink Victorian to me. Not at all. Not anymore. Not even a flickering one.

I saw a three-story brown office building.

Pretty sure it was an office anyway, at least on the bottom floor. It had thick slats of vertical brown siding, similar in style to the old seventies doctor's office near Spoke 9, where the nurse gave me the juice boxes.

The building had a yard.

Not a big one, and not one with grass, but there was ground between the sidewalk and the building. About four feet worth. A mixture of charred black rock and gray ash, mostly, but with veins of something red and orange and glass-like running through it. It reminded me of the ground the construction crew was digging up over by the Hotel Burning Bright, but without the gooing yellow sulfur.

But the craziest thing?

The place had its own entrance.

Like the brown building was an old apartment complex on the Pit-facing side, and an entirely different establishment on this here back side.

An establishment with its own entrance.

A backdoor entrance.

Not a solid escape door, either, like on the back of the Physical Services Parlor, and all the other buildings in the City that had back doors. But a door with a glass window pane and bronze etched lettering on the glass.

Like an official, use-me-if-you're-a-customer business entrance.

On the back of the building.

It was unheard of in the City, even before the Pit Mandate. I'd learned that in training.

The lettering on the window was hard to read as Annie pulled me past it. And I noticed that she wasn't asking me about what I was seeing if I wasn't seeing a pink Victorian, like she was. She had no interest in what I was seeing at all.

Which had to mean that what she was seeing was just too good.

I suddenly no longer needed to be dragged along behind her.

"Where are we going?" I asked. Even though I should've known.

We reached the edge of the building. Annie looked around and then darted into the passageway between it and the building next door.

"What do you see next door?" I asked.

"Blue Victorian," Annie said.

That's what I saw too. Solid and true. No flickering. The back wall abutted the sidewalk and rose in a straight line, three stories, to a scalloped roof. It had a rear exit door, but it was solid blue and covered in cobwebs. Clearly nobody ever used it.

But Victor's old building was flickering again. I could sometimes see the side of a pink Victorian.

This side of the building had a couple belowground windows toward the back of the house. Annie was sitting on the paving stones with her feet dangling in the well of the one nearest me.

"Come look at this," she said, scooting over to make room.

The ground where Annie sat and the window she peeked through, it was like her presence, her interest in that spot allowed me to see it. That spot was entirely pink Victorian, complete with scalloped fish scale siding.

Around that spot, though, the rest of the building flickered, pink and brown.

I walked back out to the sidewalk.

The back of the building was still an old brown building. No flickering.

So which building was Victor's old place?

I kept calling it an apartment complex, but Carl had called it an apartment *house*. He'd said Victor's place used to be an old apartment *house*. And that to some people maybe it still looked like one.

Did he think I'd see what it was now or what it used to be?

Thanks to Annie, it seemed, it didn't matter. I was seeing two things.

Both of them could be described as an old apartment building. But only the pink Victorian was an actual house. And it matched all the other Victorians on the street. One of which was probably Carl's.

"What are you doing?" Annie asked.

And I realized that she was seeing what the house used to be. Seventy-six years ago, Victor Kane had lived in a pink Victorian apartment house.

So what was I seeing?

It was too hard to explain what I was doing, and Annie's tone sounded slightly annoyed, like she didn't really care what I was doing, she just wanted me to stop doing it. I returned to the side of the building and sat down next to her, with my feet in the window well.

"Look," she said.

36

The below-ground window's glass was covered with soot and ash, but someone—Annie, most likely—had wiped a circle clear of grime. I used my forearm to make the circle even bigger. But it didn't help me see much.

The basement wasn't pitch dark, but it wasn't brightly lit either. I had no idea how Annie was seeing anything at all.

Then again, maybe she was seeing something entirely different from what I was seeing.

"It's dark to me," I said. "What am I looking at?"

"It's dark to me, too," she said. "But look."

She leaned forward, butt rising off the paving stones, feet landing in the window well. She crouched and peered and pointed through the window, at a sharp angle, toward the back of the basement. I had to lean into Annie to get a good look.

The back wall was not a flat, plastered wall. It was exposed rock, like the yard, one floor above it. Craggy black and gray, with veins of that bright red and orange glass-like stuff. I noticed a few spots of bright yellow sulfur, too.

Annie was staring at me. "Why aren't you more impressed?"

"No, it's cool," I said.

"No. Too late for that. If you really thought it was cool, you'd be wigging out like I am."

She stood and dug her hand into her pocket, came out with a wad of plastic wrap. Inside were bits of red grit.

The red grit she'd used to buy her boss a sandwich.

The red grit that acted like money.

She had my interest. "You think it's the same?"

"Yes, I think it's the same! Even if I didn't, look at it! It's glowing red. If I didn't already have an inkling what it was, I'd be busting in there right now to mine it myself."

Before I could ask her what she thought the orange stuff was—because as far as I could tell, there were two distinct veins, two distinct colors, in the black rock, and her red grit was decidedly red, not a speck of orange—she was talking again.

"And how come you're not impressed by there even *being* a basement?"

"The training center has a basement," I said. "Floors and floors of basement."

"And no windows, as I recall," she countered. "What do you think of these windows, Corbin?" She tapped the glass. "You've clearly seen whatever's in that black rock wall before—we'll get to that later—but have you ever seen below-ground windows before?"

She had me there. I hadn't really been looking for such

windows, but now that she mentioned it, I couldn't recall seeing any anywhere else.

And the well did have a bit of a DIY feel. The paving stones that lined it didn't match the ones covering the walkway. They were misshapen, like they'd been taken from someplace else and broken to fit.

And now that I was paying attention, the frame of the window itself was blue, like it had been scavenged too, probably from another Victorian.

I pulled up on the bottom frame to open it.

"I already tried," Annie said. "It's stuck. Or locked. I'm gonna go see if I can get in."

She hopped out of the well and headed down the alley.

I stood to go with her.

"No, you stay."

"You don't want me to come?"

"And have you scaring people into locking their doors?" She flashed me a grin over her shoulder to say she was kidding. "Just stay there. I've got a better chance of getting in if I go by myself. But if you don't see me in three minutes. Come save me."

"I don't like the sound of that."

"It's fine," she whisper-yelled back at me as she turned the corner. "See you in a sec."

I continued watching the end of the alley, listening for the flickering Victorian's front door to open, for light conversation to follow.

But instead, I started hearing an electronic buzzing sound.

I glanced at the basement window.

It was gone.

The building was a brown building. No flickering pink Victorian at all—without Annie, I couldn't see it.

Ah hell, so how was I gonna know if she got in, now?

I climbed out of the well and ran down the alley, hoping Annie was still standing outside a flickering pink Victorian's front door and I'd be able to see it and her.

But there was no one on the sidewalk.

The Pit-facing side of the building was a three-story apartment complex, solid and brown. The first floor had small apartment windows on either side of a green front door with a centered glass window.

I saw no one inside. Just a hallway straight ahead, with stairs on the right, going up.

I tried the silver knob and the door opened.

I ran down the entry hall, looking for stairs going down.

The hall ended at a T. The halls on either side had two apartment doors each, but nothing else. No stairs going down.

But the T was short. It did not stretch to the back of the building. Which, I remembered, had looked like an office when the building was brown.

I headed back outside and around the brown building, still not seeing any sign of the pink Victorian or the window wells or Annie.

But as I neared where the window had been, I once again heard the buzzing sound. Like hair clippers, except the buzzing sound cut out every so often, in no discernible pattern. *Zzzzt. Zzzt-zzt.*

I rounded the corner, staying on the sidewalk, not wanting to walk on the rock yard with its veins of red and orange, and approached the building's back entrance via the four-foot paved walkway.

The signage etched on the door's glass window was small. Like it was designed to go unnoticed, to not capture anyone's attention as they walked on by. Like it was only meant to confirm for someone specifically looking for it, and walking up the walkway, that they'd found the right place.

The bronze lettering read *Physical Services Parlor*.

37

Physical Services Parlor? Like, Darryl and Angela's Physical Services Parlor? Did they have something like a franchise?

Probably not. It was more likely that all places providing physical services were called the same thing. Regardless, I peered through the window and didn't see anyone inside.

I tried the handle, and the door opened. Strange. The scent of sulfur was heavier in here. So was the buzzing sound. A light flicked on automatically.

The walls were green. Maybe even the same shade as Darryl and Angela's. The room was about the same size as their anteroom, too.

Straight ahead was a closed door, but to the left I found an open set of stairs going down.

"Annie?"

I took the stairs two at a time, palms brushing the walls on either side of me. I expected to come out on the left side of the craggy black wall, and I did, but the room was not the one I'd seen through the window.

There was no window.

There was also no Annie.

The room was big, clearly running the whole length of the lot, and the exposed-wall trend had been carried out onto the floor. I couldn't walk any further into the room without walking on black rock. One of the veins of orange had been uncovered and traced to the center of the room, where it liquified into a tiny caldera, about four feet across. Like a mini Pit. It popped and bubbled, sending up smoke and ash.

But the room didn't reek of the smell. Some kind of ventilation system seemed to be sucking it up toward a vent in the ceiling.

I figured this explained why the neighborhood was so smokey and ashy outside. Not because of the City's Pit, but because of Victor's.

But he didn't just have his own Pit. He had his own heat-worshipper tree.

It was stunted, no taller than me, but it seemed healthy. Happy, even. Leaning as it was toward its own personal heat pit.

A red bucket sat beneath it, collecting the tree's sweat.

I didn't get it. What was this place? The sign said *Physical Services Parlor*. What did a personal pit and a heat-worshipper tree have to do with Twister services or Dust Devils?

And where was Annie?

The electronic buzzing stopped. In its place, I heard conversation. Coming from upstairs. I took the stairs two at a time.

The light turned on as I reached the landing. I saw no one in the small green room.

But the conversation was louder. I could almost make out words between a few more electronic buzzes.

The only door in the green anteroom was the one across from the entrance door. I tried it.

The door opened silently onto a hallway that looked long enough to run the whole length of the building. Which made no sense. I'd definitely seen apartments on this floor on the other side.

But what really made no sense was that I recognized this hallway. The temperature was cooler in here. The wall to my right was gray concrete. The wall to my left was green plywood. Exposed bulbs were strung every four feet along the ceiling. The end of the hallway looked like a dead end from where I stood.

But I knew better. I knew this hallway. I'd just never seen it from this end before.

"I know," I heard someone say in a pacifying tone, "but let's finish this batch and then I'll go check the bucket."

I knew that voice. It was male, and kind, and not as low as I always expected it to be when face-to-face with the guy.

"Darryl?" I said.

The conversation went silent. I didn't hear anyone moving, either.

I'd never been this far down the hallway before, but I'd seen Darryl disappear into a room somewhere down here. I ran my hand along the green plywood, nudging for a hidden door.

A couple feet ahead of me, and without my help, a door opened.

Darryl peeked out. But he didn't look back at me; he

looked the other way, down the length of hallway leading to the front of the store. I could see the thick rolls at the base of his meaty head.

"What was it?" said a woman's voice. Too bright and musical to be Angela.

"I guess nothing."

"Darryl?" I said.

Darryl jumped and looked back at me. "Corbin? Dude, yo, what are you doing here?"

He looked over his shoulder, at the woman in the room, then back at me. Fear colored his face. He stepped into the hall, letting the door fall shut behind him. He was wearing a black-and-white horizontal-striped eighties scoop-neck tank top and tight surgical gloves up to his armpits.

"How'd you get in here, man? The front door's locked, and I didn't hear the bell."

I skimped on the details. I told him about how I was following a lead on an assignment when I opened a door.

"That door," I said, pointing at the door behind me, the one I'd thought, until now, opened onto the Management Building, across the street. "Except, I was over near Spoke 5, twelve blocks from the Pit.

Darryl's face blanched. "You're here as part of an assignment?"

He glanced at the closed door to his right. The woman hadn't said anything since I'd started talking, but I imagined she was listening.

And that thought was affirmed when she opened the door.

Darryl tried to block her, tried to nudge her back inside, but she palmed his muscled chest. He stopped fussing and stepped aside.

The woman wore a white cable-knit sweater and a gray wool skirt. In this heat. But it didn't seem to affect her much. Her wavy, sun-blond hair fell softly around her shoulders, and the roots were still light and bouncy. I already knew who she was, but I still dropped my gaze to her feet, looking for strappy white heels.

But her feet were bare. She stood with all her weight on her left foot. Her right knee was bent, and only the tips of her toes brushed the floor. I could see the back of her ankle.

The skin was red. And the tattoo was faded to almost nothing, except on the parts that were puffy with shiny fresh ink.

I looked back up at her face. "You're Am—"

Faster than I thought he could move, Darryl wrapped an arm around my head and slapped his other meaty palm over my mouth before I could finish saying *Amlathea*.

I couldn't move. Darryl had me in a headlock that had me thinking he could snap my neck at any moment. I stared at him with shocked eyes.

"Don't," he said. "Not here. Not ever, but especially not here."

Then, to her, "You shouldn't have come out here," he said. But his tone wasn't angry. If anything, it was sad. And if I wasn't mistaken, a sheen glistened in his reddening eyes.

38

Amlathea smiled sympathetically at Darryl. "He'd already seen me. It's why he was given the assignment."

She turned and walked back inside the room.

Darryl let go of me and straightened my shirt. "Guess you might as well come inside too, then," he said.

So I followed them both inside Darryl's room.

It was similar to Angela's room, or the room I thought of as Angela's, the one at the other end of the hall. It had exposed two-by-fours and a concrete floor. But it was bigger. There was plenty of room for the three of us. And instead of a massage table, there were two chairs. Two tattoo chairs. One was a slimmed-down black recliner, currently laid out flat, for the client. The other was a circular black stool with an elbow rest, for Darryl.

I pointed at the tattoo gun sitting on a long slender table set against the wall.

"The first couple times I heard that," I said, "I thought it was hair clippers."

"It might've been," he said, grabbing a set of hair clippers off the same table, further down. "I do hair as well. We're a full-service physical services parlor."

He rolled the circular stool between his legs and flopped down on it. His muscular thighs barely fit beneath the elbow rest.

"Do you look as miserable as you do because you've decided you're going to tell me things?" I asked him.

He snorted and half smiled an affirmative, amused but not. He sat hunched over the armrest, arms folded on top of it, and he stared at the floor, not meeting my eye.

Amlathea sat perched on the edge of the laid-out client chair, her upper body leaning forward, arms braced to either side of her legs, which she crossed at the ankles. She winked at me.

"Well, then, in appreciation for that, let me start," I said, and I pointed in the direction of the Management Building across the street. "Those guys knew about your"—I pointed at Amlathea's tattoo—"and they knew you were meeting someone at the hotel. But my boss seemed surprised to hear either of your names when I told them who I saw there and how it turned out."

"You told them," she said. A question that wasn't a question.

"Yeah," I said. I wanted to say more—that I was new here, that I didn't know what I was doing, that I wouldn't do it again—but I was still new here and I didn't know what I was doing. I didn't know yet what I might still have to do.

"Is that all?" Darryl asked.

"For now. You go."

Darryl shook his head and his lips pinched together. If he was sad and dejected before, he was inching towards pissed now.

"I'll go," Amlathea said. "But I have conditions."

Darryl inhaled a big breath and sighed it out, the pissed expression on his face relaxing. I didn't know what to make of that, whether it meant that what was coming next for me was good or bad.

I gestured for her to go ahead with her conditions.

"You can't tell anyone—"

"Then why tell me at all?"

"—about Darryl."

"Oh." I looked at Darryl, thinking he should feel relieved, but he looked pissed again. More pissed than before.

"They want to know where you're getting your work done," I said, pointing again at her tattoo. For some reason, like her name, I felt like I shouldn't say the word. Like the walls had ears. Even though I could see the two-by-fours. Maybe that's why I could see the two-by-fours. "They asked about that specifically. So what do you want me to tell them?"

"Something else?"

I snorted. "Right. Okay. Maybe you can help me with that," I asked Darryl.

He glanced at me, but he didn't say anything. I took that as a yes.

"What else?" I asked.

"Your... condition," she said. She waved a hand in front of

her own body, indicating her torso, and gave me a strange smile. I would've said it was a sad, sympathetic smile, but her eyes were most definitely sparkling.

Was that mischief? Was that... well, considering where I was, was that some kind of demonic flashing? Was that even a thing? Jeez, I hoped not.

But I knew what Amlathea was referring to.

My heart pounded.

"The striations?" I said. "The cancer without the tumor?"

Darryl looked up from his brooding, and the confused look he gave Amlathea told me Darryl hadn't told her about my condition.

She knew about it all on her own.

Did that mean she could see through the Illusion? Did that mean—

"Can you fix me?" I said, my desperation causing my voice to squeak. I had done my best not to think about my condition, to tell myself all would be well. I just had to wait for my appointment. I just had to be patient.

But if she could fix me, if this could all be over now.

"Fix you?" she said. "There's no fixing you."

Darryl turned his confused look on me, only this time it was blanching into fear. I could almost feel the striations growing inside me.

"What about Cherise Montaire?" I said.

"That's my condition," she said.

I shook my head. "I don't understand. Am I dying? *Can* I die again? Hell, I don't even know if I died the first time. One minute, I'm mowing the lawn, next thing, I'm on a table, bright lights and people looking down on me. They say I'm in the City. But that's gotta be a euphemism, 'cause I tell you what, it's not a name. It tells me nothing. I don't even know where I am. I've *guessed*. The bubbling Pit of hellfire is a pretty good giveaway, if you ask me. But I don't know for sure. I can walk through walls. Not without consequence, clearly, but I can do it. That's a silver lining, I suppose, ripped to shreds by my condition. And now you tell me, what, that you don't want me to meet with Cherise Montaire? The one person I know of who can fix me?"

I'd been standing this whole time, but my rant had exhausted me. I looked for another place to sit, couldn't find one, too tired to walk to one anyway, and just sank to the floor, the two-by-fours causing my shirt to ride up my back, my shorts to give me a wedgie, but what did it matter?

Amlathea said, not unkindly, "She can't fix you. You're not broken."

"I've seen the striations," Darryl said, "the blinking. The growth."

"Change," she said, nodding. "Not destruction."

"So I'm not dying?"

"Not in the sense you're familiar with, no."

"Something worse?"

"That's a matter of perspective," she said. "And perspectives run the gamut in the City."

"Yours is that it's not bad," she said.

"Mine is that you're lucky."

I puzzled at her, then glanced at Darryl. The scowl on his face as he looked up at Amlathea told me this was news to him, and so likely false news at that.

"But the striations," he said. "The blinking."

She smiled at him as if to say *And?*

"We got him the appointment with Cherise."

Her brow crinkled. *And?*

"Then what's your ask about her and his striations?"

"Simple," she said. "Corbin will meet with her and then tell me what she says."

"That's it?" I said.

"That's it."

"Why?"

She shrugged. "Let's just say I'm curious."

I sighed. "Fine. Is that all?"

"Depends what else we talk about now."

I got that. I was all over the place in my head, in my stomach—in my body, apparently—but I understood her position. She needed to protect herself. From something. For some reason. Like everything around here, I wasn't privy to the details. But she wouldn't know how much of a threat I posed until after she heard what else I had to say.

"Fine. Why is your tattoo already faded? It was bold at the hotel."

Amlathea and Darryl shared a look. It was the same look Darryl and Angela had shared when they'd decided not to talk to me.

But Amlathea gestured for Darryl to go ahead.

"You're the artist," she said.

39

Darryl straightened out of his sulk and unfolded his arms, leaving his elbows on the rest and clasping his hands together out in front of him. He pivoted the stool so that he was facing me.

The pause was long enough for me to register the quiet, the cool, the lack of sulfur scent, and I suddenly wondered where Angela was.

"The ink's not intended to last." He shook his head. "No, that's not right. We'd like it to last. But its purpose isn't decoration. It's safety."

"Safety."

"She..." He started to say, then he turned to her. "I can't tell this," he said.

"I'm not from here," she said to me.

I waited for more. When it didn't come, I said, "Okay. I'm not from here either."

"You are, though, in a way. These buses and buildings and things all look familiar to you. Different, but same."

"So you're saying you're not from Earth?"

She considered it. "Sure. Yeah. Let's go with that."

"You talk like you're from Earth."

She grinned. "Thank you."

I snorted a laugh. Nothing quite like giving lots and getting back lots of nothing.

"So you're not from here," I said. "What's your point?"

Darryl said, "The ink keeps her rooted here. Safely. Well, as safely as she can be."

"Are you the only one who does it, who uses it?"

Darryl narrowed his eyes at me. "Why do you ask?"

"They asked, in my assignment—"

"The red folder?"

"Yeah—where she gets the work done. They make it sound like they're just looking for a referral. But then you use words like *safety*, and I'm wondering if what they're really looking for is how to put a stop to it. Why would they care?"

"By *they*, you mean Management?" Darryl said.

"Yeah."

"Remember what I said about the gamut of perspectives?" Amlathea said.

"Yeah."

"To have so many perspectives, you need just as many people. And all of them care."

"So you're saying Management is just one perspective?"

"He's quick," she said to Darryl, poking fun at me. Then, to me, "I'm excited to see what you have to say about Cherise."

"Great, happy to help," I said, deadpan, and my mind flashed forward to meeting with Cherise tomorrow at the Pit—and then it flashed backward to when I'd climbed the Pit with Annie.

Annie.

"I've gotta get back to my friend," I said. "Can we get to the point?"

"Your friend?"

"Annie. I told you"—except I hadn't—"I was looking for her when I stumbled in here."

Amlathea's brow wrinkled with concern. "Can she get in here?"

"Doubt it. She sees a pink... wait, how am *I* in here? Why can I see this place?"

"So she's probably prowling around Victor's old place futilely looking for you? You need to go." Amlathea hopped off the table to hustle me out.

"Wait," I said, pushing myself up the wall to standing.

Darryl followed Amlathea's lead, awkwardly climbing out of his stool and rolling it out of his way. He came toward me.

"Wait," I said, holding up my hands and backing against the wall, between two two-by-fours. "They want to know what Victor wants with you."

But I was no match for Darryl. He slotted his meaty hands under my armpits and pried me bodily from the wood.

"The door, please," he said.

Amlathea opened it. Darryl carried me into the hall.

"I'll leave," I said, but Darryl didn't put me down. I dangled in his hands. "But those are Management's two questions. They want to know where you got your tattoo and what Victor wants with you."

Amlathea opened the door at the back end of the hallway.

I saw flashes of the Management Building, across the street, intermixed with flashes of the brown building's green anteroom and its entrance door with the bronze etched lettering.

Amlathea smiled innocently at me and said, "Who said it was Victor who wanted to connect?"

40

Darryl set me down outside the door.

But I didn't land back in the green anteroom on the backside of the brown building that sometimes looked like a pink Victorian, where I'd last seen Annie, where she'd probably be looking for me, and where she was probably stomping around in her purple Docs, already pissed that I was nowhere to be found.

I landed on the sidewalk, across the street from the Management Building.

Think fast, Kohl.

I guessed I'd just have to make it work.

I pulled Management's report form from my back pocket as I ran across the street and into the Management Building's lobby, to the report slot. I grabbed a pen and started scribbling, skipping all of the form's questions about weather and whatever, and writing just my name and the answers to my assignment's two questions.

Victor's not the one who wanted to connect with Amlathea.

Amlathea got her tattoo at

I tapped my pen on the form. I'd promised Amlathea I wouldn't mention Darryl. But more than that, I didn't *want* to give up Darryl.

But then I had an idea.

If I couldn't see the hospital that was over by the Hotel Burning Bright anymore, then chances were Management couldn't see it either. They'd see a post-mandate glass building.

Amlathea got her tattoo at a brown, pre-mandate building three blocks clockwise from the Hotel Burning Bright and three blocks further from the Pit.

There. Assignment done.

I stuffed the form into the return slot, then headed back out the door.

People don't like you running in the City, so I turned the movement into something more like a skip, a gallop, anything to get me back to Victor's old pink Victorian as fast as I legally could.

Except a pink Victorian was not what I found.

Down the street, still a few buildings away, I saw the old brown apartment building, solid and still, with the green front door.

Dammit.

Whatever. I started yelling, anyway. "Annie? Annie?"

I reached the edge of the building next to it and rounded the corner, down the alley.

The side of the brown building was flickering pink.

Thank goodness.

"Annie?"

But it wasn't Annie's tiny frame and pixie cut I found pacing around the closest window, arms folded, feet stomping at the paving stones, knocking the top ones into the well.

"Annie?" the woman said. "Is that the name of your little friend with the purple hair and purple boots?"

My chest tightened. "Yeah. Is she here?"

"She left, and good riddance."

I hadn't passed Annie on the way here. How long had I been gone? "Are you sure? Is she okay?"

"She's okay. So long as she doesn't nose around here no more. Mabel may not mind, but I do. Girl's mad at you, though."

I bet. Not that I blamed her.

"Thanks," I said, turning to leave.

But something caught my eye. Something in the furthest window well, the one Annie and I had peered into. I turned back to take a look, but the woman eyed me. I got the hint and got busy leaving again.

But I hung a right out of the alley and went around the building, through the other alley, to the back side. The building was brown all the way around.

Standing at the back, I peered around the corner, down the side of the building with the window wells, where I'd just been talking to the woman. She was walking toward the front of the building, with her back to me. The side of the building was still flickering pink.

I figured it would continue to flicker pink so long as she was here. But I had to be fast. And silent.

I hurried on tiptoes to the closest window well. Paving stones had been kicked off the top and into the hole, partially blocking the glass.

It was dark inside the basement, and I wasn't at the right height or angle to see the vibrant veins of red and orange on the black rock wall.

But for a split second, just before the flickering pink building shifted to solid brown, and for a lingering moment afterwards, I did see something. A dark, cool-boy haircut and a chiseled face.

Victor, looking out at me.

And he did not look happy.

41

Maybe I could catch Annie at work.

I headed back to the Management Building, keeping an eye on the sidewalk, lest Victor crack it open and drag me down again.

But I made it back to the lobby without incident. I didn't feel lucky about it, though. I couldn't shake the worry that Victor was leaving me alone now because he had something worse planned for me later.

I took the lobby elevator up to Annie's floor, but she wasn't at her desk.

Maybe she was at the cafeteria.

I took the stairs down, but the door to the second floor wouldn't open.

What the...? I jammed on the release bar, but it just wouldn't budge. Did they ban me from the cafeteria again?

I headed down the stairs to the lobby and rode the elevator back up to Terry's floor.

Carl's tidy glass desk was dark and empty.

Terry's door was closed and locked. I knocked, but no one answered.

I took the stairs back down to the lobby, stopping at the cafeteria again, just in case, but to no avail. I'd been locked out. They'd banned me again.

But why? I hadn't taken any food from the cafeteria since my one and only purloined ham sandwich.

And I'd turned in my report.

But maybe Management hadn't gotten it yet and already considered it late. Annie had told me I was already late. I'd thought she'd been joking, but maybe not so much.

Whatever. I'd visit Terry and get it squared away in the morning, before my appointment with Cherise Montaire. And as for Annie, I'd call her when I got home. Maybe we could meet up after she finished work.

I headed to the Pit to catch the Red bus home for the night.

The bus came trundling around the curve just as I got to the stop. Nice. Perfect timing. Maybe my luck was looking up again.

But I couldn't get on the bus.

The people who'd boarded in front of me got on just fine. But when I lifted a foot to step on, my toes kicked an invisible wall.

"What's going on?" I asked the bus driver, kicking the invisible wall to show him what I meant. You could hear it. *Thud, thud.*

He shrugged at me. "Step aside," he suggested.

I did, and the people behind me got on just fine.

Well, hell.

Good thing I like to walk.

I hoofed it home, trailing behind the Red bus, which wasn't much faster than me. Which I supposed was good to know, but what the hell? Why wasn't I on it?

It had to be about the report. Maybe instead of not getting it, they *had* gotten it and didn't like my answers.

Or lack of answers. Maybe this was punishment for skipping most all of the form's questions.

The bus beat me home, but not by much. My legs were beat after running all over the place all day, and I trudged up the stairs to my floor, then down the hall to my apartment.

There was a yellow post-it note stuck to my door.

Report to Terry Peaches' office at 11:00.

I pulled the note off the door and read it again.

Okay, I could do that. Easy. The note's orders were already my plan, just on a different timeframe. Although, eleven o'clock was kind of an odd time. Right before lunch. And it would give me less than an hour with Cherise Montaire. Still, that was more time than I usually got with my doctor back home. And it was nice to know that Management still considered me part of the team, even though I was probably going to get an ass chewing when I arrived.

But the last time Terry wanted something from me, he'd left me a message on my answering machine. Seemed a lot of effort to leave me a paper note, even if all he did was assign the task to some peon. So why not just call me and tell me him—

No.

I tried my door but it wouldn't open.

Dammit, *no!* My phone was in there! How was I supposed to call Annie?

And my clothes. My shirt! My *Lucky* shirt. Why wasn't I wearing it?! If I ever got back into my apartment to get it, I swear, I was never taking it off again.

And my juice boxes!

And what about my shower?

I sniffed my armpit. Ugh. I'd never needed one more.

And where was I going to sleep? My bed sucked, but it was mine.

Okay. Think, Kohl.

Should I bother my neighbors?

About what? Whether they saw who left the note? Did it matter? It was either Terry Peaches or someone I wouldn't recognize anyway, most likely the latter.

Still, one of my neighbors might take me in for the night. Never mind that I'd never met or seen any of them before.

I knocked on the other three doors on my floor, but no one answered. So much for that idea.

I sank to the floor in front of my apartment, my back to the door, my forearms on my knees. I supposed I could just sleep here for the night.

I tipped onto my side and gave it a try. Curled myself into the fetal position. Closed my eyes. The floor was hard. And the parchment map in the inside pocket of my board shorts was lumpy beneath me and was cutting into my thigh.

What I really wanted to do was rest my poor legs. Have a seat on my couch and put my feet up on my coffee table.

I rolled onto my back and kicked my legs up against the door. I supposed it was the next best thing. I stretched my arms out to either side and sighed.

Maybe someone would come home soon.

My mouth was dry. I worked my tongue to get some saliva going. But that only made my stomach growl.

No food.

No bus.

No home.

No shower.

No clothes.

No phone.

No Annie.

I supposed it was a good thing I didn't have a dog, or I'd feel terrible right about now and be a country song cliche to boot. Or so I've heard. I've never really listened to country.

But this wasn't forever. It was just until tomorrow, just overnight. Kinda like camping. But without any gear. But that was okay. It wasn't like the weather was bad. Hot, uncomfortable, sweaty, absolutely. But I'd be okay. I even had a roof over my head.

And by this time tomorrow, it would all be over. My chastising from Management. My meeting with Cherise Montaire. By this time tomorrow, it would all be done with, and I'd be okay.

Right?

42

I sat on an indigo bench in Purgatorium Park at Spoke 6, near the Indigo bus stop, just outside the ring of heat-worshipper trees. Light gray smoke billowed from their beloved caldera and stunk up the air. The gritty black dirt that covered the park grounds crunched under my foot as my knee bounced. My stomach felt queasy from more than just hunger and the expanding striations.

I'd gotten here early to meet Cherise Montaire, but you wouldn't have known it from the bright yellow sky shining down on me like high noon.

On Earth, the birds would have been singing and looking for worms. The sun would have been just starting to lighten the horizon.

Here, in the City, there were no birds. No worms, either. And definitely no sunrises. The Pit roared as it boiled and popped in its three-story caldera, and the only other living things besides people were the trees. Their sweat hissed as it dripped onto the black grit, adding a sweet nectar scent to the ubiquitous rotten sulfur.

There were actually quite a few people out this morning. Or maybe they came out this early every morning. I sure didn't. Most of them were exercisers. Joggers, walkers, stretchers. All of them wearing some manner of workout shorts and T-shirts.

I looked right, toward Spoke 5.

I looked left, toward Spoke 7.

Maybe Cherise Montaire would be super early like I was. Maybe I should find a bench that faced away from the Pit instead of toward it.

Maybe you should relax, Kohl.

I pried the parchment map out of my pocket. Unfolded it. I'd used it last night for the few hours I'd slept as a pillow, and the creases were becoming more delicate and threatening to tear.

I studied the cluster of upside-down *C*s.

The few singularly placed upside-down *V*'s.

The patches of dashes.

What was the point of this thing? Why had Management given it to me? As far as I could tell it had nothing to do with anything. I'd answered Management's questions about Amlathea without it.

The humps, the upside-down *C*s looked like hills. But they also looked like the pinecone buds in the grayish-green field, and the scales of a fish, and the scalloped siding on the pink Victorian.

The upside-down *V*s looked like mountains. But they

also looked like sharp teeth or the tips of horns, like spearheads, and like the conical shape of a heat-worshipper tree.

The dashes looked like grass, or maybe rays of heat, like the corona of a sun, or the glint of something shiny.

And the lines that looked like a windy road, was that what they were? Or were they something else entirely?

I blew out a sigh and leaned my head back. I'd studied the parchment's markings until my eyes glazed over. But I was still no clearer about their purpose.

I checked the time on my watch against the time on the Management Building's digital clock tower. After lying on the hallway floor outside my apartment for a few hours, I'd gotten bored, and nervous about being late, and so I'd started my trek toward the Pit. I'd gotten here hours and hours early. My butt was sore from so much time spent on the bench. But both my watch and the clock tower said it was finally getting close to early lunchtime.

I only had a few more minutes to wait for Cherise Montaire.

I folded the parchment up and straightened a leg as I shoved it back into my pocket.

I looked right.

I looked left.

The people walking past me now were all dressed for the day in slightly dressier shorts and shirts. I caught the eye of anyone who came close enough and smiled at them, just in case they were Cherise Montaire.

Are you my savior?

Are you *my savior?*

I got a variety of responses, from smiles to puzzlement to frowns, but no one joined me on the bench.

Then I saw a woman wearing baggy black pants and a billowy, brightly colored blouse, like someone had splashed her with all the primary colors of paint. She was a heavyset woman, but the baggy fit of her clothes made her look heavier than she probably was. The blouse flowed and billowed around her so much, I thought she had to be holding out her arms.

And maybe she had been, at first. I hoped that maybe she was waving at me, smiling, excited to see me, to help me. But as she got closer, I noticed she was keeping her head down. She had wild auburn hair, as wild and billowy as her shirt. I placed her in her fifties, but I could've been off by twenty years in either direction. She walked awfully fast, but her face had seen a lot of sun.

And I just knew it was her. Cherise Montaire. I rose off the bench to greet her.

She looked up from the sidewalk for just a second and glanced at me. She smiled. And there were so many things in that smile.

Recognition.

Friendliness.

Wisdom.

But the smile only lasted a second.

Her eyes left mine and trailed down my body—dragging the corners of her mouth down with them and into a frown. Her brow crinkled and her eyes widened until I could only describe her expression as one of horrified shock.

Her eyes flashed up to meet mine. Just for a second. Just long enough to offer a silent apology.

She turned and darted across the street, away from the park.

Away from me.

"Wait!" I said as I ran toward her.

The Indigo bus was stopped at the bus stop. She ran straight for it, running behind it, through its exhaust, and stepping up onto the curb.

I was further down the street. I headed for the front of the bus, figuring I could run around it and catch her at the door.

Through the bus's front window, I saw her board. She stared out at me, the terror still on her face.

I trailed my hand along the bus face to slow myself down and keep my balance as I made the sharp U-turn, to climb the bus's stairs. I led with my head as I lifted my foot—and smacked into nothing. I stumbled backward onto the sidewalk.

"No!" I tried again, pretending the ban barrier was nothing more than a glass wall. I tried to step through, to push through. The invisible wall blocking me from boarding the bus might as well have been a Kevlar boulder the size of the Pit. I was never getting past it.

"Step back, please," said the driver, like he saw this kind of thing every day. He kept his eyes on the road, his hand on the gear shift.

I did as he asked, because what else could I do?

The woman with the wild hair and the colorful blouse chose a seat a few rows back from the door and peered out at me. I couldn't read her weathered face. There was too much going on. Fear. Sympathy. Shame. She didn't try to say anything to me that might help this all make sense.

The bus pulled away from the curb and turned the corner, down Spoke 6. I watched it go, then followed after it.

I told myself I was following it because I had to go to the Management Building anyway to meet with Terry, which was true, but not the whole of it.

I could feel the blinking. I'd been feeling the striations, the stretching stretch marks, for what felt like days now. But feeling the blinking was new. Like a pulse of dull pain I feared would eventually turn sharp. And now I would just have to live with it.

Or die from it.

The worst part was that I didn't know which.

I tried to keep pace, but my choppy, heaving breaths were affecting my gait. The bus slowly pulled ahead of me.

The woman appeared in the window that stretched across the back of the bus. I knew it was her, Cherise Montaire, because of the shirt, that happy, colorful shirt.

She stared at me, her palms pressed to the glass. I stared back at her, waved back at her.

But when the bus stopped again, she didn't get off.

43

Four blocks from the Pit, with the bus an indigo dot in the distance down Spoke 6, I hung a right and stopped by the Physical Services Parlor. I was cutting it close to my meeting with Terry and probably threatening the reinstatement of my food and housing privileges, but apparently my motivational mechanism thought my condition took higher priority.

The parlor's glass door was locked, so I banged on it hard enough to rattle the glass. Maybe Angela or Darryl could explain to me why Cherise Montaire had abandoned me at the Pit. Or what I was supposed to do about my condition now, now that I had no appointments to look forward to.

But nobody came to the door.

My stomach growled. I could smell something cutting through the sulfur scent and it smelled deliciously like pizza. Tomatoes and basil and yeast.

I checked my watch again. I could spare a few more minutes to wait for Darryl or Angela, but I found myself turning away from the parlor and heading toward the Management Building, figuring I might as well head to my meeting with Terry.

A health condition may trump housing and gruel, but apparently nothing trumps pizza.

And the sooner I had my meeting with Terry, the sooner my privileges to the cafeteria would be reinstated, and the sooner I could eat and get home for a proper nap. I deserved one. I'd had a long and strenuous few days.

You know how when nothing's going right and so you step up the bravado and the bad humor in hopes that you can mentally muscle your way through all the crap to what you want, to what you need?

I needed my apartment. I needed to eat. I needed Management to stop randomly taking away my basic necessities. But I could feel that my certainty about them giving back what was mine was nothing more than a facade. If I thought about how this might all turn out for more than a second, for longer than it took me to tell myself, *sure, yeah, everything'll be better in an hour*, I felt the worry.

What happened to the person who'd had my apartment before me?

Was I about to find out?

The shoe-goo marbled sidewalk passed beneath my feet. I reached the end of the fifth block and looked right, wondering if I should knock on the Physical Services Parlor's back door.

I decided against it. Darryl had made it clear he didn't like me coming in that way. And I didn't want Management to see me entering through the back door anyway, what with their thirty-three floors staring down at me from across the street.

And the street was busy, filled with people in shorts and collared shirts funneling into the Management Building. And no wonder. The smell of pizza was better than advertising. It was like lasagna day, only even more intoxicating and even more busy.

But I would get none of it until after my meeting with Terry. Maybe not even then.

I glanced up at the second-floor window, at the corner on the left where my table was, wondering if I'd ever get to sit at it again.

And I saw purple-tinted hair.

"Annie!"

People on the sidewalk turned and stared at me.

"Annie!" I called again.

"Why don't you just go in and talk to her," some guy said before darting between cars.

"Because I can't," I yelled after him.

He glared back at me. Like how dare I answer his snide and obviously rhetorical question. And at a yell, no less. Unheard of.

I supposed I was probably violating City norms. Most people usually kept to themselves. Didn't draw attention. Definitely didn't call out for others.

Annie probably couldn't hear me anyway. The windows seemed pretty soundproof.

But I didn't care. I stood on the street corner, waving my arms, and called again.

"Annie!"

She didn't hear me.

But someone else sitting near the window saw me. I waved at him, then pointed at Annie. I mimed her overalls and her purple pixie cut. The guy got out of his chair and got her attention for me.

She looked over her shoulder, out the window at me, pizza slice in hand.

I waved both arms high in the air and grinned.

I'd found her.

She glared back at me. Narrowed her eyes and made a face. An angry mug.

Then she shook her head and grinned.

I grinned back. "Meet me downstairs!" I yelled. I knew she couldn't hear me, but maybe she could read my lips.

I could read hers.

She mouthed, "What?"

I pointed at the lobby and said it again. "Meet me downstairs!"

I stepped off the curb and started running across the street. I'd found Annie. And she wasn't entirely mad. Maybe my luck was turning.

Oh, it was turning, alright. But not in the direction I wanted.

I saw Annie stand and look out the window.

"Meet me downstairs," I told her again, pointing at the lobby. I was halfway across the street now. Cars slowed to let me pass.

And the ground opened up in front of me.

The pavement just cracked and fell away, like a sinkhole.

The crowd screamed and sucked in a collective gasp. They elbowed each other and pointed at the gaping hole in the ground.

"It's Victor!" they yelled.

"Victor Kane!"

"Watch out!" they yelled.

That warning was for me.

But I was already in motion. My foot stepped down onto nothing and kept going, pulling me with it. I tumbled into the hole, wondering if this was why no one in the City was allowed to run.

44

I fell in what felt like slow motion.

Maybe because I never came to a stop.

Just as the street closed over the top of me, something snaked around my waist and yanked me backward at lightning speed.

I jackknifed in half. Nose to knees. My arms and legs flopped in my own wake like a set of useless tails.

Dirt and darkness passed by me in a blur, scraping up my back as it pushed up my shirt and got in my shorts.

But better backwards than forwards, I supposed.

I made no turns, just plowed straight back.

But having just come from a bench at Purgatorium Park, I knew precisely where that direction led.

And those five blocks passed by fast.

The moist, flaky soil became hard and gritty. It crackled around me. Black instead of brown. The loamy, earthy smell gave way to an odor like soot and brimstone. The scent was so strong that facing away from it didn't keep me from tasting it on my tongue.

And then I made a sharp turn. Not left. Not right. Down.

My arms and legs trailed behind me higher than my butt.

He was taking me under the Pit.

45

irt gave way to open air, and I skidded to a stop on hard, craggy rock. I unfolded from the jackknife and lay on my back, catching my breath.

I was on the floor of a shallow cavern. Orange and red veins webbed across the black rock ceiling. Something slick and yellow dripped and sizzled on the ground. The air smelled fresher than expected. But then, pure sulfur is odorless.

"Have you made your decision, boy?"

Still lying on my back, I tilted my head upwards, scraping my scalp against the rock, and looked upside down at Victor Kane. He wore a cream linen shirt and khaki cargo shorts hemmed at the knee. The side pockets were bulging. His arms were folded and he stared down at me, impatient.

I rolled onto my front and pushed up to standing.

"Are we under the Pit?" I asked.

"You bet. And don't make me prove it to you. Answer the question."

"What decision?"

"Whose side are you on, boy?"

"Um… my side?"

Victor narrowed his eyes, but then he laughed and uncrossed his arms. "Management won't accept that answer. Not an angel's chance in hell. But me? I kinda like that answer."

"Good?"

"But being on your own side doesn't mean I don't still need you to do something for me."

"Like what?"

"You interrupted me four days ago."

"At the Hotel Burning Bright? When you were meeting your lady friend?"

"That's not funny, boy," Victor said, and his tone told me that while he may not be about to kill me and might even find me somewhat amusing—that could all change in an instant. "And not accurate, either. The woman and I have an arrangement. Not that kind," he added.

He crossed his arms again and paced the cavern, tilting his head when the ceiling was too low for him to stand.

"I'm going to tell you something," he said. "And then you are going to do something for me. Management will want a report about it. But you will not give them one. And you won't make anything up, either."

He gave me a pointed look that told me he knew I'd thrown the old hospital clinic under the bus. I hoped I didn't get them into any real trouble. But if he had so many eyes and ears, what did he need with me?

"You won't mention a word," he continued. "To anyone. In exchange, I will give you something you *can* tell them that should keep them off your back a little while longer." He stopped pacing and faced me. "Deal?"

I looked around the dripping cavern. I had no way to get home on my own. So I didn't really have a choice but to do whatever Victor wanted.

But instead of pointing that out to him, I figured I'd stay on his good side and prove to him that I didn't have to say things just because I had the insight.

"Deal." I tensed and cringed away from him. "Does it have to do with the Pit?"

"Not this pit."

I pointed at the ceiling. "Is this not the City's Pit?"

"It is. You wanna see?" He poked a finger into the rock ceiling. Red molten hellfire dripped and then gushed into the cavern, hitting the floor and then splashing onto my shins.

I jumped back, trying to stay out of the way. "No!" I cried. "I don't want to see."

He put his arm down.

"Wait!" I cried, thinking his finger was the only thing bracing the dam. But the gushing stopped entirely.

I brushed the burning spray off my legs, off my shoes, then stayed hunched for a second, hands on my knees, catching my breath.

"I'll help you," I said. "You don't have to threaten me. You could've just asked."

"Could I have? You would just *help* Victor Kane?"

"The guy who can open walls and travel underground? The guy who might teach me to do the same if I get on his good side? Yeah. That's a guy I'd like to know."

"But I'm a Victor."

"So is Victor Tamales. Have you had his tacos? He gave me one for a quarter. I've been craving them ever since."

Victor laughed. "A man who sees the bigger picture. Even while living the fearsome details."

"Fearsome? Are we not past that yet?"

"No."

I sighed. "Okay."

Victor laughed. "You're a rare breed, kid. But to your point, I couldn't have just asked you. If Management thinks you're helping me willingly, they'll name you Victor. You'll lose your position. You won't be any use to me. But if I force your compliance, they'll see you as valuable. Maybe even give you a promotion. They'll reward you. And that'll make you invaluable to me."

He pulled something from his back pocket. A flask. He unscrewed the lid and handed it to me. "But I do appreciate the sentiment."

I took a sip.

Water.

Cool, refreshing water.

I'd never tasted anything so good.

I wanted another sip, but I handed the flask back to him.

"Wait," I said. "Was it you who left me the note on my door?"

He quarter smiled.

"So Management doesn't want to see me? I'm banned for good?"

"Oh, they'll want to see you after this," Victor said. "Everyone will want to see you after this."

I nodded. "And that's why the note said eleven o'clock. So there would be witnesses. Did you know they were having pizza?"

My stomach growled at the thought of pizza.

Victor grinned at full watt. "I may have placed an order."

"You can eat at the cafeteria?"

"No. No buses for me, either. I'm banned, same as you. But I might get a pie or two." He grinned.

"Huh. Well, add ordering pizza to my list of things I want you to teach me," I said. "So what's the plan?"

46

Victor insisted on staying in the cavern while he laid out his plan. He said he had many hidey-holes, but in one way or another most of them were compromised. But this one he was certain no one knew about. No one except me.

"So if I hear wind of it, I'll know who told."

"I won't tell."

I was sitting cross-legged on the uneven rocks. I was starving, and I figured that, whatever Victor had planned, I should probably conserve my energy.

Victor was pacing.

"The woman—"

"Amlathe—"

"Don't say her name. It puts her at risk."

"Okay," I said, caught off guard by his reasoning. When Annie and I had been discussing the saying of names, we'd been concerned for ourselves. It had never occurred to me to be concerned for the named one. "But how does that work?"

"It brings her to mind. And if people think she's here, people start looking for her."

"But why? Who cares if she's here? Is she not always here?"

"Management cares. And, no, she's not always here. Can I continue?"

"Yeah. Sorry."

"The woman and I meet on occasion. Usually at a hotel. Always after a rain. She comes at great risk, and I take great risk to help her. But four days ago, Management sent you. I don't know how they knew. But they did. How much notice did you get about your assignment?"

I shrugged. "Fourteen hours, maybe. I got home and there was a message to check into the hotel. That I was looking for an exchange between a woman with a sea-goat tattoo and someone else."

"So, they know about the tattoo."

"Yeah. But that's about all they know."

"And you thought the person she was meeting was me?"

"You're the only person she met."

"And Management thinks that, too? That she was meeting me?"

"Yeah."

"Good. Better than the alternative."

"Was she not meeting you?"

"No."

"Then who was she meeting?"

He didn't answer. Didn't even acknowledge the question. He was pacing again. And he looked worried.

I hazarded a guess. "Have you not seen her since that morning?"

"No. But I haven't heard any news about her. So I'm assuming she's okay."

"She's okay."

Victor stopped pacing and his head whipped my way. "What? How do you know?"

"Um," I suddenly had a worry that I shouldn't have said anything. But then I remembered that Amlathea herself had said that she was the one who had wanted to meet with Victor. "I talked to the driver of the front loader you pushed her into."

Victor had the decency to grimace and look guilty. "And?"

"He said he dropped her off at a hospital a couple blocks away. I went to check it out after I got out of the fields."

I paused, waiting for a reaction from Victor. But he offered no guilty grimace for what he'd done to me.

I continued: "But instead of a hospital what I found was more like an old pediatrics clinic. They seemed to know Amla—your friend, though. Although they denied it. Didn't like me asking about her. The nurse kicked me out, and then the building turned into a typical post-mandate glass building."

"I saw that," Victor said.

"You did?"

"Yeah," he said. And he didn't sound happy about it.

"Did you know your old house is both a pink Victorian and an old brown apartment building with an office at the back?"

"Yup."

"Which one's your old apartment?"

"The Victorian."

"Did you know not everyone can see the brown apartment building?"

"Yup."

"Do you know why?"

"Yup."

I waited for him to say more.

He didn't.

"You want to tell me why?"

"Nope." Then, "So you haven't actually seen her. But you did talk to people about her. And you probably told them her name, too, right?" He shook his head. "So something still could've happened to her." He bit his thumb and tilted his head, considering. "But I haven't heard anything. That's something."

"I saw her yesterday," I said. "So she was okay as of yesterday."

"You saw her? Where'd you see her?"

"Um." I didn't want to get Darryl in trouble. "I'd rather not say?" But my voice rose at the end, making the statement sound more like I was asking permission. And I supposed I was. Pretending to be nice to me or not, Victor had brought me here and I wasn't getting out of here without him.

Victor narrowed his eyes at me. I instinctively inched further away from him.

But then he seemed to decide that not knowing was best for everyone.

"Did she seem okay?"

"I mean, yeah, I guess. Good spirits, good humor. All in one piece. I don't really know her. Is that what you mean?"

"Yeah. Okay. So that was yesterday?"

"Yeah."

"What time?"

I shrugged. "Late afternoon?"

He nodded, trying to convince himself. "Okay. Okay, good. So she's okay."

"What's the plan, Victor?" I said softly. "What were the two of you trying to do at the hotel?"

"Sometimes mistakes are made," he said. "She tries to correct them. And I try to be someone worthy of her corrections."

He inhaled a deep breath through his nose and blew it out through his mouth. Then he put his hands on his hips and faced me. "Okay, then, kid. Time to make it rain."

47

Victor said he'd never made it rain before. And he wasn't really going to make it rain now. But he had to make it seem like something was drizzling down from the sky. It was the only way he could think of to send the message to Amlathea to meet him again at the Hotel Burning Bright.

"Except it won't be me meeting her. It'll be you. You can see the brown office building, the old doctor's office. You'll be able to help her."

"Wait. After the nurse kicked me out, it wasn't an old doctor's office anymore. It was just another glass building. And trust me, I wanted to see the clinic. They sent me home with juice boxes."

"I'm gonna be honest," he said. "It's not great that it shifted on you. But you still saw the brown apartment building, right?"

"Yeah. Flickering with a pink Victorian. And that was after I saw the clinic."

"Flickering because someone else was there?"

"Yeah. Yeah, when I was alone it was brown, solid brown."

Victor nodded, blew out a breath. He seemed more nervous than I was. "Okay. Okay, then, we've got a chance. Either way, you're all I've got. Here."

He dug in one of his cargo pockets and came out with a pair of sunglasses, his rimmed hat with the neck flap, and a pair of gloves.

"Take these," he said, handing them to me. Then he pointed at the black rock wall. "Get going."

"What?"

"It's been four days, five. She's gotta be running out of time here."

"Okay," I said, putting on the gloves and hat. It was too dark to wear the sunglasses. I slid them into my back pocket. "How do I get to the Hotel?"

"Run."

"Run? How? Where? You can't take me?"

"I gotta make it rain, boy. We gotta do this fast enough that Management's still worrying about where you went long after we're done."

"But..."

I placed my gloved hand on the black rock only to yank it back hard, my skin screaming. The glove looked fine, but it felt like the rock had burned my palm. It was hotter than a stove burner set on high.

I looked back at Victor, unable to mask the fear and dread and pain and damn-fool plain cluelessness about how to do what he was asking me to do.

"It's just another glass wall," he told me. "Go, straight that way." He pointed a few degrees to the right of where I'd burned my hand. "You'll know you've arrived when you hear the construction crew. The hole they're digging should be deep enough now that you'll walk right out into it if you aim right."

"But..."

"Let me put it to you this way, boy. I didn't get you out of those fields. And I'm not getting you out of this cave. Wouldn't even if I had time. You want out? You go. Go now, while it still matters whether or not you make it."

48

In training, after some of us managed to make it through the glass wall and they'd separated out those who couldn't, the trainers sat us down and gave us some tips for getting through other types of wall materials.

The tip I thought of now was the one they'd mentioned about novelty. I already knew I could walk through a wall. I'd done it before. I could do it again. So ability wasn't the problem. If I was hesitating, it was because something about the wall was new.

"Maybe the material. Maybe the location."

Maybe the fact that it was ten blocks thick, give or take?

Either way, something about the wall was new and therefore scary. "Totally understandable," they'd said.

Their solution?

"Just run at it."

But I don't think the training staff had this kind of wall in mind. Half a mile's worth of black craggy rock with orange and red veins and spots of oozing yellow sulfur.

The melting point of sulfur is more than two hundred degrees Fahrenheit. I'd learned that on a family trip to Yellowstone.

Earthly ponds rimmed with bright yellow sulfur deposits that I can admire safely from afar and at my leisure?

Pretty cool.

Hellish black craggy berm a half-mile thick and dripping molten hot yellow sulfur that had already burned a hole in my shoe and that I had to press my poor body into?

Not so cool.

But I wanted out of here.

And I wanted to save the day.

And I am nothing if not a willing student.

So I sucked in a lung full of air like I was going for a deep dive—because, let's face it, I was—and I *just ran at it*.

I led with my hands. My knuckles, to be precise. It seemed a better idea to burn the backs of my hands instead of my palms, just in case, you know, I actually made it through and needed to grab onto something later.

My run turned into more of a lunge. One leg straight back, the other one bent, both legs trying to give me leverage to push my hands into the rock.

If glass is easy and decorative desert rock is like molasses, then passing into black volcanic rock is just this side of impossible. Almost like a Management ban barrier.

Except I was making some progress.

I was almost wrist deep.

And the best part was that it no longer burned.

And that gave me the motivation, the surge to push harder.

And the rock yielded. I imagined its atoms and mine twisting sideways to accommodate each other in the same space. On Earth, that would sound ridiculous. But I wasn't on Earth anymore. I was in the City.

And I was getting ahead.

I looked over my shoulder to see if Victor was watching, if he was proud.

But he was gone.

That shook my focus for a moment.

What if I got stuck?

What if I didn't make it?

But I was making it. I was chest deep now.

I sucked in a fresh gulp of air and buried my face in the rock.

49

A few steps into the rock and I started to get disoriented. All my previous walk-throughs, I would have been out by now. Ten times over. Twenty times over.

The rock moved around me like grainy molasses in winter. Every step was a fight.

But I just kept on kicking.

Another step.

Another step.

I just had to keep going.

Just keep going, Kohl.

Victor had said if I continued straight in this direction, I would come out in the construction site's excavation hole. I pinned all my hopes on his word. Because if he'd lied, or if he was just plain wrong—*Don't think about that, Kohl.*

Just keep going.

Just keep going.

But the Hotel Burning Bright was several blocks away. Ten or so, give or take.

I didn't know how many. I'd never counted how many. I'd always just looked for the bright pink facade.

If I'd known how many blocks away it was, I could've done the math, could've counted my steps. I could've given myself something concrete to focus on, to accomplish. I could've known when to expect my exit.

But I had no idea where I was. How far I'd come or how far I still had to go. All I could do was keep going.

I listened for the sounds of excavation equipment. But I didn't hear a thing. Not even the rock passing by me. It was like a sensory deprivation chamber down here.

Black.

Silent.

Odorless.

Only the taste of ash and the occasional sharp scratch on my arms kept me clued to where I was.

Deep underground, far below the city.

Wait. How could Victor be telling the truth? He had to be wrong.

I'd climbed the Pit with Annie. The bottom of the caldera was several stories down. I doubted the excavation crew was digging that deep.

So how could I come out in their hole?

The question alone made my chest tighten up, never mind the answer. And whenever my chest tightened up, it heightened the sensation of the striations, their movement inside me. I could feel them stretching. Growing.

And that feeling, that reminder, only made my chest tighten up more.

Instinctively, I sucked in a gasp.

But my lungs didn't get much air. Down here, there was no air.

And I thought of something Darryl had told me. That thing about the fish being plucked out of the pond, into open air, only to be thrown back, now aware of the water.

I exhaled, trying to do it calmly, like normal, and not like I was freaking out.

Then I let myself inhale, smooth and controlled.

It was a habit. Breathing was something I'd done for twenty-eight years back on Earth.

But was it something I needed to do here?

Was I *really* tasting ash?

Or did I just expect to?

Victor traveled through dirt. I'd seen it. I'd been in it. Loamy, moist dirt. Plus, he had that bubble, that empty bubble of space around him.

So why was I pushing through rock?

I fought for my next step, and my next, like all the steps that had come before. My knee led the way. My foot hinged forward, toes pushing a little further so that my foot could stomp down.

But suddenly my kicking toes met no resistance.

I'd been pushing forward so hard that the sudden increase in momentum pulled me forward.

I tumbled out of the rock into open air. And was pelted by hot, molten rain.

50

Victor had caused a downpour, alright. But there was no calling this stuff rain. Not the earthly kind.

It smelled like rotten eggs and brackish swamp. Ash and dollops of lava and big black chunks of tephra hit my skin like thrown gravel. The feeling of it was almost nice, given the disorientation job traveling through half a mile of volcanic rock had done to my body, twisting my cells all out of joint. My insides burned with electric aftershocks. Even my clothes clung to me like they'd been wrangled by the Illusion into becoming an uncomfortable part of my body.

But the falling debris hit so hard it felt like maybe it was knocking some of my cells back into place. If I made it through this, a Twister service would be the first thing on my agenda, I tell you what.

I squinted up at the yellow sky, then fumbled in my pocket for the glasses Victor had given me and put them on. The sky was smokey gray, but it glowed blindingly bright in the direction I'd come from, where a pyroclastic cloud mushroomed over the Pit.

I viewed all this from the bottom of a two-story hole in the ground. The sides were black rock, with only a couple veins of red and no sign of anything orange or yellow.

The site and the streets and the buildings beyond were silent save for the volcanic debris pelting the City like a hailstorm. It must've been going on for some time now, long enough for the construction crew to abandon their equipment and take cover.

Thankfully, they'd been in the middle of digging out this hole. The big yellow excavator was still down here, its long arm bent in half. The bucket rim was touching the ground, in mid-dig. But the arm's bent elbow was pointing skyward a short distance from the edge of the hole.

I climbed on top of the cab and shimmied up the arm, holding tight to the metal hydraulic system. The tip of the elbow was further away from the hole's edge than I'd thought. But I made the leap anyway. I landed on my stomach, legs dangling, elbows all scraped up. It took some strain and struggle, but I managed to pull myself out.

And, man, did my arms feel the fatigue. If I made it through this, I'd have to ask Darryl where he went to the gym.

Stay focused, Kohl.

I looked around, spotted the Hotel Burning Bright's pink exterior, and ran through the storm, shielding my face with my forearms.

How was I supposed to find Amlathea? I didn't want to call out her name.

I ran across the street and down the sidewalk toward the hotel's sliding glass entrance.

Erich, the guy who'd offered to give me information about acceptable forms of payment but only for a price, was behind the front desk. He had his face pressed against the floor-to-ceiling glass, and he flinched every time a big piece of falling rock made a dent in the sidewalk.

I waved to get his attention.

When he saw me, he backed away from the window. I thought he must've left to go hit a button to open the sliding glass doors for me, to help me get in faster. But the doors didn't open. And when I stepped in front of them, they remained closed. I had to grab the doors where they joined and pry them apart.

"Thanks for nothing," I mumbled as I stepped inside, brushed off as much dirt as I could, and generally made a mess just inside the doors. Then, to Eric, "I'm looking for a woman. Blond hair…"

I stopped talking because Erich was staring at me with wide eyes, and he had his back pressed against the wall like he wanted to sink into it and hide.

"What's the matter?" I asked. It couldn't be me. He hadn't been scared of me when I'd come in to talk to him a couple days ago.

Erich jutted his chin toward the back of the lobby, then inched along the wall like he was trying to scoot further away from me.

There were a handful of people waiting out the storm in the hotel bar. Enough that the hotel had put a man behind the counter to serve up drinks. The beer dispenser hissed and gurgled as he poured from the tap. Most of the customers wore steel-toed boots and hard hats. They sat at the high-top tables, hunched over pint glasses and talking quietly. I spotted the construction site's foreman sitting with part of his crew. If he saw me—and I thought he did; he was looking right at me—he didn't acknowledge me. So I didn't wave.

I scanned the four red wingbacks, the elevators. I tried to poke my head into the breakfast room, but I hit an invisible wall. Another ban barrier. No food for Kohl.

No Amlathea, either.

Your plan isn't working, Victor.

And never mind that I only knew the first step of his plan and had no idea what to do once I actually found her.

But where was she? I couldn't help worrying that maybe Victor was right and something had happened to her. Maybe Management found her after Darryl finished her tattoo and she left the parlor.

But if she wasn't here, then what had Erich been nodding me towards?

I went back to the desk to ask him.

He was on the phone.

When he saw me, his eyes widened and he backed away again. But he didn't hang up.

"Who are you calling?" I asked. In my mind, I pictured Management. Terry, in his blue shorts suit, stomping his little feet into the hotel lobby and dragging me off by the shorts to who knew where. Someplace awful, no doubt. "Put the phone down," I said.

"She told me to call."

"What?"

"Your blond woman. She gave me a phone number and told me to call when you arrived. I'm calling her, sir."

"'Sir'?"

"Yes, sir. But she isn't answering."

"Well, what room is she in? I'll head up."

"She isn't in the hotel, sir."

"Then where are you calling?"

"I don't know, sir. She gave me the number and left. She said to call when you arrived and to try to keep you hidden."

"'Hidden'?"

"Yes, sir."

"Why do you keep calling me sir?"

Erich's eyes widened. "I'm sorry. If you could wait in the breakfast nook, that might be safer for all of us."

He made a pointed glance at the construction crew in the bar.

They were watching us. And I didn't like how they were looking at me. I scratched my head.

And touched the hat. Victor's hat. The unmistakable rimmed hat with the neck flap. After the journey through the rock and all the disorienting it did to my cells, I'd been so physically uncomfortable everywhere that I'd forgotten I was wearing it. Wearing his gloves, too.

I turned back to Erich. "Who do you think I am?"

Erich's eyes widened. He kept the phone to his ear, but he backed away from me again.

"What would it take to get me a room here?" I asked.

"Not much, sir. Just please don't hurt me."

"How much is not much?"

"Do you want a room? I can put you up—"

"No, I just want to know what would buy me a room."

"Depends who's on the desk, sir. Lee told me he took a pair of shoes once, but he got demoted for it. To housekeeping. They said if he was going to steal, they rather he do it from the customers. I don't know what the manager takes."

"What do you take?"

"I don't, sir. Too risky. But if you want a room while you wait. Just... if you could keep it secret."

"So there's no way to legit rent a room without Management's approval?"

"I don't think so, sir. Not that I'm aware of."

"What about red grit?"

"Red grit, sir?" Erich shook his head, clearly stressed that he didn't know what I was talking about. If he had, he would've told me.

Well, maybe not me. But he was eager to tell Victor. He was afraid of Victor Kane.

"Never mind," I said, drumming impatient fingers on the counter. I'd learned what I wanted to know. "Still no answer?"

Erich looked at the phone like he'd forgotten he was holding it. He pressed it to his ear. "It's still ringing."

He held the phone out to me, but I waved it away. "When the woman left, did you see which way she went?"

"Yes." Erich pointed to the left, down the sidewalk, towards the construction site.

"How long ago was that?"

Erich cringed and clutched the phone. "I don't know, sir. Twenty minutes, maybe?"

Twenty minutes. Had Amlathea passed by the construction site as I was climbing out of the hole?

But why didn't she wait for me here?

Why would she venture out and brave Victor's rain?

I didn't know. But I felt I had to go find her rather than wait for her here. I didn't know how long Victor could keep up this rain. Or how long the city could put up with it. The sidewalk outside the hotel was pitted and pot-holed. Any more damage and it would be unwalkable.

"When she answers, tell her I'm here. I'll check back in ten minutes."

And I headed out into the storm.

51

Rocks and lava rained down on me as I reached the end of the block.

Across the street, the construction site was flickering.

It was just a split-second blink every few seconds. Not enough to see two different places, just the construction site. If I hadn't seen flickering before, I probably wouldn't have even noticed. So what did that mean?

Another question for another time.

I ran across the street toward the flickering site.

And I saw her.

She was kitty-corner from me, on the next block up.

She had her forearms over her head, trying to shield her face from the storm. Her blond hair was a flat mess. She crossed the street to the construction site, then turned towards me, on her way back to the hotel. She was running, probably as fast as she could, but she was still slow over the uneven ground. And her strappy heels weren't helping her any. One of them was broken, the ankle strap flapping. Her poor feet.

I picked up the pace and ran across the street at an angle, leaping over larger divots in the road, to meet her at the corner of the sidewalk.

Amlathea! I called her name in my mind, unwilling to say it out loud, not after Darryl and Victor had both told me not to, but also feeling like if I didn't call out for her, then I wasn't doing enough.

Amlathea!

And she looked up. She seemed relieved to see me. But almost immediately her expression changed. Confusion.

She knew I wasn't Victor Kane. She stumbled into a pothole.

"He told me to meet you," I yelled through the sound of pounding hail. "He told me to help you."

I reached her and bent down to help her up. Her white sweater was covered in ash and cinders and burn holes. "Are you okay?"

I could see that she wasn't okay. The debris falling from the sky hurt and left ashy welts when it hit my skin. But on her, the damage was tenfold. Her arms were covered in burn blisters.

"Here, take the hat," I said, ripping it off my head and stuffing it onto hers, wondering if instead I should try to fasten it to one of her poor arms to protect her skin. I pulled off the gloves and the glasses. "Take these, too. Do you want my shirt?"

She shook her head, still looking down, hunching against the storm. "Thank you."

She put on the hat and glasses, slid on the gloves. Then looked up at me. "Thank—*you*."

"Hi."

"What are you doing here?"

"Helping you. Victor asked me to."

"*Asked* you?"

I shrugged.

She nodded, like she knew the score but didn't hate him for it. "That's very charitable of you."

"I want to help," I assured her.

"I'm glad. Let's get inside."

"Inside where? I don't think the Hotel Burning Bright likes my patronage."

She smiled at my stupid joke. A beautiful smile. It brought out cheekbones that complemented her slightly droopy nose tip. I could see why Victor was smitten.

"I don't think they'll mind you now that you're no longer wearing his uniform." She hooked her arm through mine and steered me toward the hotel.

All this time I'd been talking to her, my back had been to the construction site. But when I turned around, arm in arm with Amlathea, the construction site was gone.

"What the—wow. Are you seeing this?"

"You see it?"

"I see a park. A real park. Like the kind back home."

With grass and trees and a pond so clear I could see the fish. It wasn't any grass or tree or fish I could name, but the general look of things was familiar. There were birds singing in the trees. And something like squirrels and rabbits.

And it wasn't just the construction site. It was the roads.

It was the buildings beyond. They were all blinking intermittently with the park.

And there was no Pit in the distance, no falling debris.

I stepped closer, tried to walk on that grass, tried to chase those squirrels.

My arm slipped away from Amlathea's—and the park all but disappeared, becoming nothing more than a curious flicker.

"It's you," I said, turning back to her.

Amlathea had her forearms over her head, getting pelted by the storm. I looped arms with her again—and all around me, the park returned, the water babbling, the wind blowing softly. I helped her navigate the choppy sidewalk. It blinked in and out with the park, making walking difficult.

"You're why I can see the park," I said.

"And you're why I can see that big hole in the ground," she said. "It is a big hole in the ground, isn't it?"

"Yeah. It's a construction site. Big earthmover equipment everywhere. I don't know what they're building."

Although, judging by the presence of a basement, I figured it would probably be another Management building.

"Are the workers present? I don't see any workers."

I told her they were in the hotel at the bar.

"All of them?"

"I mean, probably. I don't know them personally, so I won't know if anyone's missing."

Her brow wrinkled and she bit her lip, clearly distressed.

We made it across the street to the corner of the hotel's block. The storm showed no signs of letting up.

"What does Victor help you with?" I asked.

"He helps me see."

We reached the hotel's sliding glass doors. They were still open from when I'd pried them apart. But she stopped us from going in.

"That's it?" I asked.

"For now. For today."

"But then how did you get into the hotel without Victor earlier."

"You mean earlier today?"

Actually, I didn't. I meant when I'd first seen her meet with Victor, before he'd opened a hole in the wall and then pushed her into a front-loader bucket. But now that I thought about it, Victor *had* been there. He'd been behind me somewhere, waiting to meet her. So—

"Yeah. How did you get in and talk to the front desk guy? And if you need Victor to see, then how come you made it all the way to the hospital in the front-loader bucket? How come it didn't all become park?"

"Clearly, I don't need *Victor* to see," she said, squeezing my arm. "I can see what another sees, same as you. But Victor—it's not just about the seeing."

"So you like him, too?"

"What?"

Oops. Her tone was genuinely confused... but not put off, I didn't think. Guess that topic was something they hadn't discussed together yet.

Good going, Kohl.

"If it's not just about the seeing, then what are you looking for?"

"I don't know," she said. "But with you here, hopefully I'll know him when we see him."

52

She stepped through the open sliding glass doors and into the hotel lobby. Still arm in arm, I followed a step behind her.

The crowd in the bar had gotten livelier since I'd left. The tables were accumulating empty glasses as the construction crew started on new ones. They talked louder, occasionally throwing up hearty laughs. The bartender had turned on a couple of TVs. Both of them showed the news with sound and subtitles. The Channel 7 weather girl reported from Purgatorium Park about the storm. As far as I could tell, she was just stating the obvious. She offered no theories about why it was happening. But she did say it seemed to be abating.

"You—I know you," Erich said from behind the front desk. "You're not—"

"Who?" Amlathea said, in a tone that warned him the only acceptable answer was silence.

Erich got the message. "Glad you found each other," he

said, putting on his hotel attendant persona. "Let me know if I can be of service."

"What now?" I whispered. I glanced outside. The weather reporter was right. The Pit was still spewing up effluvium, but not as bad as it had been. "The storm's going to end soon."

"Do you see anything?" she asked.

"What do you mean? I thought Victor helps *you* see."

"He does. By seeing what I always see."

"What are you seeing?"

She shook her head. "Too dangerous. This is already too dangerous. Just look around and tell me what you see. Start with him." She pointed at Erich, flipping through some papers behind the front desk. "What do you see?"

"Erich? Hotel desk clerk. Red uniform."

"So you know him."

"Yeah."

"And he looks the same as usual."

"Yeah."

"How about these guys?"

She pointed at the group gathered in and around the four red wingback chairs.

"I don't know them."

"And nothing strikes you as odd about them?"

"I mean, they're here. I don't know why people forced to live in the City would need a hotel in the City—"

"So, nothing," she said. "How about in that room?"

She walked us closer to the breakfast nook.

"I can't go in there."

"Why not?"

"Because when they're mad at you, the people who force you to live and work in the City take away your room and board."

"That's awful."

"Tell me about it."

"What did you do?"

"I don't know. But I'm guessing I'm still doing it. Helping you, and all."

"Right. Sorry about that. Can you see in there, at least?"

I peered into the breakfast nook. There were a few people in there, but they all looked like your average short-wearing City dwellers.

"Nothing out of the ordinary," I said.

Amlathea sighed.

"What?"

"He's either not here or I actually do need Victor to see."

I couldn't do anything about the second possibility, so—"Where else should we look?"

"I don't know. I thought he was from the block next door. But you said there wasn't anyone there."

"You mean he works on the construction site? What do you mean you 'thought' he was from there?"

"I thought I saw him in the park. This whole past week, I thought I saw him there. He's just a little bit brighter than the rest, bright enough to leak into the park. But with the storm... you said no one was there."

"Wait, you're looking for the construction crew?" I pointed into the bar. "They're all sitting in there. You can't see them?"

She squinted into the bar.

"Is it flickering?" I asked.

"Yeah. But… I think there's too many people." She let go of my arm, then quickly reached for it again. "Yeah. There's too many people. You say they're in there? The people from the block with the hole?"

"The construction crew, yeah. They're the ones laughing the loudest. With the hardhats and all the empty glasses on the tables."

She was shaking her head.

"You don't see it."

"No," she said, her tone worried.

"Well, tell me. What am I looking for? I don't care if it's dangerous. The sooner we get this done, the sooner we're out of harm's way."

"If only it worked like that," she said. "I don't know what you'll see. But it'll be different. Unexpected."

"Well, let's go."

I led her toward the bar, stepping around a pillar.

And someone in the bar lit up like a glow stick.

"I see him."

"You see him?"

"He's glowing. Like rays of light are emanating from him."

She laughed.

"What?"

"That's what you all look like to me."

I stared at her, wondering why she hadn't just told me that.

But maybe Victor had told her something different. I wondered what he'd be seeing if he were here.

"Why does he look like that?" I asked.

But I knew the answer. Or part of it. I let go of Amlathea's arm just to confirm it for myself.

Sure enough, the man stopped glowing.

And I recognized him.

"That's Ed," I said. "Victor said sometimes mistakes are made. Ed's not supposed to be here, is he?"

"Can you get him to come outside?"

"Hey, Ed!" I called.

Ed looked my way. I waved him over. He was sitting at a low-top table with a couple other guys who were watching the news. He scraped his chair back and stood. He had a little red water glass in his hand.

"Now what?" I asked Amlathea.

She hooked her arm in mine again. "Can you still see him?"

"He's glowing again, so he's bright on the eyes. But, yeah. I can see him. What do you want me to say?"

"Nothing. Just get him outside."

Which was the easiest thing in the world.

"Some storm, huh?" Ed said, as he walked toward us.

"Yeah. Have you seen the roads?"

"Only on TV," he said, and we walked together toward the open sliding glass doors, Amlathea still holding tightly to my arm. I thought Ed would stop just short of stepping outside. But then he said, "Whoa," and continued out the door, carefully stepping around the holes and uneven ground in the broken walkway.

"Now what?" I asked.

"Thank you," Amlathea said. She let go of my arm and walked toward Ed.

Ed stopped glowing. But the closer Amlathea got to him, the brighter he started to glow again.

She said something to him, but she spoke quietly, and I couldn't hear her over the last bits of debris falling from the sky.

Ed looked back at his crew still sitting in the bar. Some of them casually watched him in return. Then he looked across the street to the construction site, an expression of fondness and farewell on his face.

He nodded.

Amlathea smiled that beautiful smile.

The brightness faded, taking the two of them with it.

And the construction site stopped flickering.

Guess that was that, then. I sighed at my job well done.

"You can stop the storm now, Victor," I said to myself.

And it did.

I looked around on the ground to see if Victor was watching me from somewhere. The street was so covered with holes that any one of them could've been Victor's. Except none of them were closing back up.

I shrugged it off and turned back to the hotel, hoping that maybe I, too, could get a drink from the bar. Maybe nurse it while I thought this whole thing over. What did it mean for Ed to leave? What did it mean that I was still here? Would I ever see Amlathea again?

But those were ponderings for another time.

A message was ringing throughout the City as if yelled from the sky.

"Corbin Kohl, please report to Management. Corbin Kohl, please report to Management."

53

"*Corbin Kohl, please report to Management. Corbin Kohl, please report to Management.*"

Instinctively, I looked left, toward Spoke 6, five blocks from the Pit. I could see the Management Building's thirty-three glass-windowed floors from where I stood in front of the Hotel Burning Bright. The digital red clock counted time at the top, against a yellow sky that was slowly clearing of smoke.

It was 2:26 in the afternoon.

I wasn't late for anything. Victor had said that he was the one who had left me the note to meet with Terry Peaches.

But he'd also warned me that Management would want to meet with me after this was over.

I just hadn't expected their request to be so soon.

"*Corbin Kohl, please report to Management.*"

Or so urgent.

Or so embarrassing.

I looked inside the pink hotel's open sliding glass doors at

Erich, behind the desk, and at the construction crew still inside the bar, their drinks forgotten.

Had one of them made a call? They were all looking at me. But their interest looked more out of confusion and curiosity than because one of them had played a part in what was happening to me now.

"Corbin Kohl, please report to Management."

I started walking. It was easier said than done. Big chunks of concrete were gouged out of every flat surface and left nearby as additional obstacles to overcome. Any spots that weren't chewed up were slippery with grit and ash. Red dollops of lava were still burning themselves out all over the place. I steered clear of those.

I was about ten or so blocks from the Pit. A couple blocks off the nearest spoke. Spoke 9. Which was in the opposite direction from the Management Building.

I headed for it anyway. It would be faster to walk down a spoke than to round the curve ten blocks from the Pit, or to try to weave through the streets.

"Corbin Kohl, please report to Management."

The voice of my summoning rang out for all the City to hear. It was uncanny. Like the big G-Man himself calling down for my attention.

But this wasn't exactly His realm I was in, was it?

That was confirmed when the message changed.

Just as I turned right at the fifth block, they dropped the *please.*

"Corbin Kohl, report to Management."

Should I be running? I picked up my pace a bit. But I

didn't see any occasion to run. And not just because it was damn near impossible, what with the road and sidewalks all torn up.

How did I want to play this? Was I in a hurry to get to the Management Building, to please the powers that be? Or was I going to dilly-dally. Maybe give Victor a chance to give me whatever it was he'd had in mind when he'd said he had something for me to give to Management. Something to keep them off my back.

I looked for him, but I didn't see him peering out of the ground. Maybe the damage done to the roads was preventing him from performing his trick.

Or maybe he'd lied to me. Maybe he'd never intended to help me.

He was a Victor after all.

"Corbin Kohl, get to Management now."

By now I could see the Management Building's front doors down the street. The smell of fresh pizza still lingered in the air. I wanted to slow down, to keep my cool, to pretend I was still in control of this thing, of myself. But I found myself moving faster.

There was still a crowd relative to non-pizza days, but the street wasn't as busy as it had been this morning.

I entered the building and caught the elevator.

And Management knew I was here. I pressed the button for the twenty-first floor, and the doors shut, cutting off the message.

"Corbin Ko—"

54

The elevator doors opened onto Terry's red waiting room.

"Hey, Carl," I said when I found the old guy slumped in his chair behind his desk, his hands folded up high on his chest. He opened one eye, grinned like he was trying not to, and slowly opened the other eye.

"I hear you've been up to no good," he said, still grinning.

I cringed. "You heard that in here?"

"They heard that out the end of Spoke 12," Carl said.

I nodded, coming to terms. It meant that Annie had heard it, too. So did Darryl and Angela. And Cherise Montaire.

"I take it you went to Kane's old place," he said.

"I did. Thanks for the tip."

"Don't thank me yet." He nodded toward Terry's closed door. I should probably get my talking-to over with. But since the summons had stopped, I was feeling less pressured for time.

And I wanted to thank Carl.

"You went through a lot of trouble to get that printout for me, didn't you? The one for his old apartment."

Carl was so slumped in his chair that his shoulders were already touching his ears. But he still managed a shrug. The movement bobbled his head.

"What was in it for you?"

A thousand years of emotion and struggle and history passed over the ancient man's face. I caught sadness. Determination. Hope. But there were more. He narrowed his eyes a bit at me, which I took to mean *don't ask anymore about that, for both our sakes*. And then he attempted to perk up his grin.

He wasn't mad at me for asking. But he didn't want to talk about it. Not here, anyway.

"Well... thanks," I said.

Carl grunted. "You better get in there."

55

I knocked on Terry's door.

Rather than tell me to come in, Terry opened the door himself. He was wearing his royal blue shorts suit with his red tie. Brown dress shoes. No socks.

His were the knees of the burl variety.

"So you're okay," he said. And if I wasn't mistaken, it was said with a sneer and a hint of disappointment.

He turned away from me and stomped across his red plastic carpet with a sigh.

I closed the door and followed him as far as my usual spot, equidistant between his desk and the exit.

Outside his floor-to-ceiling windows, the sky above the Pit, five blocks away, was the clearest yellow I'd ever seen it. As if Victor had used up a few hours'—or, if I was lucky, a few days'—worth of smoke and sulfur smell to make it rain.

Terry took his seat behind his glass desk. He turned to one side and drummed his fingers on the glass, his chin almost resting on his shoulder as he studied me.

I stood at parade rest and kept quiet.

"Management received your report," Terry said. "I'm told you half-assed your responses. I'm told you listed a *hospital* near Spoke 9 as one of your discoveries."

It wasn't a question, so I didn't answer. But my stomach churned. I'd lied and listed the hospital as the location where Amlathea had gotten her tattoo. At the time, I'd been worried about Annie and had just wanted to get the report done. But the way Terry said the word *hospital* with such distaste, such disbelief. I hoped I hadn't gotten the nurse or anyone else who worked at the doctor's office in trouble.

"Would you like to amend your statement?" he asked.

Did I? What would I say? I didn't want to tell him the truth. I didn't want to tell him she got her tattoo right across the street at Darryl and Angela's Physical Services Parlor.

But the hospital... was I digging its grave?

I closed my eyes. *Yes or no, Kohl?*

"No."

"Are you sure?" Terry said. "We have a confirmation team, you know."

He smiled at me, because of course he knew I didn't know.

"Our confirmation team couldn't find such a place," he said. He tilted his head. Probably waiting for me to squirm.

But I wasn't surprised they couldn't find the place. It was why I'd chosen it. It had been a gamble.

But it had paid off.

I tried not to show my relief that the hospital was safe. I stared back at Terry, trying to keep my gaze even and not challenging. I didn't want Terry to know that I knew about the City's flickers. Not everyone knew. I knew Annie didn't. And apparently no one on the confirmation team knew about them either.

I had a feeling Terry also wasn't in the know. About a lot of things. He'd said the hospital was listed, not as the place Amlathea had gotten her tattoo, but as one of my *discoveries*. An awfully vague word. Like he knew just enough to question me about my answers and no more.

Like he still wasn't privy to the assignment and accompanying information that had been given to me in the red folder.

And his next question confirmed it.

"Mr. Kohl, you also merely reversed the perspective of another question," he said, awkwardly, like he was repeating someone else's words. "Management would like an answer."

"And do they want me to give it to *you*?"

Terry narrowed his eyes. "Let me remind you, Kohl, of something you seem to constantly and willfully overlook. And that is that I can make your life hell. You work for—"

Terry's phone rang. He jumped about a mile high, then fumbled for the handset.

He brought it to his ear, his hand and voice trembling a little. "Yes?"

He listened for a moment, then turned his back to me and tried to speak quietly.

"Yes, I have some. ... Of course. ... I was getting to it. ... Yes, of course. ... Of course. ... Yes, of course. My apolo—"

He pulled the phone away from his ear, stared at it,

huffed, and set it back in its cradle. I assumed he'd been hung up on.

I looked around the sparse red and glass room, but if there were listening devices present, I didn't see any obvious candidates.

Terry opened a file cabinet, rifled through the drawer, and pulled out a document.

He turned toward me and slid the piece of paper across his glass-top desk.

"Am I supposed to—"

"Yes. Take it," he said.

I walked to Terry's desk, picked up the paper, and returned to the center of the room. Slowly. Slow enough to see that the paper was a two-page spread with questions front and back. A blank copy of the assignment report form I'd already filled out once.

Management wanted me to fill it out again.

I took all of this as a *no*. I wasn't supposed to give any pertinent information to Terry.

I allowed myself a small victorious smile before putting away, stuffing the form under my arm, and facing Terry again, resuming parade rest.

I awaited dismissal. I assumed the meeting was over.

I was wrong.

Terry stared at me for many long seconds. Studied me. Looked me up and down. Narrowed his eyes at me. I couldn't tell what he was thinking. But it obviously wasn't good.

Outside his office, I heard the elevator rising up through

the floors. It dinged. Opened with a whir. Shut with a clank. Continued on.

Finally, Terry said, "Many people saw you tumble into a hole in the ground outside this very building this morning."

Another non-question. So I didn't answer. But my stomach was in knots.

"They say it was Victor Kane. Was it?"

A baseline lie-detector question. Because I couldn't exactly say no. As far as anyone knew, there was no one else it could have been. So unless I wanted to make someone up, the only answer was—

"Yes."

"What did he want?"

When in a bind, state the obvious: "To make a scene?"

"Why?"

"How should I know?"

"Where did he take you?"

"As you said, into the ground."

"But *where* in the ground?"

I couldn't tell Terry about Victor's cavern beneath the Pit. He'd specifically said no one knew about it. That if he heard anyone mentioning it, he would know I had told. Given how he'd treated me so far—and I thought he kinda liked me a little—I didn't want to find out what he'd do to me if I got on his bad side.

Think, Kohl.

"Again, how should I know? I was *in the ground.*"

"Mmm." Terry nodded, unconvinced. "But you're here now. So where did he let you out?"

"He didn't. But I remembered the construction site by the Hotel Burning Bright. My first assignment," I reminded him quickly.

But I don't think he needed it. He knew I'd come out near the hotel. However they tracked us, they must've noted I'd slipped off their radar when I'd disappeared into the hole. So they watched for me to pop up again. And I'd popped up near the hotel. This was another lie-detector question. And to Terry's dismay, I'd just passed.

"They're digging a hole on the construction site," I continued. "So I walked to it."

"You walked to it."

"Through the dirt. Like it was a wall." I rubbed my shoulder, so he'd understand. But unlike walking through a wall, where I led with my shoulder, the pain of walking through half a mile of dirt was everywhere. Head to toe. But I felt it more strongly on my front than on my back.

"I'm hoping to get a Twister service after this," I added, trying to gauge how much longer this meeting would take. And whether or not I would actually be allowed to leave.

"And you made it," Terry said, clearly not believing me. Even though this part was true.

Obviously. Because I was standing here.

"I have a good sense of direction," I said.

"Uh-huh."

He stared at me. Drummed his fingers. Out the window, at Purgatorium Park, I could see tiny people. They seemed to be doing their best to clean up the mess.

"Okay, Kohl. You're dismissed. But"—Terry smirked at

me like he had me, like he was about to win this battle after all—"you'll need to fill out that report to Management's satisfaction before you leave. Ta."

56

I trudged out of Terry's office, shut the door behind me, and leaned against it. I pulled the form out from under my arm and looked it over. If the ban barrier could keep me out, I had no doubt it could keep me in.

Stuck in the Management Building but banned from the cafeteria. Ugh.

How was I going to answer Management's questions to its satisfaction?

"Corbin?"

I looked up at Carl. He was sitting upright, with his back away from his chair. He struggled with both hands to pick up a small package on his desk.

"This was dropped off for you."

"For me?" I stepped toward him and took the package. It was wrapped in brown paper and about the size of a paperback book, though not as dense. My grip on it squished it together. "Who from?"

Carl shrugged and settled back into his chair. His

shoulders rose up to his ears. He folded his hands together over his sternum. "Don't know. I was sleeping."

The corner of his mouth rose in a grin.

I started to rip off the paper, but Carl said, "Maybe open that elsewhere."

He lifted a gnarled hand and pointed at the stairwell.

"Okay. Anything else?"

"That should do you," Carl said. "No, wait."

He struggled to sit up again.

"Can I help?" I asked.

"Yeah. Top drawer."

I went around Carl's desk and opened the top drawer on the right side of his desk. He had a few pens and a few pads of paper of different sizes.

"Take a pen."

"Okay." I took a blue click pen. "This one okay?"

"Sure."

"You want it back?"

"Nah."

"Okay. Thanks, Carl."

He raised his eyebrows in response, then snuggled into his chair and closed his eyes.

57

I headed down the emergency stairs and stopped at the first landing that couldn't be seen from any of the egress doors. I sat on the second step from the bottom and tore open the package.

It was the parchment map.

It was all folded up, but it was the parchment map. The *For Corbin Kohl's Eyes Only* parchment map. I could tell by the stiffness of the paper and the foxing on the edges.

I patted my shorts pocket, where I'd kept it, but—yeah—my pocket was empty.

Holy hell.

Who had found it? And how had they known to return it to me?

I unfolded it and a note fell out. The penmanship was barely legible, the letters thin and sharp.

Suffice to say, you dropped this. And if you're receiving it, it means Management has let you go. Which means your report answers were good enough.

Don't change them.

But do give Management something extra. They'll like that.

They'll like you for that.

And I'll like you for that.

Tell them you've been thinking about it, and you think this parchment might've been the under sheet to the original drawing of a certain sea-goat tattoo you saw on someone's ankle. You think the drawing leaked through. The upside-down-V horns. The upside-down-C curves of the scales on the fish tale. Etcetera.

You might be wondering how this could be, given how stiff and waxy the parchment feels. But they made it that way. This drawing is old, and they've attempted to protect it. You, of course, aren't supposed to know that. But they will. They won't question it.

GIVE THE PARCHMENT BACK TO THEM WITH YOUR REPORT.

Now, do I need to tell you how to destroy this note, or are you smart enough to figure that out on your own?

Smart enough. Definitely smart enough.

And hungry enough. I tore the note into bite-size chunks and started chewing. What note? There was just enough pizza smell in the stairwell that I could pretend I was just a dumb, hungry kid enjoying a slice of pizza.

I popped another paper bite in my mouth and unfolded the blank report. And I drained a good amount of the blue ink in Carl's pen, filling out all the questions. Every single one. Even the dumb ones about the weather. *It was hot. Duh.*

And as for the one that asked about rain, *rain* was not a word that could describe anything that fell from the City's sky, in my opinion. So as far as I was concerned, at least for the purposes of this report, *I've never seen it rain.*

Victor had said that if Management let me go, it was because my assignment answers had been good enough. And really, how could they not have been? How was I expected to know what Victor wanted with Amlathea or where she got her tattoo? I'd been here a week. Any information should've been impressive to them.

But they'd still locked me out of the cafeteria.

And the bus.

And my studio.

I had to believe it was because I hadn't filled out the whole report. I'd rebelled a little. And they didn't like that.

For the last question, which asked if I had anything else to add, I told them what Victor had said about the parchment. That I thought the ink in a drawing of the sea-goat tattoo had seeped through the page and onto the paper below. The parchment paper.

The scale was larger, of course. I made note of that. But when I looked at the parchment again, I thought the explanation was more than plausible. There were a few markings that didn't quite fit. But, then again, I never got a close-up look at Amlathea's tattoo.

But I didn't think the explanation was the point. The effort I was making was the point.

Returning the parchment was the point.

I took the stairs down to the lobby. I slid the parchment inside the folded report and then slid the report into the return slot.

Now, do I assume all is well, and thus restored, and get myself a slice of pizza before it's gone baby gone? Or do I head over to the Physical Services Parlor and get myself a Twister?

58

The choice was made for me. Management seems omniscient, if you ask me, but apparently it needs time to read the reports. No pizza for Kohl.

Angela and Darryl were both at the Physical Services Parlor when I arrived for a Twister service. The glass front door was unlocked, and the hidden door in the green pressboard wall opened as soon as the welcome bell dinged over my head.

"Corbin," Angela said, coming through the door first. She wore a black tank top and short white shorts. She had great legs. I may have looked at them a little too long. But I don't think she noticed.

"I'm so sorry," she said. "And it looks like you need another Twister, too. Come in, come in."

She grabbed my hand and pulled me into the hallway, continuing to apologize in a way that had me wondering what had happened to the surlier Angela I knew.

Darryl, in another low-scoop tank top with thin straps,

this one magenta, said nothing. Just held the door open and gave me a sad, concerned face: His brows pinched together. His top lip flattened against his bottom.

"What, the announcement thing with them calling out my name? How is that your fault?"

Darryl said, "No, dude. Your meeting this morning."

My cancelled meeting with Cherise Montaire. For a busy, stressful second, I'd forgotten about my condition.

"She took one look at me and ran away," I told them.

"We know," Angela said. "She called."

Angela nudged me into her room and up onto her padded table. Darryl tried to follow us inside, but there wasn't enough room. He ended up standing in the doorway, with the saloon door open out to the hall.

"She did?" I said, scissoring my dangling feet back and forth. I was too anxious to lie down. "What did she say?"

"Uh," Angela said. She glanced at Darryl, passing him the train of thought, then dug through the shelves underneath me for her Twister.

Darryl said, "She said she can't help you yet."

"'Yet'? What does that mean?"

Angela plugged in the Twister and turned it on. Aimed its roar at me. She was grimacing, probing at my right arm.

Darryl said, "She said to give her a call when the striations reach your head."

"My head?!" I didn't know what to feel. Angry that I couldn't get a cure until things were terrible or relieved that I hadn't reached that point yet. "So they haven't reached my head?"

"No," Angela said, walking around the table and poking at my back. It might've been nice under other circumstances. "It's mostly in your arms."

"How will I know when it reaches my head?"

I could feel Angela cowering behind me, not wanting to answer.

In front of me, Darryl smiled at me sadly. "You'll know, dude."

"Soon?"

"No," Angela said quickly. "It's still active, but it seems to have slowed. I've never seen anything like it. Cherise said you were touched by an—"

"Angela," Darryl warned.

"What?" Angela said. "It's what she said."

Darryl shook his head. Another warning about the dangers of repeating certain things out loud.

But it seemed to me, between the two of them, they already had told me, thanks to Angela's name. Or namesake.

"No, it's okay," I said. "I think I get it. And I think I know what happened."

I thought back to that morning when I'd followed a woman with a tattoo and a guy wearing a doofy hat and a key pair of gloves through a wall, only to touch the woman's blond hair just before she was pushed into a front-loader bucket. And I remembered the long, shoulder-length gloves Darryl had worn when he'd given that same woman another tattoo.

And I remembered that that same woman—the woman who'd taken kind and simple Ed from this hellhole, the woman who even Victor Kane couldn't help but worry about, the woman who needed a tattoo to hold her down here in the City—that same woman had told me she thought my condition was lucky.

"And I think it's all gonna be okay."

59

I invited Annie over to my place. It seemed like the nicest thing I could do. I had juice boxes after all.

After Angela set me right with her Twister best she could, Darryl said he'd walk me out. I thought that was weird, but I wasn't about to tell him not to accompany me. Turned out he wanted to talk about Amlathea. I found it interesting that he wanted to do it without Angela overhearing.

Darryl told me that he would pass on to Amlathea that Cherise Montaire had skipped our meeting but had offered to help me when my condition worsened.

I'd totally forgotten I'd promised Amlathea I would do that.

I asked him how he was going to get in touch with her, since I'd just seen her vanish with Ed. But Darryl said no worries, he'd take care of it.

Darryl was a good dude.

I headed back over to the Management Building feeling pretty good, all things considered. My condition probably wasn't as bad as I'd initially thought. Victor seemed satisfied with me for now, so I should probably be able to walk around for a while without him tripping me up. I even seemed to have a few more friends in Carl, Darryl, and Angela. Things were pretty good, indeed.

The cafeteria was still blocked to me when I checked it on the way up to see Annie.

"You're okay!" she cried when she saw me. She popped out of her chair, ran around her desk, and gave me a big hug. "Did you hear them calling for you? Course you did. *Corbin Kohl, get to Management now*. I was like, *how*? He was *taken*, you dimwits."

She let me go. "I heard some of the other assistants talking about how they've *never* heard the PA system throughout the City before. *Never*. Throughout the building? Sure. Never throughout the City. I'm so glad you're okay." She wrapped her arms around me again. "What did they want?"

"To talk about my report."

"You didn't answer all the questions, did you?"

"My bad."

She squeezed me tighter, then pulled away and slugged me in the stomach. "And that's for ditching me at the house *you* asked me to investigate with you. Rude."

I told her I was sorry and that I'd explain everything another time, some other *place*.

"Yeah, yeah. You owe me," she'd said.

And now I was paying up.

I took most of my T-shirts out of my closet and laid them on my coffee table, along with two grape juice boxes.

I'd missed out on pizza day. It had taken Management two days and a reminder to Terry that I hadn't eaten anything for even longer to get my ban lifted.

"Oh, have they not removed that yet?" he'd said, oh so innocently. "Guess you've been locked out of the bus and your apartment, too, huh? Sorry about that."

I had been locked out of the bus—my poor legs—but the extra night locked out of my studio reminded me that I had an alternative homestead.

The library.

I spent my second night there. Never did see the person who changed up the display or left the card catalogue open to *soil*. But I thought I might've had an insight into what the person was telling me. Even if the insight did come a little late.

Soil, to my mind, was healthy dirt. Dirt you could grow stuff in. And healthy dirt needs water.

Around here, Victor seemed to control what passed for dirt.

And he'd said he and Amlathea always met after a bout of what passed for rain. I had a feeling she had something to do with causing the strange drizzle.

So maybe my secret librarian's hint was that Victor and Amlathea weren't the bad guys after all. Maybe together they'd eventually improve this place, turn all that volcanic rock into soil.

Or maybe I'd just been so hungry I was making sense out of nothing.

Either way, after my get-together with Annie, I'd be

taking a spare shirt and shorts and half my juice boxes to the library. It didn't have a shower or a refrigerator, but it did have a bathroom. And if I ever got kicked out of my studio again, the library was a better home than nothing.

And as for the ban lift taking a couple days, that turned out to be interesting, too. It revealed that Terry and Management were definitely at odds about me. After my reinstatement to the cafeteria, I charged in ready to eat everything in sight, gruel or not, and the guy behind the sneeze guard went into the kitchen and came back with a personal-sized pizza.

"Compliments of Management."

A knock sounded at my door. My first visitor since I'd been in the City. Not to mention the first knock I'd ever heard on my floor.

I opened the door.

"Nice place," Annie said as she strode in. "I like this shelf separator thing. You've actually got a bit of a bedroom and a living room. And a coffee table? Not me. I've got nothing but a bed and a hot plate. So what are we doing?"

"I need your help," I said, gesturing her toward the couch. "I'm guessing your penmanship is better than mine."

"No doubt. I liked art back in the day. Charcoals mostly." She sighed wistfully. "What do you need me to write?"

I showed her my shirts all lined up on the coffee table. I figured I should save for dressier occasions the white-turned-ash-gray polo I'd worn to the Hotel Burning Bright the day I'd first seen Victor and Amlathea. Just in case. But the *NOW YOU SEE ME NOW YOU DON'T* shirt I'd worn to check out Victor's first apartment with Annie and a couple others I wasn't a fan of were all laid out on the table.

"Juice box?" I said, handing her one.

"Yeah. Where'd you get this?"

I told her. I told her about the flickering hospital and the flickering pink Victorian. She was mad I hadn't told her sooner, but she understood that sometimes not knowing is better, around here.

"But if I ever need to know, you need to tell me. Promise you'll tell me."

"I'll tell you."

And I told her what I'd learned from Erich, the front desk clerk at the hotel, about her red grit. "It's a thing, a money thing. But I don't think it's commonly known among the masses. It's like it's kept secret by the upper echelons and not distributed among the peons."

"But it was shown to me."

"Yeah it was."

She made a smug little moue and fluffed her pixie cut like a proud peacock, then grinned. "So what are we doing here? 'Cause I get the feeling you want me to write on your shirts."

"Yeah. In big capital letters. With grape juice. I figure I'll never wash it well enough to get the stain out. You can use my toothbrush. Or your finger?" I shrugged.

"I'll just use the straw," she said. She sucked up some juice and plugged the top hole with her index finger, keeping the purple liquid ready inside the tube. "What am I writing?"

"One word," I said. And outside the window, I thought I saw something in the yellow sky twinkling down on me.

And maybe I did. After all, I was pretty sure I'd once heard an angel call me this word. I pointed at my chest with both hands, where the five-letter word was already printed on my favorite green shirt, armpit stains and all. "Lucky."

AUTHOR'S NOTE

Thank you for reading! I am thrilled that you picked up this book, and I hope that you enjoyed it. If you want to see more books like it from me, **make sure to leave a review!** Reviews help me in many ways, but especially when I'm wondering what to write next.

Also...

I have a newsletter! I send out updates, exclusive content, and other goodies to subscribers about once a month. The monthly newsletter is free, and you can sign up at meganbledsoe.substack.com. Or you can use the QR Code at the bottom of the page.

Make sure to read the newsletter's welcome email. At the bottom, there's a link to a page of goodies that's just for readers of this series. The password is **orwherever**, all lowercase.

Talk to you soon!
Megan

MORE BOOKS BY MEGAN BLEDSOE

Glitching the Matrix: *a novel . . .*
The Metanaut: *a supernatural thriller*
Girl, Incorrupted: *a love-horror story*

THE *CORBIN KOHL IN HELL* SERIES
fun low-fantasy mysteries
Corbin Kohl Adrift in Hell
Corbin Kohl Baited in Hell
Corbin Kohl Cornered in Hell

ABOUT THE AUTHOR

Megan Bledsoe takes inspiration from the world's unexplained but still undeniable phenomena. She used to be an attorney but now writes in the Pacific Northwest, where she lives with her family. She is the author of *Glitching the Matrix*, *The Metanaut*, *Girl, Incorrupted*, and the *Corbin Kohl In Hell* series. Find her online and join her newsletter at meganbledsoe.com.